love BROKEN

J.D. HOLLYFIELD

Editor: Lawrence Editing
Formator: Champagne Book Design
Designer: Okay Creations

To all the skeptics.
Love is, indeed, blind.

I guess the old saying is true.
Everything in life happens for a reason.
And in an instant life can change, taking your entire world,
flipping it three different ways to Sunday and land in a
direction you never expected to be facing.

And that direction can change everything.

Well, I say screw age old bullshit because now
I'm totally fucking lost.

LOVE BROKEN
J.D. Hollyfield

chapter ONE

The Waldorf-Astoria Hotel—Chicago

My arm's getting a workout as I raise my hand, *once again*, to grab the cute bartender's attention. Motioning for another round, in no time, he's sliding another cocktail in front of me, and I graciously accept. I'm close to clocking in five hours of drinking and people watching at the bar of the Waldorf Hotel, one of Chicago's top-notch hotels, taking in the insane scene around me.

What's so insane about it, you ask? Where do I even begin?

Let's just begin with the sold-out hotel that's filled with hordes of people, all here for the same reason. Books. So many books. Did I mention they were all *romance* books? Readers from all over the globe gathered for an all-week event or in "*book terms*," an author signing. An event I was invited to.

I know the first thing you want to know is who the hell I am and what brought *me*, or as Journey sang it best, *the lonely girl livin' in a lonely world* to this event. Well, it's about time we got acquainted. My name is Katie Beller, but the world, as of late, knows me as romance author, Bailey Swan—the famous name behind the words.

I look around the packed bar, people huddled in groups, girls wearing matching T-shirts, and readers flaunting over their favorite authors. I've just spent the last hour by myself sipping on my vodka tonic, eavesdropping on a reader who drilled her author buddie on how she started her career. With eyebrows yay high, I think to myself I *definitely* don't have a clever story like hers.

Mine's simpler. The "one late night decision and my life changed" kinda simple. It goes something like this. *On a dark and dreary evening...* Okay, too dramatic? Got it. So, one night after a long shift at work, I came home at way past two in the morning. I sat down and wrote a bunch of words. By some bizarre force—which I blame on a tilt in the universe—this story became a *New York Times* best seller. How, you ask? No fucking idea.

I don't have a great literary background story for you on how my book hit the big time, or any "awe" love story that pushed me to write it. To be honest, I'm a bartender at a local hole in the wall in downtown Cleveland, Ohio, and I just get to hear and see a lot of shit.

Talk about inspiration.

Was it the love stories after love stories I listened to each night that drove me? Eh, I wouldn't call it *that*, but it did consist of stories. Some good, some bad… Mostly bad. Hear enough of them and you begin to form your own judgmental opinion of that four-letter word and how people define it.

A squeal pierces through the air as a reader fan-girls over one of the many cover models in attendance. Just another reminder there was something about love that just made people so crazed for it. Deluded to what it truly meant, or felt like. Was it about a night of hot, passionate sex? A mistake one or both won't ever be able to go back on? Probably. But *love*? Who knows? Like I said, I'm just the bartender serving the lonely, the brokenhearted, the misconstrued people of the world their drinks to loosen them up, taking the shots they offer me, and by the end of the night leaning my elbow on the bar, holding my chin up, wishing I were them.

Okay, wait. I take that back. I definitely do *not* wish I were them, getting lucky at two in the morning by a random stranger who's been spilling lies and bullshit in their ear all night in hopes they'll fall for it and end up back at their sketchy apartment having random "I'm going to regret this tomorrow" sex.

No fucking thanks.

Do I wish I were one of those girls who get swept off their feet by Mr. Romeo? Who treats his girl to the movies and perfect dinners? Maybe. Do I want to be swept off my feet with those special trigger words whispered softly into my wanting ears and made sweet endless love to until the sun comes up?

Ehh, okay, sometimes.

Fuck, okay, yes, I want love.

But I'm me. And *that* kind of love just doesn't look like it's anywhere in my future. Plus, I work in a bar and watch what people define as love nowadays, and you just don't see the luster in it anymore.

And whatever. I'm fine with it. I mean, I'm going on twenty-eight and haven't had as much as a flutter, a stolen breath, or even an endless night's sleep when it comes to love. I've had boyfriends, one-night stands, and offers, but none were it. *The* it. The one you know has forever written all over him.

I've just come to the conclusion that I'm love broken.

It's not that no one will ever love *me*. I just don't have the mechanism to love back. I mean, I *love*. I love my parents, my friends. My bird, Gerdie. I just don't know how to love deep. Like that deep love that burns. A girl once sat at my bar and told me how the love she felt for her boyfriend hurt so bad it was like being filled to the rim with hot lava. She couldn't explain it any other way. I thought that sounded quite painful, but I got it. Love can be fulfilling. It's what it's there for. The end of a lifelong search to no longer be alone.

But that same girl sat at my bar two weeks later and cried her eyes out because her fulfilled love ran off with his hairdresser.

So much for fulfilling love.

I think I'll pass.

I'm sure you're wondering how someone with an empty heart like myself could sit down and write a love story in the first place. Well, I'm right there with you. I mean, what do *I* know about love? I know it hurts, that most of the time it *doesn't* last, and it's messy. I don't need to experience it to know I'm okay without it. But working at a bar for the past seven years, I've heard it all. The good, the bad, the ugly. Love isn't always neat, or beautiful. It *is* ugly and messy. So I wrote a book because I just thought people needed to finally know that.

So, the next question I know you're wanting to ask is, for

someone so down on love, does my book even have a happily ever after? Well, it depends on what you consider the perfect ending. Sometimes reality and that fairytale ending cross. And sometimes you just get that ending that completes you enough to say this life will do. People need to wake up and realize they're always so worried about finding "happily ever after" that they panic and end up settling for that "this will have to do" ending. Maybe the one person who has no idea what true love really is, is holding the most powerful advice of them all.

Seven months ago, I came home from work. And before even washing off the sweat and grime, I sat down, opened my beer-label-covered laptop, and popped open Word. My brain was drowning in thoughts and opinions. Why do women always fall for the bad guy? Why do they fall so fast? Why do guys pretend feelings don't matter when they reel in a girl, with all those sweet words and free drinks, and then the guy never calls again? I guess I had a spike of anger and needed to let the world know. Write a letter to those lame love columnist people at the paper and send it in, threatening that they better post it, or the world of love was soon to be doomed. Strangely, that letter turned into ninety-seven thousand words and before I knew it, I was chin deep into a story. Was it my story? Or was it every single heartbroken girl's story who sat at my bar and confessed their dreams, crushed love, or failed success stories? Who knows? But it was mainly about a girl who just couldn't sit back and take any more of this fake, broken love bullshit.

Because love *was* broken.

It may never be fixed for me, but God help me, it could be for others. As I'm already a lost cause, girls out there needed to know there was hope outside of the fake pickup lines, fake smiles, and fake loves.

When I wrote *Love Broken*, I never expected it to go very far. I just wanted someone to get a fucking clue and maybe tell their girlfriend. Maybe she would tell her friend, who would tell her sister, and in the end, there might be a handful of women making a change about love. One less wasted one-night stand on the guy with empty promises, or a girl who finally waits to find the one meant for her instead of the one meant for the moment.

What I *didn't* expect was a cult-like following of women to read my book of words and start a hateration on dead-beat men. It was like overnight I went from being a nobody working at a bar to—well, still a nobody because no one knew Katie Beller. They knew the invented pen name, Bailey Swan, as the words of the wise. The love guru. And overnight, Bailey was famous.

The first couple of months after the book published I stood behind my bar listening to women dissect it. How Bailey just nailed it. Why hadn't they seen it the whole time? How they were going to take Bailey's advice and hold out for the one, read between the lines of those fake endearments, and be better at their choices in men.

And everyone wanted to be Bailey. They wanted to have her experiential brain when it came to men and swore she probably had the best life. Romance all girls wanted. She was probably married with her prince charming and three perfect little children. Little did they know, she was a plain Jane with some bad choice tattoos, straight brunette hair anyone would pass on, and a normal figure that has almost never seen the inside of a gym in her entire existence.

I turn to see another male model sitting with his back to me on my left. I don't need to see his face to know he's wooing the girl on the other side of him. Her star-crossed eyes tell me everything I need to know. She's already head over heels for this guy. Blond, voluptuous and doe-eyed. By societal norms, she's beautiful.

Me, on the other hand, sorry to disappoint, but I'm nowhere near this perfect portrait the world is painting of me. I'm normal. I'm five foot four, and nothing to call home about. I have tits, but everyone has tits. Are they the "perfect perked breasts" you read about in your smut books? How the hell should I know? I don't review tits for a living. I serve booze. I've never worn a belly shirt, and that's because I have a belly. When pot bellies become an "in" thing I'll be all over it, but for now I will keep my cute little pooch behind closed doors. I'm your average size six, with my seventy-five pairs of ripped skinny jeans and tank tops under my band and random quote T-shirts. If I get fancy, I put on a cute black dress with my favorite pair of combat boots. That's me. The one no one picks.

Wah-wah. Oh well. I'm over it. I'm on to saving others now.

When my best friend, Kristen, insisted on me joining this massive book event she hosts every year, I turned her down.

Well, at first.

"Katie, this can be huge for your career! To meet all your fans and get the praise you deserve!"

My response to that? "Nah, I'm good."

I wasn't looking for fame or power. I didn't need the spotlight to feel I got my point across. I just wanted to put out my book, make a point, and move on. Serve more booze to people who appreciate me. Because everyone appreciates their bartender.

Also, they didn't want to meet me. They wanted to meet Bailey.

"Katie, everyone writes under pen names. It's the way of this world. People have lives to protect. You don't have to tell anyone your real name. You come as Bailey Swan. Simple as that."

"Yeah, and when they see a skater girl instead of a Stepford wife, what happens then? Who breaks off the riot of picketing housewives and single women who feel scammed?"

Kristen's infamous sigh rings through the phone. "Katie. You're beautiful. You are you. You don't need to be anything but yourself. When will you see that?"

Umm, *when I stop proving myself right that men don't see girls like me as the ones. They see me as the friend, the buddie. Not the one you bring home to Mom.*

"Katie, I know what you're thinking. And stop. You haven't found love because you're so anti it. Stop rallying the troops to fight it and maybe you'll surprise yourself."

I laugh. "Oh, okay, so I should let one of my best drunk customers sway me? How about Jack? The drunk construction dude who swears he was born to teach me a lesson in bed. How about I let him teach me about love? Maybe he'll surprise me."

"Katie, that's not what I meant." More sighing, more eye rolling, that part on my end. "Listen. Just come out. If you don't like the tour, you can drop. I won't commit you to the whole tour, just the first two weeks. If you hate it, then you can bow out and go back to feeding the rising statistic of alcoholism."

Okay, I laugh at that. She's right. People drink too damn much in this world. I can't really complain because their bad habit pays my rent, but I'm definitely shocked people haven't caught on that booze doesn't fix life's problems.

"Please? Please, please, please!"

I don't say no right away.

Ew, why aren't I saying no?

Am I actually considering this?

I am considering this.

"Come on. You can do it. Just say yes..."

Stop! Get out of my brain!

"Ew. Fine." *What?*

"YES! Thank you, Katie, you won't regret this, I promise! This will be great for your career!"

Not if I'm deaf because she's screaming through the phone.

Yeah, I wasn't so worried about my career, as I was about the demise of my self-esteem.

What had I just agreed to?

chapter TWO

I agreed to mayhem, that's what.

In the past five hours I've been here, I've determined the book world is crazy. So many talented people who write books and the amazing amount of people who read them. It might be a whole new world for me, but to *these* people, it's their dome. Their utopia. And to them it's a complete rush.

I watch authors who have their cliques, ones who've been in the industry for years, and ones who are just meeting for the first time. And it's crazy how social media brings so many people together. Something I need to get on, it seems. I don't do the whole Facebook thing because honestly, I don't have a list of anyone I care to hear about when they poop or what they ate for breakfast, lunch, and dinner. I hear enough of people's life stories at work. I don't need to read about it all day online.

Since sitting down, I've been approached by readers and authors asking if I was somebody. Every time the name Bailey Swan tried to fall off my lips, I choked. Instead, I'd said "no, just a friend of Vodka" and continued to sip on my drink. Apparently, I was a big fat chicken too and couldn't tell anyone I was an author. I didn't know any of these people, nor did I have an author buddie to latch onto. Kristen was MIA, so I chose to be a wallflower and not expose myself. Well, expose Bailey Swan. I told myself if I didn't give myself up now, I still had a solid twenty more hours before the signing started, so I had *that* amount of time to back out and catch the next flight home. I'm sure my boss, Dex, who got stuck picking up my two weeks' worth of shifts at the bar, would at least be happy to see me.

Once it hits one in the morning, I decide to give up and call it a night. I'm not going to out myself as an author to anyone down here, and the vodka isn't pushing it either. I thought maybe I would just get drunk enough to start blurting out who I was, but the drunker I got, the more I hid inside my shell.

I stagger to the elevator, after stumbling past a screaming group of girls chasing a model, and then trip into my door. Using three credit cards, my license, and a Chipotle gift card, I finally use my actual room key and stumble inside.

"Hello, room! I'm Bailey Swan! Nice to meet you all. Would you like my autograph or to shun me? Who wants to go first?" I giggle, throwing my purse to the floor. It opens, and out pours my phone and a pile of change. I picked up a scheduled list of authors at the check-in booth and told myself

I was going to spend my night online, setting up a Facebook account and learning who all the authors were. As much of a hermit that I've realized I've become, I do want to try and make some friends.

Of course, before friend making, a shit-ton of room service needs to be ordered.

"Hello, Ms. Swan, I hope your stay has been enjoyable. What can I help you with this evening?"

"Yes, Bailey Swan here." I chuckle. "I want food. Can you still bring me food? Pizza? Can you make me a pizza? I like pizza." God, I'm drunk.

"Yes, Miss Swan, room service is still serving."

"Great!" I holler, like Tony the Tiger in heat, and jump on my bed. "Dude, you rock, thank you. Can you bring me two pizzas? Oh, and how long? If toppings take a long time, then no toppings. I'm cool with no cheese. Does dough take a long time to cook? Wait… Do you just have any old pizzas I can have?" Someone feed me *right* now.

"Miss Swan, room service should take about forty-five minutes. And my apologies, we are unable to serve old pizza."

Boooo. Reminder to sober self: complain to Kristen about horrible choice of hotel.

"Okay, fine. But hurry. I haven't eaten in eight days. I need pizza." More like eight minutes, since I stole the bin of olives sitting on the bar and chowed them down on the elevator ride up.

I think she tells me goodbye, or I just hang up, because I drop the phone and spend the next five minutes jumping on the fluffiest bed ever, until I wear myself out, or slip in my case, and fall onto my back.

"Ahhhh…" I sigh to myself. I throw my hands over my

head and they hang off the bed. "I can get used to this fancy author lifestyle." Laughing to myself, I turn to lie on my stomach and without realizing how far down I am, I roll right off the bed.

Humph!

"*Ouch*," I grunt, rubbing my poor head. "Okay, maybe not so much," I grumble when I hear shuffling outside my door. My ears perk up instantly, and I sit up looking at the clock. "Wow, that was fast." I crawl to my hands and knees and sloppily make my way to a standing position. "So, fine. It definitely pays to be Bailey Swan. Super-fast room service." I stumble to the door, because *no one* waits for pizza, then whip it open. "Man, that was—*Whoa*!" I squeal as I'm pushed back into my room, another body coming with me, and the door shutting instantly.

"*Hey*! What are you doing? My pizza is out there!"

"What? Who... wait, who are you? What are you doing in *my* room?"

I take in the fuzzy male form in front of me. "*Your room?* This is *my* room! And you just got in the way of my pizza!" My hangry side is shining through and I need to get to my pizza. "Sorry, pal, you're in *my* room. Now if you don't mind, you need to leave because I have a pizza coming over and we would like our privacy."

He regards me strangely, but then the banging on the door recaptures his attention.

"No, wait. Don't open that. It's not safe out there."

I look at *him* now strangely. "And why not? Pizza doesn't bite. I do. Now move."

He jumps in front of me, putting his hands up. "Please, just wait. If you open that door they'll attack. I've been running from them for the last twenty minutes. I just spent the last ten hidden in the stairwell."

Now I'm *really* looking at him strangely. "And why? Did you steal something?"

"What? No. They want my picture, autograph, my *babies*. They're insane!"

Seriously, what kind of event does Kristen run here? I continue to stare at him until it begins to make sense. "Oh, wait. I know you. I saw you running down the hallway earlier. From a flock of drooling women."

He nods. "Yes, that was probably me."

"Well, you run like a girl."

His eyes widen, eyebrows up. "*I do?*"

I'm going to also leave out how on point his tight butt looked running in his fancy jeans. I shrug my shoulders. "Yes, now if you'll excuse me, I really need to open that door." I go to sidestep him, but he blocks me.

"I beg of you, please. Just let me hide here for a couple of minutes. I swore this was my room." He looks down at his room key, then up at me. "What room number is this?"

"How the hell should I know?"

"Well, it's your room."

Good point.

"I don't know. Five-eleven I think? Maybe six-eleven. What floor are we on?"

He looks mildly confused. "My room is five-thirteen. I'm actually next door. Our rooms connect. I was trying to get into my room and must have mistakenly tried using my key in yours."

He looks at me.

I look at him.

"Okay, well, good thing it's not a far walk for you. If we just open that door you can literally hop to your room and I can grab my pizza. We both win."

"I, it's just that if we open that door, they're going to attack. Most likely bombard your room. They're probably already eating your pizza. They're hungry. One tried to bite me."

"They tried to *bite* you?"

"Yes, I'm telling you."

Beyond my drunken haze, I do notice the distress on his face. I stare back at the door, trying to make peace with the pizza I'll never get to eat, and I sigh. "Fine."

I turn around and walk toward the bed. I open my arms and like an angel, I float—okay more like belly flop—onto the bed. One bounce and it takes me sliding off the damn side again, and back onto my back.

"Whoa, are you okay?" My temporary roommate runs to my rescue, bending down. A wave of his cologne smacks me in the nostrils and I'm not sure whether to love it or cry. "You smell like apples. Do you have any in your pocket?"

"What? No, sorry. I don't have any food in my pockets. Can I help you up?"

I look at him while he kneels over me, sticking out his hand. His hand looks perfectly manicured compared to my missing nails that I may have chewed off on the flight here.

"Eh, no. I'm cool down here."

"Oh, okay. Well, how about I sit down here with you? Keep you company until the mob disappears. Then I'll leave you be and sneak into my own room."

I shrug. Not that I care.

"So, what's your name? I'm sorry I barged into your room and never told you mine."

"It's Kat—I mean Bailey, the name's Bailey."

"Hello, Bailey, I'm Charlie Bates."

Okay, so you know what happens next. I bust out laughing.

"Bates? As in the motel? I love my *mother*, Bates?"

He shrugs, not expecting *that* reply. "Well, yes. I guess that too. I'm the featured model for the tour. Hence the mob. Did you not recognize me?"

I open one eye as wide as I can. I mean, he *does* have smooth skin. Perfect hair. Chiseled cheekbones my bird would probably beg to peck at. His green eyes stare into mine, waiting for an answer. One I don't offer because I turn and barf on the floor.

"Seriously, I'm sorry. I didn't mean for you to get sick." He apologizes, as I walk out of the bathroom after brushing my teeth.

"It's fine. It's not every day I barf. I have a lead stomach, so it must have been all the bouncing I did earlier." Or the pound of olives. *Yuck.*

Charlie seems to be studying me, making sure I won't barf again. "Are you sure you're okay?" he asks for the billionth time. And for the billionth time I pinch myself, wishing this to be a bad dream. Not that I care that he's a sexy model. I'm immune against all things pretty. But now I have even less in my stomach, and since the pizza is out, I'm going to have to live off the mini bar snacks until morning.

Since my room only has one bed, I've taken up residency at the head of the bed, while Charlie Bates, the model, sits toward the bottom as I take down a bag of ten-dollar M&Ms and he grabs a tube of Pringles.

"Okay, Bates, spill. What is it that you do? Just look pretty for those hungry wolves out there and take pictures?"

He laughs a sound that I strangely enjoy. I shake it off, because I'm immune, and wait for his response.

"No, that's not all I do. I play small league hockey back home. This is just kind of an extra gig for me. It pays well, and the ladies seem to enjoy my look, so when I get offered jobs like this one, I take it."

Hmmm, sounds fishy. "And what does one do on tours like this? Stay in shape by running the whole tour from his fans? I mean, you can't be *that* special."

He chokes on his chip. Covering his mouth to avoid any more chip splatter, he replies, "No, well, I didn't say I was special. I guess with these things, women enjoy the models. The ones on the covers. The covers they escape to."

"And what is it they are escaping from exactly, Bates?"

He looks at me. "Reality."

I think I scare him when I bust out laughing. Like holding my stomach while kicking my legs out, almost karate kicking his Pringles out of his hand, laugh. "*Reality*? Are you kidding me?" More laughing. "Bates, you think your pretty looks help women *escape* reality? Don't you mean deter them further from it? You..." I wave my finger around his frame. "You are the main reason women have such ridiculous expectations. Women search for *you*. Not the average guy, who is, in reality ninety-nine percent of this universe. You give women an image of how their men are supposed to look. Which is *not* real. You aren't giving them an escape, you're giving them false hope!"

His eyebrows crease. His shoulders stand straighter. "I certainly do not. I come here, and I interact with my fans. Express how thankful I am that they enjoy my face on their covers and storybooks. That's not me creating a false reality."

I sit up. And because I'm still semi drunk, I crawl over to him and sit on my feet, poking him in his hard chest. "This." I continue to poke.

Over poke maybe.

Wow, he's like solid.

Poke, poke.

"Okay, I get your point."

Oops.

"All I'm getting at is *this* is not what men really look like." I twirl my finger at his chest. "I bet you have what? A negative fat percentage, right?"

He looks like he's thinking about it. I roll my eyes. "Never mind. How about this…" I take my hand and tug at his perfect thick head of chestnut brown hair. *God, it's like fucking silk.* "Shit, what products do you use?"

He takes my hand, wrapping his large fingers around my tiny wrist, trying to dislodge my grip out of his heavenly locks. "Okay, I get it, can we not pull my hair out?"

"Oh, sorry, but again." One last attempt, I grab at his chin, lifting his face up to expose his contacts. While looking for the outline, which sadly I don't see, I catch him watching me. "What? And what kind of contacts do you wear? They're good ones."

"Bailey, I don't wear contacts."

"Are you sure?" I ask, feeling silly because his eyes, those don't look real. Magical eyes are never real. I pause for a moment, searching his face. His perfect features, his straight white teeth, his nose, which may be a little too big for his face—I also may be making that up to fault him—and then back to his eyes that are still staring at me. Realizing I'm still holding on to his chin, and at some point, he manages to wrap his arm around my waist, I panic and let go. "You... people like you don't exist in real life. And if you did, they don't exist for people like me." *Did I say me?* "I meant! I mean people in life. As a whole. Everyone."

It's obvious I'm now suddenly uncomfortable. I try and back away, but his hand is still on my waist, which I want to ignore, but it's burning a neon sign into my skin that blinks "his touch is kind of amazing."

"Why does someone like me not exist for you? You're beautiful. I'm sure any man would be lucky to have you."

And, bubble popped.

Exactly.

Red flag number one in the rule of broken love. False praises!

Letting out a huge scoff and rolling my eyes, I push his hand away and crawl back up to my side of the bed. "Nice try, Bates. I don't fall for that fluffy bullshit. Save it for the drooling mob outside." I lie back down on my pillow fort and grab for the remaining bag of candy. I have to admit, he almost got me. That sexy, model lure. I kind of get why women go bonkers over these guys. Because they *are* seriously flawless. This guy sitting on my bed, who has crumbled chips all over his lap, is like what girls dream about. What they masturbate at night over. Not me, but the ninety-nine percent of other women. I masturbate to Tito's vodka and X-Files reruns.

Charlie Bates is just another reason why women are so love broken. I wonder what his poor girlfriend thinks when he's out doing these. "So, what does the girlfriend think of your crazed fans? Does she mind all the heavy petting going on?"

"I don't have a girlfriend."

Okay, I embarrassingly choke on an M&M.

"Geez, are you okay?"

"Yes! Yes. Stay where you are. You're not going to use your sneaky model ways on me. You say no girlfriend? I don't believe it. What? Can't be held down? Too much action to stay with one poor woman at a time?"

He looks at me, I think as if I'm kind of a bitch, which I am, but answers anyway. "It's complicated, but no. I want to be with someone who wants to be with me for me. Not what I entail."

I'm sitting there, my mouth open, and a chewed-up M&M falling out of it.

"Did I break you?"

What? Oh. "No. Pfft. No. But I need a better explanation, Bates. That doesn't cut it."

He settles more onto the bed so he's completely facing me. "Well, as you said, I'm a name. My look sells. So does my prominent hockey career. I have a nice nest egg and for some, let's say the reader world, I'm a household name to romance readers. Someone like you may want me just for that reason. May never care to get to know me for me. You might never care that I'm obsessed with the cooking channel or despise movies that have no plots. You just want to look pretty next to me."

Full "O" face.

Open and jaw to the ground.

"Well, am I right?"

"Oh my God, you most certainly are not! I'm far from a *fame chaser*. And I don't... you don't. You do *nothing* for me. Sorry. Not even a little twitch of excitement." *Oh God, why do I sound so unsure of myself?* "Listen, Bates, I get it. You want to be loved for what's on the inside. We all do. I get it. And what's on the outside isn't what a girl needs. Whatever..." I stop talking because for some odd reason, he begins crawling up the bed.

"Dude, what are you doing?"

He makes it way too far into my personal territory, and I'm trying to tell myself that's not his minty breath I smell and feel on my nose.

"I'm just testing out your theory. You say I'm not your type. So I just want to see if you are truly immune." He leans forward as my eyes threaten to fall out of their sockets, they're so wide.

Is he going to seriously kiss me? Holy shit! This hot dude in my room, covered in Pringles crumbs and muscle, is going to kiss me.

God, he smells good.

I hate Pringles.

His eyes are like fucking orbs trying to suck out my soul.

Maybe this wouldn't be such a bad thing.

"I have a feeling that if I kiss you right now, Bailey, you would not only let me, but you would find extreme enjoyment in it."

Aaannnd nope.

Red flag number two. Cockiness, man! No girl likes a cocky guy.

I lift my arms and push at his seriously steel chest, and he goes flying backward. Possibly a little farther than I expected because he summersaults off the end of the bed. As I hear the loud thump, I panic and jump to the end.

"Holy shit, are you okay?" I watch him grip his head. "Seriously, so sorry. I didn't expect you to pull some tumbling act right off. Are you hurt?"

Rubbing at his wounds, he shakes his head and sits up. I try and reach for him, but he doesn't accept my hand. "Okay, *She-Man*, I get it. Immune."

I don't say anything else. He gets up and brushes the crumbs off his pants, when we both hear the knock on the door.

"Room service," the voice calls from the other side of the door.

Charlie walks over and looks through the peep hole.

"So, unless they're lined up alongside the wall, it looks to be clear."

I get up off the bed. I brush off my dignity and try fixing my wild head of hair, then walk over to meet him by the door.

"So hey, sorry about—"

He cuts me off by grabbing my face with both hands and kisses me. Not just a light, thanks for the hospitality kiss, but an all-out rough kiss. I stand frozen, completely caught off guard, until something inside me takes over. My sellout side gives in and I sigh, leaning into his grip. Just as I open my mouth to participate, he pulls away. Releasing my face, he opens the door to the googly-eyed hotel staff.

"Ahh, you must be the pizza. Good thing you came just in time. She is *really* hungry. She was about to maul me."

I'm... I'm... I'm not working properly. I look at him, trying to speak. Maybe yell. Slap him? Offer him some pizza? I have no idea. But he doesn't stick around to find out. He turns to the staff and gives her a wink to die for. Like literally, that damn staff employee practically leans into my pizza plate, as he walks the two feet to his room, uses his key, and disappears inside.

Fuck him.

Fuck broken love.

chapter THREE

Did you know you can be in a five-star hotel and still hear whistling through the hotel walls? Fucking bullshit, right? And why the hell was *he* whistling, anyway? He didn't win anything. I told him I wasn't interested.

Fine, he kissed me. So what.

It's not like I... Like I... *God, I enjoyed it.* But that's not me. I don't do boy toys.

I got up bright and early to take a shower, trying to wipe off the hangover along with the thoughts of my late-night intruder. I need to focus on today. It's a big day for me. It's the day I expose my own self. I think about the past seven months and how I've hidden behind a name. As I said, I don't do any social media, besides what Kristen pushes, so it's not like I've been living this fake life. To anyone out there today it's just a name. And people *love* making assumptions of who's behind the mask. The title. The cover. Some accused me of being a male writer, hiding behind a female name so my book would sell. Some said I was probably some overweight hermit who has never even had a real orgasm before. And then there are those worshippers who expect me to be this perfect household name, in my ironed white dress, preaching about love.

In my story, I write about a girl named Abby. A plain, quiet journalist who writes her very own *Dear Abby* column for her local newspaper. She spends her days reading letter after letter from the devastated women of the world who have fallen for fake love, only to be brokenhearted in the end. They beg for her advice and plead the need to understand the what, how, and why of their failed relationships. She responds to all the letters offering her best advice, knowing none of these women will take it. She knows if that love glitch in society never changes, then *no one* will ever change. So she decides to take it upon herself to teach men a lesson.

Abby decides to go undercover and creates a fake Facebook page posting a fake profile, pretending to be someone she's not. She pretty much catfishes all these guys into falling for her. Through the story you learn about her own issues with her image and love, how she can't find love because of all the stereotypes in the world today. She sets up this fake profile to prove her theory right. Men spend too much time focusing on what's on the outside, and women allow it. Of course, during her venture she meets a guy. And in this guy, she finds love. But he loves the image she creates. She doesn't know how to recreate herself in this fake person. And when she confesses who she really is, he doesn't like her anymore. The one person she opened her heart to, and he breaks it.

But in the end, it's her fault. Because she tried to be something she wasn't. She learns from her mistakes and learns to believe in herself. Because someone out there wants to love her, not a stereotype. In the end love finds her. That typical cliché that if you stop looking for it, it will practically smack you in the face. I just wanted people to stop reading the "how to get someone to love me guide" and be who they really were. I just didn't think it would start such a revolution.

A knock on my door interrupts my thoughts. I finish pulling up my black dress and go to peek out the hole. Kristen is standing outside my door, bouncing up and down.

"Hey," I say, opening the door for her.

"Hey! You almost ready? You have a crazy crowd down there. Hope your signing hand can handle it." She beams.

"Well, I doubt that, but I guess." I'm not feeling the excitement Kristen is.

"Hey, what's wrong? Why don't you look happy? This is going to be great! People are going to love you!"

"Yeah, but what if they don't? What if they take one look at me and call me a fake?"

Kristen's smile fades. "Katie, if anyone thinks that, then they're the wrong ones. You wrote a very powerful book. You wrote a great story and a billion people read it and agreed with you. They took your words and entrusted your advice into their own life. You're a mentor to a lot of women. It doesn't matter what you look like, which may I add is beautiful!"

I laugh sarcastically. "Oh yeah, me and all my plain glory."

Grabbing at my shoulders and leaning in close, she says, "Katie, why are you so negative on yourself? You're a true beauty. I don't know when you'll ever realize that. You stop people mid-step when you walk into a room. You don't have to be dressed like a supermodel to be adequate. You are your own beauty. Now, stop being so hard on yourself. And prepare. You are about to get mauled. I called for security to walk you down."

"You're kidding me."

"Nope. Like I said. You're a loved woman. Now grab your stuff. It's showtime."

There are so many things in life people may never see or experience. But an author signing needs to be on everyone's bucket list. Because this is a mad house. When I was younger, I barely read. I skimmed through high school books, and cliff notes were my best friends. I wasn't one who hung out at the library or had my nose jammed in a book. It just wasn't really my thing. Even now, I can't say I spend much time doing it. If words are involved, it's me telling them or writing them. I didn't write that book to start a career. I wrote it to help make myself maybe feel better about what I wasn't doing right, or because of issues with broken love I may always be single. I just wanted to say I was okay loving myself if no one else did.

But these authors? Ones who write their heart and soul into their stories for readers to suck in and devour? It's kind of crazy amazing. As I walked through the mob of readers, I read T-shirts with names on it. Photos of models, one in particular that I recognized. Quotes, covers, poster-sized faces. They had it all. And the books. They had more books than I've ever seen.

Once Kristen and my entourage of security got to my

table, it was like the entire room became quieter. People seeing the author herself for the first time stepping up to her podium. And when I turned to take in what was coming for me, it was something I couldn't even explain.

So I'll just say surreal. Faces stunned. Smiling. Shit, some were crying. But when the screaming and waving began, I kind of felt weird myself. A little drunk, maybe? But I was completely sober. Maybe I was high and didn't know it.

Just as I'm about to smell my own breath for booze, someone hovers too close behind me.

"Ready to get mauled?" A deep voice tingles inside my eardrums.

I turn and almost brush noses with an all too close Charlie Bates.

"Bates..." I regard him with no care. "Looks like you made it through your night in one piece. You kinda look like shit, though. Up too late *whistling*?" I poke. His laughter seeps into my skin and I want to scratch at it. God, I hate that sound. It's so magically annoying.

"It was hard *not* to whistle while I thought about how my night ended. I had to go back to my room and take a cold shower... Amongst other things, to relieve—"

"Gahhh! I don't want to hear it! Go away, Bates. Don't you have some girls to swoon?" It's like my insults don't even bother him. That smile just gets bigger. Before he can answer, Kristen walks up.

"Oh good, you two have met! Charlie, this is my best friend, Ka—I mean Bailey. Don't bother with the charm, she's immune. But your tables are across from one another, so we'll have to work the lines to accommodate you both. Shouldn't be a problem, and as long as it works today, the remainder of the tour should be fine." She's looking at both of us while we both stare one another down.

"Um, am I missing something?"

"No, I met Bates last night. Kind of a creeper. But don't worry, we'll be fine."

Kristen opens her mouth to respond. Then closes it. Opens. And then closes it again. Charlie just laughs at me, confusing her even more.

"Great, well, I'll be on my side of our fantasyland if you need anything, *Bailey*."

I offer him my most annoying look and turn away.

Kristen claps her hands, taking in a deep breath. "Okay! Well, Charlie, I wanted to let you know I needed some information from you to send your check, but I couldn't find any information for the PR company you're using."

"Don't. Don't worry, just have it all go through me. I'll take care of it," Charlie replies.

Kristen nods. "All righty then! Show's starting! So, both of you have a great signing!"

When Kristen said the show was about to start, I wasn't nearly prepared for what she truly meant. There was no signing 101 class that could have prepared me for what I was about to experience.

When the first reader approached my table, she practically passed out telling me how much she loved my book and asked if she could hug me. *I* practically passed out because I had no idea how to respond.

How are these other authors all cool and collected? I feel dizzy on my feet with nerves, and with each fan, I barely spit out a sentence that makes sense. I'm shocked they're not leaving their books on my table as they leave.

Even as another reader makes their way up, I'm trying to silently practice a constructed sentence in my head.

"Hi. Oh my God, I'm so excited to meet you—"

"I'd love to." *Dammit.* She didn't ask me anything yet, did she?

"I'd love for you to sign my—"

"Happy to meet you too." *Just stop.*

I shake my head a few times, hoping my brain reshuffles.

Let's try this one more time. "I'm sorry. Hi, I'm Kat— Bailey. Bailey, mmkay?" What?! "As in hi, I'm nervous. Don't mind me." Someone needs to put me down. And out of this poor reader's misery.

The reader is looking at me like I have two heads. Shit, I'm royally fucking this one up. "You're nervous?" she asks, shocked.

"Well, I'm sweating at an unhealthy rate, so I'm hoping it's that or I should see someone after this thing."

She laughs, which makes me feel somewhat human again, and I jump in. I wipe my hands on my dress and stick my hand out. "Okay, let's try this again. Hi, I'm Bailey. And I promise I'm normal."

No handshake in return, though. Nope. Fans don't shake hands. They hug. Same with the next and the next. Hours later and my line wasn't even dying down. Like, was this real life? They were just words. And people were repeating lines from my book like a mantra, telling me their own real-life stories of how it helped them.

As one totally hip reader said, it was so fetch.

I've also never hugged so many people in my life.

Annoyingly, every time I went in for the hug, over their shoulder I would make eye contact with Charlie. And it was as if he was ready every time, offering me an eyeful. He would wink at me, pull his shirt up just enough so I could get an eyeful of some abs, brush his palms against his chest. Geez, anything cliché about a hot model, he would do it. And thank God, I didn't fall for any of it.

Yep. Thank God.

Did I also mention it was getting unnaturally hot in the room? I was sweating, and I had a constant flush to me, all due to the heat. *Nothing,* of course, to do with my across the hall neighbor. He wasn't helping by sending someone over every twenty minutes with a postcard of him with no shirt on. No surprise, it was signed Bates Motel. I just rolled my eyes and tossed them into my garbage. By the end of the day I swore I was going to own more of his swag than he was.

When the signing is finally done, I run like hell to my room. I rip my dress off and throw myself into a cold shower. I seriously need to remember to complain to Kristen about turning the damn heat down.

The banging on the door gets me out of the shower sooner than I expected. Annoyed, tired, and in need of much longer alone time, I get out, throwing a towel around me, and whip the door open.

"What?" I bark at the annoying person on the other side, the very *one* I want to avoid. "What do you want, Charlie?" I sound theatrically annoyed, so he hopefully pays more attention to how annoyed I may be and less on my eyes that are checking out his sexy physique and dashing smile. I seriously didn't just use the word dashing, did I?

"I come bearing gifts." His charm makes my stomach feel all funny, which I hate. What's worse is he's holding a box. He doesn't need to tell me what's in it.

I can smell the gooeyness of cheese and dough and... "Is there pepperoni on that?" Dammit, I'm starving.

"And extra anchovies," he says, wiggling his eyebrows.

"What's wrong with you?"

"Nothing. I was making a joke. You know, *Loverboy*? Total eighties classic?"

"Yeah, no."

"What? How've you not seen this? Pizza guy turned gigolo to earn money for college. Women call and the secret is to ask for extra anchovies—"

"Are you insinuating I'm looking for a male lover? And, dude, I am *not* older than you!"

His smile falls super quick. "Shit, no. I wasn't saying that. It's just a movie quote. I was trying to be funny. I—"

I don't wait to let him finish. I slam the door in his face. But not before wanting to secretly suck that cute pout off his face. Maybe squeeze his tight ass I had to stare at all day. Possibly finish off by eating a piece of that pizza that smelled amazing.

"I was just joking!" he calls through the door.

Sadly, I'm not. Goddammit, the ass on him.

"Thank you so much. It was a pleasure meeting you as well—"

"Excuse me."

My current fan and I both turn toward the interruption. I, of course, see an interruption. My *reader* sees dripping sex on a stick. I can't help but roll my eyes as Teresa from Indiana ogles Charlie Bates. WHAT *is* it with this guy? I mean, I already know the answer to that question. No need answering. If those eyes don't suck you in first off, it's going to be that voice, then his abnormal kindness. No need to even go into how great he smells.

"Ladies, I was just walking by and I couldn't help but notice how beautiful you two look. Mind if I get a quick photo?"

"What? No!" "Oh my God, yes!" We both reply at once.

Charlie smiles wide. I turn and gape at Teresa. *Traitor.* Either way, it doesn't stop him from slying his way in between us and squeal when he wraps his arm around my waist pulling me into him, all snuggly against him. I try and pull away, but he squeezes me tight.

Leaning down, he whispers quietly in my ear, "You smell exquisite." And pulls away just as fast. "This is going to be a great picture, don't you agree, Bailey?" He smiles wide just as the flash captures my growing frown.

Bang, bang, bang.

"Mr. Pepperoni here, open up. I have extra if you hurry!"

I take a huge swig.

"It's all warm and gooey, ready to be devoured."

And another one.

"Each bite satisfying your every pizza lover's desires."

AND ANOTHER.

I toss another empty mini liquor bottle on the floor. "Just go away," I whisper to myself. "And take the mental visual of you naked with pizza hanging from your lips with you, dammit."

He's been at it for almost ten minutes. I mean, that pizza probably isn't even that warm anymore. Trying to feed me lies.

"I heard USA is playing all Adam Sandler movies. They go great with cuddling and pizza."

"*La la la la* I hate cuddling." *But do I?* I mean, I could like it…

"Ahh, there she is, the woman of the hour. Come on. Open up. Innocent night of movies and pizza. I was joking about the cuddling part. I mean, unless you—"

I throw my shoe at the door, shutting him right the hell up. I need him to get out of my head.

"You can be big spoon if you wa—"

My other shoe goes flying.

"This pizza is getting cold. You know it's best when the cheese is dripping hot and you risk it overflowing in your mouth."

That's it.

I pick up the phone and dial the extension to the hotel bar.

"Remington's."

"Yes, I need to speak to the blonde in front of you." I have no idea who's at the bar, but I'm going to take a wild guess there's at least one, and she's a Charlie Bates fan.

"Sure thing…"

"Hello?"

"Hey, girlfriend. I have some secret info for you. Charlie Bates is outside room 511. He's looking for a group of girls who want to have some fun. Think you can help him out?"

"Oh, hell yes."

"Great. So hurry. He's only going to be outside the door for about three more minutes."

The line goes dead before I can even finish. I hang up the phone and lie back in my bed, opening another mini bottle.

"Come on, Bailey. I promise, I don't bite. Just the pizza. The amazing thick crust—"

"Charlie Bates!"

"Oh, shit. Come on, let me in!" *Bang, bang, bang.* "Shit, shit—"

Something drops. I guess it's the pizza, along with his pounding footsteps as he takes off down the hall. I can only assume, because that's where the howls of female voices disappear to.

"You wasted a very good pizza last night."

I jump at Charlie's unexpected presence.

"What do you want, Bates?" I ask, pressing the elevator button to go down. I take a peek and he's standing there, looking all sexy with his hands in his pockets, his smile on point. I shake my head because I just referenced him as sexy, which is super cliché, and take another stab at the call button.

"Not a thing, Miss Swan. Just heading down for a day of fun. Thought we'd elevator pool. You know. Save on electricity."

I laugh. By accident. Because that wasn't funny.

"Did I just get a laugh out of you, Miss Swan?" His brows rise, accentuating his eyes.

Stop staring, Katie.

Right.

"No, I choked. That's how I sound when I choke. My gum. I choked on my gum."

"But you're not chewing any gum."

Observant bastard. "Whatever, you win. Congrats. You're a wee bit funny."

His smile, which is the devil, causes a break in my brainwaves, and I find myself smiling back at him. The elevator door opens and he holds it, waving for me to go first. As I step in and proceed to press the button, he stops me.

"Now how rude would I be if I made you drive? Allow me, Miss Swan." He leans over, purposely brushing his arms across mine as he hits the button to the lobby.

"Shall we?"

And I can't help but shake off another smile as the door shuts.

The antics of Charlie Bates went on for days.

From the nightly knocks on the door with pizza, to the "elevator pooling" as he called it. Don't get me started on that devilish smile, the way he laughs, or the whistling. That goddamn whistling.

Each night I covered my head with my pillow, shielding my ears from the magical sounds of his voice and the word pizza. I drank my mini bar clean of all its bottles, and each morning I hated him even more because I felt like hell for mixing darks with clears. But each morning he would be there at that damn elevator all smiles for our share-a-ride down to the lobby. And each time he would talk. And talk. And talk!

This went on for three whole days, until I couldn't take it any longer. And dammit, he loved knowing he was getting to me. He knew every time he turned on that shower, I pictured him touching that perfect cock I'm sure he has and stroking it as he insinuated the first night. And all *I* wanted to do was fucking stroke it! I wanted to do so many things! Ahhh! What was wrong with me? He was evil. That's what conclusion I came to. He was nice, and sweet, and evil.

On day three I opened my door. I just couldn't leave the pizza out there any longer. I'd had a long day and got stuck signing almost two hours after the show because there were so many people! Charlie was right there with me, and since we were both stuck, he had no one else but me to send his postcards to. And I was so damn sick of seeing his postcard chest. I actually started convincing myself that maybe it was time I saw the real thing. Just take a little dip in the fantasy world. I would be fine. I could play in his world and easily pull myself out. I wouldn't get sucked into the bullshit of fake men and fake love. I mean, I didn't even *like* him. How can it get out of hand?

So, I finally opened the door. And there he stood, holding the pizza that smelled like heaven, with his smile matching the beauty of the pizza. And to further sell me, a bottle of vodka. He had officially, semi, kinda, sorta won me over.

And without a word, shockingly, he walked in with that damn smirk on his face. We ate pizza in silence, and I just stared at him while trying to figure out his game. Did we just go at it once we were done? Does he get me super drunk first, so I loosen up? I just couldn't figure him out. I mean, I would have been fine if he just left the pizza. I'm sure he has a long list of blood suckers in the lobby he could spend his time with.

But he stayed. And we ate pizza.

Just as I'm almost through with my fourth piece—don't judge, it was a long day—I finally throw the white flag up and lean back against the bed frame. As I let out a huge breath of air, I notice Charlie staring at me.

"What do you want, Bates?" I ask, acting nonchalant.

"To find my certain kind of someone," he says, quoting a line from *my* book.

"You read my *book*?" I ask, shocked and sitting forward.

"Yeah. I wanted to know what all the hype was about. Why, are you shocked?"

"That you can read, yeah. I thought you were just a pretty face." I fight to hide my laughter.

"Ahh, so you're admitting you think I'm pretty," he pokes, sliding closer up the bed.

I catch his move and lean back against the bed frame again. "Well, sure, you're like a cute little puppy people can't help but wanna pet. But little do they know you're probably lacking obedience, and you're a biter. I bet you pee in the house too." *Where the hell am I going with this?*

He smiles, then more movement. He's getting closer.

"Well, I can only admit to one thing and that is, I do possibly bite."

Oh, fuck. Stay away from me.

He scooches an inch closer.

Please don't come any closer.

Eliminating the final space between us until our thighs are touching, he picks up my plate and moves it to the side. Leaning in, he inhales my scent.

"You aren't my type, so this is doing nothing for me," I whisper, my eyes fighting not to close.

"I know," he says, leaning the rest of the way in and kisses me. His lips, like soft silk, caress my mouth, licking my lower lip as he gently bites down. He lifts his hand, placing it around my neck, wrapping his fingers just below my hairline, and increases the pressure of our kiss.

I kiss him back. Because, who wouldn't? His mouth is perfection. His taste, his lips. "I am not enjoying this at all," I mumble as I press my lips harder onto his.

"I know you're not," he moans, increasing the pace as his tongue meets mine. Each stroke sends me just a little bit more on the worried side, that I seriously *am* enjoying it. Enjoying him. I'm not sure how it happens, but my hands work their way into his hair and they pull him closer, forcing him to practically straddle me. As the moans filter through the room and our kiss starts getting out of hand, he suddenly pulls away. Confused, and halfway in heat, I look at him, waiting for him to suggest we get naked.

"Thank you for having dinner with me. I hope it was everything you ever imagined it would be." Then he completely pulls away, taking that fucking smile with him, and stands. He turns my way, catching my stunned expression. "I'll leave the vodka here. I heard mixing clears and darks is not a good idea. See you tomorrow, Bailey Swan." And then he walks to my door and leaves.

Then I hear the goddamn whistling, followed by the shower.

Fuck those lips.

And fuck his advice.

chapter
FOUR

W e've been on the tour for only a week, and I want to quit and go home. The book tour itself is amazing. I guess I never really put much thought into the impact I'd make when I published my book. The stories that are being told are truly heartwarming. On more than one occasion a reader has put me in tears, and I swear I've become a godparent to a handful of readers' first-born children.

As much as the spotlight is fun, I miss the bar. I miss my simple life. A life where no one paid much attention to me, unless I was underserving them. And sometimes they didn't even catch that. I've also had enough of *him*. Charlie fucking Bates. It's like he's taking everything in my book and trying to reenact it! Every night, he shows up with his damn pizza and feeds me. I don't know why, but each time I let him in. More or less I let the pizza in. We eat practically in silence as I scowl at him and then when we're done, he attacks me. He kisses me until I can't even remember why I don't like him and then he bids me a nice night. As in *leaves*! I swore after last night I wouldn't let him in anymore. After our showers practically turned on at the same time, I made a vow that I seriously did *not* like him and he was no longer allowed in my room. I was going to ask Kristen to move my table far away from his and literally taser anyone who came even close to my table with his postcard.

I'm walking back up to my room, my boots in my hands because my feet feel like they're going to fall off. I sense his presence before he even talks, more so because I can hear the parade of squealing girls behind him.

"Want any different toppings on your pizza tonight?" He leans in, whispering into my ear.

I reach the elevator and turn to him.

"Seriously? Just stop. Go play with your groupies and leave me alone. I'm not sure what sort of game you're playing here, but if you haven't caught on, I'm not interested. I'm not your type, Bates. And you're not mine."

He leans casually against the elevator, staring at me. "And how do you know you're not my type? You have never asked me what my type is."

I turn, rolling my eyes. "Bates, I know your type. The perfect A-lister. The blonde, perfect rack. Plump lips, probably dumb as a rock but doesn't matter because she looks super pretty and is super easy to get in the sack."

He looks like he's pondering my description and it makes me even angrier. "She doesn't sound like she likes pizza, so you're way off."

I grunt and smack my shoes against my side. Where the fuck is this elevator? "Well, I'm sure she would eat it as long as you turned a blind eye long enough for her to purge it back up. God forbid her weight goes over a hundred pounds, minus the weight in her fake titties."

I don't know why this annoys me. Who cares who he likes? It's not my problem. I'm not even in his league, or him in mine. My league is... well... who knows what my league is. It's a no-league, league.

"Bates, just leave me alone. Go satisfy one of your fans. I'm sure they'll play your games." I turn away, praying the elevator door opens so I can escape his staring gaze.

Just before Charlie can counterargue, a squeal rings out from behind us. "*Oh my god*, Charlie Bates, I finally caught you! I *must* get a picture with you."

We both turn to see a cute little blonde chirp from behind us, smiling wide, while pushing her boobs out.

I roll my eyes and turn back to the elevator. *Come on, come on.*

"I'm actually busy, so maybe tomorrow at the signing," Charlie says, keeping his attention on me. "Listen, if you don't want pizza, I can bring up something—"

"Oh, but please! I won't be able to stay for tomorrow's signing, and I really want a picture. Please, I seriously love you. And I'm your biggest fan!"

Charlie looks annoyed, trying to ignore his *biggest* fan.

"You like burgers? I hear they have great burgers in the restaurant—"

"Oh my God, I *love* burgers!" Blondie bounces up and down. "I could go with you if *she* doesn't. She looks tired anyway, and *I'm* all ready to go." She looks at me with sympathetic eyes, because apparently, I look too worn to keep his attention.

I double roll my eyes now, taking in a deep breath. Point proven. This is why people's expectations ruin lives. And also, why I know he is just pulling my chain. People like *him* don't go for tired looking people like me.

Charlie momentarily gives his attention to the girl. "Listen, I said I was kind of busy so—"

"*Oh em gee*, you should totally go, Bates!" I chirp, just like blondie. I turn, fully facing both with a smile as fake as her tan. "You came at just the right time. He has been *begging* me to find him a blond bombshell like yourself. I bet you just love a good time, right? Get your fill of the *oh so dreamy* model."

She nods excitingly.

"Great, well, perfect. Hurry and grab him so everyone else doesn't scoop him up first." Then I scream down the lobby hallway. "Charlie Bates is by the elevator and he's super horny!" I catch the attention of a billion lurkers. As they all come flocking, he turns to me looking sullen. I give him the "I told you so" look just as the elevator door opens. And luckily, before he has a chance for any rebuttal, it closes.

I'm on drink number, who cares? I just want to pretend I never met Charlie Bates. I want to go back to semi-hating relationships and go to bed considering lesbianism. Too many people in this world see a good-looking guy and think that's what they want. That *they* are the perfect guy. No one looks at the average Joe anymore and says "wow, he's my dream man." And *that* is what is wrong with the world today.

Charlie Bates might be a girl's wet dream, but he is also a heart crusher of broken dreams. I mentally tell myself fuck him as I walk past our connecting room doors and bring the bottle to my lips. Just as I pass, the connecting door pops open, causing me to drop the vodka. I scream like a banshee when suddenly Charlie steps into my room.

"What the fuck, Bates?" I gape at him in horror. "Dude, how the hell did you get that door open?"

"I opened it last night when I left. I felt the rejection getting stronger, so I had to pull a wild card."

I stare at him in complete disbelief. "What rejection? You mean the fact that we have nothing in common or that I am totally *not*—"

He's on me instantly. He picks me up, slamming his mouth to mine. Carrying me over to the bed, he crawls us both up the mattress and lays me down, never taking his lips off mine.

"Bates, what are you doing?" I ask between nips.

"Showing you just how much I'm not your type." He rips his mouth away from mine and attacks my neck. His teeth scrape the flesh, trailing kisses feverishly and marking my skin, until stopping just above my breastbone. God, his lips feel like silk gliding all over my skin. My body temperature has spiked tremendously and my hands go animalistic, claiming his hair.

"Well, you're doing a great job of it. You're going to be disappointed, you know," I moan as he pulls my tank top down, pressing his mouth to my bare flesh. Sucking my nipple into his mouth, my back arches, my hands putting pressure on the back of his head.

"I bet I won't," he hums, biting down.

"*Oh God*, you will. These are simple Cs, you know. They

don't grow or anything," I say, wrapping my fingers tighter into his hair.

"Good, I think they're perfect. And I would be concerned if you had growing breasts." He licks and moves to my other boob.

I close my eyes, trying to enjoy this. I need this. I need a good release, and I know Mr. Walking Orgasm himself can easily give it to me.

Working out my left tit, he releases it, traveling down my stomach. I instantly panic, grabbing his head again. "Seriously, no abs there, pal. Head back now."

He swats my hands away, and with his tongue, I feel the warmth of his mouth all the way down my stomach, past my navel, and to the lining of my shorts.

"You're soft and smooth, more for me to squeeze and slam into if you let me. Your skin smells like vanilla and innocence. And I want nothing more than to suck, and pinch, and devour it."

Well, fuck me. I close my eyes tightly as he hooks his fingers around my shorts and begins pulling them down. My inner battle to let him go farther down or to lift my feet and catapult him off me is going bonkers. He is going to not want you. *Who cares!* You are not his usual conquest. *Let him get the job done.* "Seriously, this is a bad ideaaaa…" I choke on my last word as his tongue strikes my center. Taking no mercy on me, he laps at my wetness, using his free hand to open my sex and suck on me. His tongue jabs in and out while his finger, his… "Oh God, maybe this *was* a good idea." I throw my head back, moaning as his finger dips deep inside.

"God, you taste like heaven," he hums, licking and suckling while he works himself in and out of me. Working in a second finger, he thrusts his hand inside so deep I can feel his knuckles at my opening. "Fuck…" he grunts as his hand works faster, his tongue becoming more aggressive. The sensation is unexplainable. My eyes aren't just closed; they're rolled in the back of my head. I'm pretty sure I've bitten through my tongue and when I release Charlie's hair, I'm going to have chunks of it in my nails. "Oh God, Bates, yes, oh God, I'm going to… I'm going, I'm…" Going to explode. And that is exactly what I do. I clench tightly around his fingers, wrapping my legs around his waist, while I go through an out of body experience.

Yeah. That good.

I haven't even fully come down yet, before Charlie's pulling back from me and abruptly standing. Pulling his shirt over his head, he tosses it to the floor. Seeing his chest for real is like a kid in a candy store. Cliché comparison, I know. But seriously, all I want to do right now is lick the shit out of his chest. Grabbing for his zipper, he thrusts it down and climbs out of his pants and briefs.

"Jesus Christ, even your dick is perfect," I hum, hoping that was said in my head and not out loud. His simple laugh proves otherwise, and all I want to do is cover my face. I do just that when the sound of foil tearing causes me to peek. Yep, the condom is in view. God, the way he slides that thing over his gorgeous cock, I may embarrassingly lick my lips. *What am I doing?* He is like the highest cut of filet, and I'm like leftover meatloaf. I begin to tense, thinking maybe this was a bad idea.

"Get out of your fucking head, Swan. This is happening. And it's happening because we are both into each other. Not because you're better than me. Even though you are. I still want you and I hope you still want me."

He thinks *I'm* better than him? "You're insane. You're going to regret this," I say, trying not to blush as he climbs on top of me, pushing my knees apart and working his way just where he wants to be.

"Trust me. I would never regret anything that is with you, Bailey Swan," he says, dipping down and taking my lips against his. He kisses me with intent. As if this is the only place he wants to be. And goddammit, I feel it. That, in this moment, this is the only place *I* ever want to be. Under this man while he ravishes me. *Oh God, I'm being ravished!* My heart does a little leap, and then stops beating altogether because it freaks itself out.

"Any more arguments out of you, Bailey Swan, before I show you just how perfect we can be together?"

Nothing but honesty shines in his beautiful green eyes. For some odd reason, I trust him. I shake my head, a small smile breaching my face.

"Thank God. Now be prepared to be convinced." He smiles and thrusts into me.

I'll admit I haven't had sex in a little bit. Okay, like over a year. But it's like riding a bike. You just never forget. The way his silky cock slides inside, the feeling of being filled comes right back. The sensations of friction consuming. My eyes close, but his hand around the side of my neck causes them to reopen.

"Eyes open, Bailey. I want to watch those beautiful eyes as they gloss over in the realization we should have been doing this days ago." He bends down and presses a kiss to my lips as he pulls out and slides back in. "Then I'm going to require you to beg for forgiveness on what you've been missing out on all week long—"

I go to smack him, but he pulls out and this time, with more aggression, slams into me. My hand drops and my head falls back, a throaty moan flowing past my lips. God, he feels so good. Each thrust, each kiss, the continuous soft grunts escaping up his throat. He handles my body as if he already has me memorized. Every piece of my skin tingles from his touch. His hand roams down my neck, to my breasts, my hips, and finally begins squeezing my ass.

"Fuck, this feels good," I confess, slowly working my hips to meet his. My hands are locked in his hair once again, a place I have quickly learned to love. I bring his mouth down onto mine and kiss him with the feverish lust that's blasting through me. Our tongues collide as we fight for closeness, his hips starting to move at a quicker pace, his thrusts less controlled and more erratic.

"I told you this was going to be a good idea," he grunts into my mouth, lifting his hips and diving deep inside. My head drops back against the pillow, allowing him access to feast on my neck. His lips, wet and smooth against my hot skin. "God, Bailey. So fucking tight." He nips at my skin, his hand grabbing at my breast and squeezing. Each touch and sensation push me closer to the edge. I won't be able to hang on much longer before I go flying.

"I'm not going to last much longer," I moan, moving my hands from his wild mane and bringing them to his tight ass. He groans immediately and flips us, putting himself on his back, while I find myself sitting up and riding him. The deepness he reaches is fucking amazing. I sway back and forth, riding his cock, my eyes unable to stay open. His rough grip is so tight on my hips, I know I'm going to have bruises. With his hands so close to my center he takes his thumb and begins rubbing at my clit, and I know I can't hold on any longer. "Oh God, Bates, I'm gonna—"

He flips us again.

"You gotta hold on, Bailey. I'm not even close to being done with you." He offers me his wicked smile and pulls out. The sexual frustration is clear across my face because my orgasm is at the tip of my fucking vagina and it wants out. He takes my body and flips me onto my stomach, lifting my hips up so I kneel on my hands and knees.

"I knew you'd look so beautiful like this," he says, smoothing his fingers along the crease of my butt. "Your pale skin, smooth to the touch, sweet to the taste." He bends down, placing his lips just above my tailbone and both hands wrap around my ass cheeks. Removing his right hand, he brings it to my neck, brushing my hair aside. "I'm gonna need you to hang on, baby. I'm not sure I can go slow anymore with you like this." His cock finds my entrance and with how slick I am, he eagerly slides right in. We moan in unison, the awareness of how good it feels. Being so deep, he begins to move in and out, a thin layer of sweat building between us.

I don't remember sex ever being this good, and thank God, I gave in. My body clenches around him. He can feel me sucking him up because he picks up the pace, his thrusts becoming brutal. In and out he slams into me, his balls slapping against the back of my clit. He unexpectedly grabs for my hair, wrapping it around his fist. With a gentle tug, he pulls my head back far enough so his lips can reach mine.

And that's when I explode.

I moan furiously into his mouth as I squeeze around his dick and come, my orgasm practically knocking the wind out of me. As I begin to come down, he releases my mouth and his fingers dig into my hips. "Fuck. God, fuck, fuck…" He repeats once, twice, and on the third pound inside me, he lets go.

Falling on top of me, we both fight to process what the fuck just happened, along with trying to catch our breath.

"Holy shit, you're like a fucking goddess. Jesus," Charlie states, out of breath as he begins spreading kiss after kiss to the back of my shoulder.

Feeling like I just released a century's worth of built up aggression, I inhale a huge breath of air. "I think I may sleep for a week after that," I reply and close my eyes, ready to get that sleep going, but Charlie is up and once again flipping me. I'm on my back, and before I can react or discuss the effects of whiplash from all the damn flipping, he's grabbing at my ankles and pulling me down the mattress. Dropping to his knees, he spreads my legs.

"I'm nowhere near done with you, Bailey Swan. Sleep is a long time away." And he wraps his mouth around my pulsing lips and goes to town.

chapter FIVE

ang. Bang. Bang.
     "Katie, are you in there? Seriously! This isn't funny."

Bang. Bang. Bang.

"I swear if you left without even giving me notice, I'm going to kick your ass."

"Someone needs to tell that woman she has the wrong room." A deep voice sounds in my ear as warm hands curl around my waist, bringing me back into something hard.

Hard...

Charlie Bates, hard.

I stifle a soft purr and find myself snuggling further into his hold. He's still in my room. And damn, I feel like I've slept for days. Maybe this *was* a good idea.

"Seriously, Katie, I know you're in there. I called the front desk and you haven't checked out! It's already a quarter past eleven and the signing's already started and I have a mob waiting for you. Don't do this to me."

A quarter past eleven? Huh?

I open my eyes, and when the bright red numbers come into view—

"*Shit!*" I swear, throwing my head back, accidentally head-butting Charlie in the face. "Dude! Shit! We're late! We overslept. Get *up!*" I jump out of bed and realize I'm naked. "Shit!" I turn, bending forward and trying to cover myself.

"I think I saw all your secret hiding places last night. No need to hide from me now."

"Ugh," I grunt, realizing he's right, and go in search of my underwear. Finding a pair under the bed, I hop on one foot to the next, trying to get them on. "Seriously, Bates, get up! Kristen is going to kill us."

He finally hops out of bed, his fucking morning wood about to poke his *own* eye out, and leisurely goes in search of his own clothes.

"Katie, please!"

Shit, stop calling me Katie!

"Kristen! It's Bailey! I'm up! So sorry! I'll be down in ten minutes!"

Charlie comes up behind me, wrapping his hand around my lower waist and pressing his lips to the back of my neck. I stop for a second and lean into his hold, until I realize what the fuck I'm doing and push him away.

"Seriously, Bates, get dressed and out of here."

His laughter's getting on my nerves. "Wow, I never expected you as a love 'em and leave 'em kind of girl. I'm wounded."

I want to turn around and punch him, but the knocking on the door interrupts that.

"Dude, let me in. I'll help you get ready faster." Kristen bangs again on the door.

Shit! She cannot see Charlie in my room.

"Dude, you gotta go. Seriously. Back where you came from, buddie." I bend down, grabbing his shirt and tossing it at him. Grabbing his shoulders, I push him toward the connecting door.

"Katie, seriously, let me in!"

"Who's Katie?"

"I have no idea, now shoo, get out—"

Charlie quickly turns, catching me off balance. Dropping his shirt, he lifts me up, pivoting and pressing my back against the wall. Slamming his mouth on mine, he kisses me like a fucking champ. His tongue dives into my mouth. I instantly moan, wrapping my fingers up and into his hair.

"KATIE!"

And then I pull really tightly.

"*Shit!* That hurts."

"Good, put me down and get out!" Finally, he does what I ask. I pick his shirt up and toss it into his room. Just before I close the door, I say, "You were great, but this never happened." And I slam it in his face.

Fuck me.

Fuck awesome sex.

My body might feel like jello after my all-night workout, but my mind is tense and in fucking knots. What the hell did I do? I mean, I know what I *did*, but why him? Why did I let some hot model get in my bed and in my head? I could have worked out my aggression on the damn battery-operated toy I brought. Or a normal Joe hanging out at the bar. Why *him*?

I shuffle the laminated postcards for the ninth time, trying to distract myself from witnessing the catastrophe happening across the room. The signing is in full swing and every time I glance his way I catch him smiling at a girl, offering her that stupid quirky smile he gives me. And every time he catches me looking, he gives me that damn wink. I'm seconds away from punching that wink off his face. I'm just mad at myself for letting him sucker me. It's like I became just another one of those foolish fans who swoon over the sexy perfection of Charlie Bates. And fuck me, he *is* sexy. Everything about him is. His voice, his hair, his smile, his gorgeous cock! Ugh!!! And I fell for it. I'm sure he's had his publicist change his room already so he doesn't have to have any awkward run-ins with me and can move on to another sucker.

I take a break from my fans and excuse myself. I need a time-out. I head to the bathroom to splash some water on my face to relax, wishing I was pouring some vodka down my throat instead. "It's fine. Everyone makes mistakes—"

"Who you talking to?"

I twist to my right to see Charlie walking into the women's bathroom. "Dude, get out of here. Last I checked you don't have a vagina."

He doesn't stop, though. He comes at me, pressing my back against the sink.

"I hope not, but you do, and I can't stop thinking about it." Both hands wrap around my face and he kisses me. He doesn't ask for an invitation, he just takes, his mouth devouring mine.

A strange spark in my chest rattles me and I don't like it. I push him off me, his eyes lighting up with mischief. "Seriously, Bates. That was a one-time thing. You know it and I know it. We are complete opposites."

"And opposites attract." He smiles, coming at me again.

I dodge his mouth and move out from his grip.

"I'm being serious. Don't feel like you owe me anything 'cause we, uh, well, whatever we did last night."

"You mean sex? Hot, passionate, nail biting, sweating, name screaming—"

"Oh God, I get it, yes! But we're done. I don't even like you."

His smile widens, and it only pisses me off more.

"Really? Because last night I think you told me you loved me."

I freeze, nervous I may have said something by mistake in the heat of the moment.

"You told me how much you loved my tongue, the way it swirled around your pulsing clit—"

I punch him.

I clearly need him to stop talking. So, I punch him. I mean, not hard 'cause I'm a wimp, but enough to catch him off guard. I think I stunned us both, but before either one of us can react, I take off.

Fuck these weird feelings.

Fuck Charlie Bates' tongue.

chapter
SIX

Charlie fucking Bates does not listen.

At all.

He didn't take a hint that I wasn't into him, or my threatening assault, because like clockwork, he comes to my door with that damn pizza. And, like the other nights, I don't answer. But unlike me, Charlie fucking Bates has sex appeal and somehow gets the maid to open our connecting door.

And he doesn't care I'm lying in bed, or that I'm staring at him about to punch him for a second time. He simply tosses the pizza on the floor and starts taking off his shirt! My mouth is hanging open, shocked at the way he thinks he can just come in here and get what he wants, is appalling to me! Even when he crawls up my bed and starts spreading kisses up my legs, tugging me out of my pajama shorts, you know what

I do? I LET HIM!

I hate Charlie Bates.

I hate that, for another night, I allow him to take me to a whole other level of orgasm. I allow him to toss me against the wall and fuck me like I've never been fucked before, until he has me screaming his name. He takes me in the shower while using the shower head to clean me off, and then *get* me off, before fucking me until his name is pure whispers on my hoarse throat. And when he's done drying me, he lays me on the bed and fucking talks to me! He talks to me and tells me about himself. Personal stuff I want to scratch out of my memory because he's making himself less the model and more a real person with real views and aspirations and making me realize just how much I misjudged him.

He just wouldn't stop.

But strangely, I also wasn't stopping him.

"That's my mom. My sisters and I surprised her for her sixtieth birthday. As you can see, that's where I get my dashing smile from." He offers me a sample, showing his perfect set of teeth.

I decide not to mention he has oregano in his front tooth because, let's be honest, I need a reason to fault him and I'm starting to struggle to find one. We're sitting on my bed facing one another Indian style, with an open box of pizza separating us. He's been swiping for the past thirty minutes, giving me a photo breakdown of each picture on his phone. "This is Ellie, my dog. I'll have to be honest right off the bat, she's my one true love. So, any girl"—he wiggles his brows at me—"would have to settle for being number two."

I take another huge bite of gooey goodness. "You have a weird fetish and plan on marrying a dog. Got it."

He reaches over and nudges me, causing me to let out a laugh. Embarrassingly, I spit out a piece of pizza in the process.

"Oops," I say wiping at my jeans.

"Here, let me get that." With his thumb, he gently wipes the smeared pizza sauce off my chin. His movement is slow. He doesn't need to take this long. Our eyes catch. "You shouldn't waste pizza like that. It's a written rule." His thumb brushes along my bottom lip. I've gone mute, no sly comeback ready to fall from my mouth. His finger is slow and calculated as it slides with ease across my lip, smearing the excess sauce. I'm frozen in place, completely unsure of what to do. My heartrate is picking up. His touch is lethal, and even more so are his searing eyes as they calculate what I'm thinking. What *am* I thinking? That pizza sauce has never been such a turn on.

"There." He pulls his finger away from my mouth. Hopefully not because I looked like I was about to chomp it off. "Simple lick of the lips and nothing's gone to waste."

I fight. And I fight. I tell myself not to do it. But it's impossible. I do it.

I lick my lips.

And it is the hottest lick of pizza sauce I have ever tasted.

"Jesus, I, uh, I'll be right back. I need to use the bathroom real quick."

Charlie is up and doing a poor job of hiding the bulge in his pants. Almost falling off the bed trying to throw his legs down, he stumbles to the bathroom, shutting the door and instantly runs the faucet.

When he finally comes back looking less strained, he suckers me into talking about myself. I tell him about the bar, about the book, and about Gerdie, my bird. He tells me Ellie and Gerdie would get along great if they ever met and then he tells me how he got into cover modeling on a whim.

The more this went on, the more I found myself letting him in. And I wasn't sure if I loved it or hated it. Each night, the small talk got longer. Deeper. He was sharing story after story, whereas I found myself doing the same. It was as if we were becoming something more than just what we were. And what the hell were we? I just didn't want to fool myself. Become that statistic I've spent half my life fighting against. Charlie Bates was perfect. I was just, well, me.

I knew we'd never work outside our little hotel room bubble. And that was just a fact. I don't even know why I bother even thinking about that. It's not like we've spoken a single word about us, or what happens in two days when the signing is over and we go our separate ways. And maybe it's better that way.

Maybe I'm just trying to mask the real issue here, which is that I've fallen for someone like Charlie. But *have* I fallen for him? He's hot, and damn does he know what to do with his hands, his tongue, and his golden dick, but still. That's sexual. It's probably just me latching on to something I have never really had before.

But with Charlie it's not only sex, it's also friendship. He's like an endless pit of conversation. He doesn't just get up and leave once we're done. He stays, and I can't believe I'm using the word, but cuddles! He continues to tell me stories about his friends, his work, and his family. His likes and dislikes. And there I am right next to him sharing the same stuff. It's like we know each other on a whole deeper level.

And I don't know whether that scares me, excites me, or pisses me off. Because in two days, I go home. And then what? Am I that thick-skinned girl who came here saying I could just take a dip on the wild side and walk away unfazed?

I don't think I can.

And that's why I need to cut ties and leave.

We're finishing up our last night on the tour. Our final author dinner is tonight, and then once we wrap up our promo interviews in the morning, we are free to go. I've tried to avoid Charlie all day because I just want to make it easier on myself when we go our separate ways. I know he's catching on because his smile isn't fully reaching his eyes. The first postcard that came my way, said, "*What's wrong, Swan?*" When I tossed that in the garbage, the next one came. "*Do you want me to turn that frown upside down tonight?*" Another one tossed.

The next one was a drawing of a stick figure—two stick figures may I add—and it looked like they were doing the spider on a swing set. Okay, fine, he got me there. I smiled and turned to him, giving him the "*really?*" look. His return smile, of course, was infectious, and I settled to just let it go. Let us have our last night.

We've been at dinner for over two hours now, which finally seems to be wrapping up. Charlie chose to sit exactly across from me, I'm sure to mess with me the whole time. Kristen is next to me, which doesn't help since she keeps catching his googly eyes at me.

"Is there something going on between you and Charlie Bates?" She leans in, whispering.

I give her my best '*pfft*' face. "Ew. No, why? Like I'm even his type."

She looks at me, but I refuse to look back. "Well, for starters he keeps staring at you like you're tonight's dessert."

I lift my head, making the mistake of looking at Charlie, and of course he winks at me and offers up that damn fucking smile. Turning away, I lift my hand, catching the waitress for another drink. "First off. I have no idea what's wrong with that guy. Maybe he has Tourette's. Facial twitching. Probably from all that fake smiling he does all day."

Kristen doesn't seem to accept my answer, continuing, "It's just… kinda strange how you both were missing the other day and not to mention you two during the signing. Are you sure there's not something you want to tell me?"

I take a sip of my current drink, looking anywhere but in front of me and next to me. Too bad I look to the other side, which is some knock-out blonde pulling her shirt down, trying to get Charlie's attention.

I sigh.

Then groan.

Then slam the rest of my drink.

I can't take much more of Kristen's interrogation, Charlie's googly eyes, or the thunder cat next to me. I get up, startling the girl next to me. I turn to Kristen. "Sorry, I'm just really tired and I need to pack. I'll catch you tomorrow before my interviews to say goodbye." I lean in and give my longtime friend a hug, who's now also confused by my abrupt exit, and before Charlie can *nonchalantly* try and stop me, I take off.

I hit the elevator button. "Hurry, hurry, hurry…" It dings and I jump in, jabbing my floor number. Just as the door shuts, a large set of hands stops the door and Charlie jumps in.

"Oh, how nice, you waited for me. All those sexual passes you were making at me during dinner, I thought you would never get up and leave. Your room or mine tonight?"

I look at Charlie, not feeling his laid-back sense of humor. I'm not even in the mood to pretend I'm okay with our situation anymore. Sometimes there's that elephant in the room and it just gets so big, you have to acknowledge it or leave. Since I'm a wimp, I'm choosing to leave.

"Sorry, Bates, I'm really tired. You're gonna have to be a big boy and sleep in your own room tonight." The elevator dings and I get out, leaving him behind.

He follows closely behind. We make it to my door, and I insert my key as he bends forward, his breath hitting my cheek. "Can I come in now or shall I enter through my secret passageway?"

I open my door and walk in. I don't hold the door. "Good night, Bates." And it shuts. I squeeze my eyes closed, wishing he were more of the jerk I originally pinned him to be. Wasn't so kind and easygoing, making this harder for me to cut ties.

I make it past the television stand before the connecting door opens. I turn to tell him to beat it, but he's on me, lifting me up and carrying me to the bed.

"Get out of your head, Bailey Swan." He kisses my lips quick, then drops me.

I bounce on the bed, and before I have a chance to start yelling he pounces. His lips cover mine, stopping any sort of hissy fit I'm about to have. His kiss is rough. Almost bruising. As if he's getting angry with me. I get angry wanting to know what the hell he could be angry with *me* about. I bring my hands into his hair and pull, knowing I'm hurting him, but he doesn't even stop me. He lifts my shirt and tears his mouth off mine and brings it around my breast. One clamp, and he bites my fucking nipple!

"*Ouch!*" I wail, pulling at his hair to release me. "What the fuck, Bates!"

"Yeah, what the fuck, *Swan*? Why are you suddenly shutting down on me? I can see it. You hardly looked my way at dinner. I saved you a seat and you sat on the opposite side!"

"Because it would've been obvious! Plus, I wouldn't want any of your groupies to know. It might ruin your image to think you were with someone."

His eyebrows shoot up, that playful smile back on his face "Oh, I'm *with* someone?"

Shit, how did that come out of my mouth? "Oh, you know what I mean. Being caught with someone like me. *I* might ruin your image."

His eyes now look wounded. "Why do you do that? Why do you always talk so down about yourself? You're fucking beautiful, Bailey. You're perfect. Why don't you see that?"

Because I'm nothing next to him. I've never been anything but just plain ole me. And us together would always make me a laughing stock. I would be the whispered gossip. The joke who caught the eyes of the beautiful Charlie Bates.

"Stop. Just stop, okay? Get out of your head." He bends down, and this time his lips are gentler. I allow him to take mine and suckle them. Our tongues meet and we embrace in something that's more than just a kiss. It's unspoken words. Maybe he's telling me it's okay. Maybe this is his way of also saying goodbye. I don't regret anything that's happened between us, despite all my reservations. But my heart is going to heave the wrath of this very bad decision. And I can already feel it.

I wrap my arms around his neck and increase the pressure of our kiss. I lift my pelvis, connecting with his already hard cock, and we both moan. The silent moment is broken and we both lose it. Our control breaks and it's both of our hands ripping at one another, trying to free ourselves of our clothes. The need for skin on skin contact is unbearable, and the second we're both free, he positions himself between my legs and pushes in.

A careless moment lost on both of us, but we don't stop. This is not slow and sexual. It's primal. We fuck and we fuck. Pulling, biting, words of passion, and lust filling the air. We take everything we can from one another until the sun breaks through the blinds and our bodies can take no more.

We don't speak when the alarm goes off, or when he sneaks back into his room to shower. Nor do I say a word when I throw my things into my suitcase and leave without saying goodbye.

I know Kristen's going to be ticked with me for ditching out on the interviews, but I'm sure I can do them through email. I check out over the phone on the way to the airport and offer to pay the shipping for half the shit I left in the room so I could jump ship. I bitch at the cab driver for his air freshener that makes my eyes water and blame the awful steak from last night on why my chest fucking hurts. I knew I shouldn't have done this tour. I know nothing about love and romance and all that sappy shit. I just know why it's bad. And why women should stop falling for it. I'm mad at myself for feeling vulnerable and letting Charlie see a side of me I've never really shown anyone. A side I never knew worked. I'm mad at myself for being a coward and leaving like I did. I could have at least said goodbye. He never promised me anything, but he also didn't lead me to believe I was just a hookup either.

To be honest, I don't know what I was. Maybe just a fool. I trudge with my suitcase through the airport, sucking in deep breaths because for some reason I feel like I'm about to cry and I know if I start, I don't think I'll be able to stop. "It's because I feel so bad I left Kristen like that," I say out loud. Pulling out my ticket, I bend down to search for my license.

"Katie Beller!"

I hear my name being yelled behind me.

"Katie Beller!"

Again, there it is. I stand and turn, surprised to see Charlie running through the airport. He makes it up to me and stops, trying to catch his breath. "Katie Beller," he says as he sticks out his hand.

"How... how did you know my name?"

"Kristen sold you out. Katie, my name is Chase Green. My *real* name. Green like the color, Chase like what I just had to do to catch you." He grabs for my hand and shakes it for the both of us since I've gone into shock.

"Katie Beller, I want to get to know you. All of you. I've gotten to spend an amazing two weeks with Bailey Swan, and now I want Katie. The real Katie. I might not be your normal type, and fuck, maybe you're not mine. But you're something I want more of. Not just the way you bite and scream my name."

I swat at him, turning a deep shade of red. We obviously have a crowd and at his words people gasp and awe.

"Jesus, Bates, what are you doing?"

"It's Green, actually. But I would like for you to call me Chase. Because that's who I really am. And I would like to call you Katie. Can I call you Katie?"

My fucking lips keep twitching, and that crying thing I was talking about earlier is seriously going to happen. I can't speak, so I slowly nod.

"Great. Great," he says, looking relieved. He hands me a piece of paper and it looks like a goddamn "in case of emergency" contact list.

"This is every single way you can get ahold of me. I know you have reservations about us. And I get it. But I want a chance. I won't push you. I get it. But God, do I want you. Let me in. Let me get to know you and show you that what we started can be something pretty fucking amazing."

I swear, if anyone's taking photos and catches me crying I'll kill them. I swipe the tears running down my cheek, the smile slowly making its way across my face. I look at Chase Green, and I see something beautiful in him. Trust.

I take a deep breath. "Okay, Chase Green, I'll get to know you."

Chase's face lights up and he goes in for the kill, offering me his perfect, beautiful lips. The crowd around us erupts into cheers and clapping.

"Excuse me, sir, but you're holding up the line. Buy a ticket or step off to the side." The security guard breaks our connection, and we pull apart.

Staring at one another, Chase steps back and puts his hands in his pockets, all of a sudden looking nervous. "Well, it was a pleasure meeting you, Katie Beller. I look forward to your call."

I smile back, feeling just as nervous. "And you as well, Chase Green, like the color. I guess I'll be giving you a call sometime."

His mischievous smile returns. "FaceTime works too. So I can see what you're doing with your hands."

Go figure. Never without his wit and charm.

"Goodbye, Chase Green."

"Till that call, Katie Beller."

chapter
SEVEN

Coming home and going back to my simple life turned out to be not so simple.

When you decide to exploit yourself, it seems social media takes that little bit of your life and turns it into widespread media footage. People who didn't know who Bailey Swan was before, knew her now. And they also had a face to the name.

When I finally made it home, my answering machine was full. I know, who the hell still has an answering machine? Well, I do. I like things simple. I'm a simple girl. I came home to thirty-two messages. Some from friends I haven't spoken to in some time, some family, a few cousins, a random ex-boy-friend, and then a shit-ton from work. They all pretty much had the same message. "Holy shit." My family all gushed over how proud they were of me. My grandmother cried for almost five minutes. It could have gone longer, but I had to abort the remainder of it.

I had friends from all eras of my life, telling me they saw me on so and so, and how awesome. They never thought I had the talent to write a book. I guess that's also why most of them are no longer my friends. The ex-boyfriend was Jeremy. He went on and on about how his girlfriend, which, later in the message he tried to retract saying she was just a friend, showed him my photo on Facebook. Had the nerve to ask if when I wrote any sex scenes I was remembering him. He told me how great I looked and that we should get together. I also threw up in my mouth, then deleted the message.

The ones I did kind of feel bad about were from the crew at the bar. Dex, who I've known for the whole seven years simply left me a message saying, "Heard you write porn." And hung up. Typical Dex just to get to the point. We got to the point the first couple months we worked together and realized the point *being* was that we really didn't click well outside of the bedroom. So, we decided to just remain friends. Not that there was any regret. Dex was smoking hot. The typical tall, buff, tattooed guy, who ran with his biker posse half the week, ran the bar the other. He had dark eyes to match his dark hair and he was a walking mystery. But that's why he got a lot of tail. Including me. Too bad I figured him out right away. Ever since our test run, he's always been protective over me. Watches over me at the bar when fights begin to brew, when drunk idiots try and get too touchy or just when he knows I need a time-out even when I, myself, don't. He always has my back. But again, that's Dex.

Moving past all the random bar patrons, which I have

no idea how they got my number, asking me out, was Randy. Randy, whose father wanted more than anything to have a boy, named his daughter the name *he* wanted no matter what sex popped out of his wife's vagina, is a knockout. She's all blond and boobs, making everyone who walks through the bar's doors look bad. She started just a year after I did and I couldn't have been more thankful for her as a friend.

Thinking about work reminds me of all the reservations I have about returning back. I think about all the explaining I'm going to have to do and possibly some apologizing. But I'm still unsure if I actually owe anyone one. I do feel like a jerk keeping this part of my life a big secret. But I just didn't want to feel the wrath of the judgement. I didn't plan for it to go this well. I actually planned for it to fail. And then no one would ever know about my explosive attempt at becoming someone I clearly was not. But then, when it exploded in a good way, it all happened so fast I didn't even know how to bring it up. People would here and there talk about the book and the infamous Bailey Swan. I wanted to hear what they had to say without changing their opinions knowing I was right in front of them, so I fed them booze and got them to talk. And damn was it entertaining.

Betty Meyer, an older single woman who works at the tattoo shop a few blocks down, got wind of the book from her sister who was getting her hair done and her stylist was talking about it. Told her she swore by the book. The author was a love guru. Told it how it really was. That it was the next "*he's not that into you*" kinda read. So, she picked it up, and when she was done, she literally kicked out her boyfriend of two years and told him until he learns to appreciate her for her, and not all the stuff she is forced day in and day out to prove her love for him, then they were done! Good ole Betty Meyer no longer does the dishes, takes out the trash, or feeds the dogs. And her man now cooks half the week! I was shocked!

Steph and Dee, twins and weekend regulars, came in telling us they both read it, well out loud to one another, and they were on a sex sabbatical. They weren't allowing any more duds into their beds until they found the real deal. No more fake lines to get them naked. I was honored they took my words so far that they were choosing to actually be better people. By the end of the night I caught an eyeful as some dude had his hand fully up Dee's skirt, but in the end, she stuck to her guns. She kept her clothes on.

Then there were people like Chrissy Baker or Stacey Wright. They just couldn't be happy for anyone. They took the book and murdered it with their opinions. Said they guarantee some overweight troll wrote it while eating Twinkies in her trailer, and has probably never felt the touch of an actual man in her life. I would have been more offended, but I actually do love Twinkies and when I was younger my parents used to take us camping in a trailer, so they technically *were* on the right track. Either way, their feedback was harsh. Poorly written book. Horrible, weak advice. How can someone who has never been in love act as the expert liaison for all love hungry women? While I wanted to take both their faces and bash them into one another, I knew they also did have a point. I *had* never been in love. But I *had* been played. I'd been used, lied to, taken advantage of and felt weak and betrayed. You don't have to know what the real thing is to know what the fake version looks and feels like. And yes, you bitches, I was the expert. Because I'd spent my entire life getting played. And when that's your specialty, you learn how to become the expert on how to avoid it.

In the end, I knew not to get upset. Because I knew deep down that Chrissy Baker's husband was actually sleeping with Stacey. And when that shit hits, smacks, and fucking splatters all over that fan, I will be here, behind my bar, silently saying I told you so. Well, I guess not so silently anymore since my gig is up.

I just knew that when I walked back into that bar, it wasn't going to be the same. I wouldn't be seen as the laid-back chick who likes to talk and pour booze. I guess I never thought about how I would be exposing myself. I guess I didn't expect a billion people to take my picture then tweet, post, Instagram, snapchat, shit, everything possible to post my face around the universe. I don't want to have to look at Chrissy Baker and *vocally* say I told you so. I want to do it behind her back while I smile and jam out to outdated alternative music.

Four hours, two layovers, and a delayed baggage claim incident later, I walk over to my bed and drop my things. I say hello to my bird Gerdie, who looks just as content as when I left him. I make little kissing noises to let him know I'm home and I watch as his feathers shiver at the sound of my voice. I got Gerdie three years ago on a whim. I had a weak moment with a guy who worked at a pet shop and while he was cleaning the counters with my bare ass getting it on, he kept talking dirty, referring to himself in the third person. At that point in my life I was experimenting in 'anyone sex.' Not just random, anyone. I just wanted sex. I wanted to lose myself to an orgasm and simply not have any sort of attachment. I didn't even want to worry if he was educated, had nice eyes, ate his vegetables, and flossed daily. I just wanted his dick to work. Hence, how I ended up being banged on the counter of the pet shop. Nonetheless, he kept talking dirty to me and lo and behold, the parrot that was "for sale" kept repeating him. Through the entire experience all I heard was this bird chirping "yeah, Jerry's gonna get it. Jerry's gonna get it." And as pet boy grunted out his release, I couldn't control my laughter. He didn't give me anything close to that orgasm I so desperately needed, but I did go back the next day and buy that damn bird.

"Guess who's home?" I sing, pulling the cover off Gerdie's cage. More kissing sounds and I see him flap his wings in approval. "Hello there, handsome. Did you miss me?" I ask, opening his cage and allowing him to climb into my hand.

"Why isn't my boyfriend calling? Why isn't my boyfriend calling..." Gerdie chirps, and I smile, knowing for the next couple of days he will be repeating anything the bird sitter said.

I allow him to perch himself on my dresser while I wash my face. I try not to acknowledge the weight in my pocket as I brush my teeth. When I change into a pair of shorts and a tank top, I stare at the discarded pair of jeans, holding that heavy weight. Seven little numbers. I shake my head and kick my pants, running over to my bed and jumping in. I cuddle into my covers, pulling my blanket practically to my chin.

"Maybe I'll wait to call tomorrow. I don't want to look all eager. Because I'm not."

"You're eager. Call, you're eager," Gerdie chirps as his nails click on my dresser, before taking flight and landing onto my bed.

"I am *not* eager. I can wait. I don't need to talk to him. He's probably not even home yet. Or flying. Or already forgotten about me. That's probably not even his real number!" Ugh, that thought kinda hurts. The feeling in my stomach, I blame on indigestion from the airport food, swirls inside making me feel unsure. Would he give me a wrong number? I mean, that *was* pretty theatrical, the whole airport stunt if he was just wanting to end things on good terms. Which we did since we had incredible sex. And he got to avoid that uncomfortable 'so, I'll see you around' talk.

"Crap, what if I call and it's the wrong number? I will die of humiliation." I look over at my jeans, taunting me.

"Wrong number, wrong number."

"Gerdie, shut it!"

"Die of humiliation, die of humiliation."

Ugh. This is pointless. I mean, oh well, if it is then I hang up. He's probably still flying home anyway. Chances are I'll get his voicemail. *Tap, tap, tap.* My fingers drum on my bed, debating my next move. Saying fuck it, I snap out of my pity party and jump up, scaring poor Gerdie. I grab for my tormenting pants and dig for the little piece of paper. Running back to my bed, I slip back under my covers. "Okay, fuck it. Here it goes…" I pull my phone up and begin dialing the numbers. I get to the last digit but can't enter it.

I stall too long and my lock goes on. "Shit." I punch in my password and go to press the last number and again, I stall.

What the hell has gotten into me? "Just dial the damn number!"

"Dial the damn number."

I look at Gerdie, wanting to smack him off my bed. If I didn't love him so much I probably would. Then I think about the conversation I had with Chase and his love for his dog.

And then it hits me.

I'm not one to call a guy. It's not my style. That's probably why I'm struggling to press that final number. It's been burned inside my brain that it shouldn't be the girl who makes that move. He should have asked for mine. *And would you have given it to him, you chicken?* Ugh, true. So maybe I need to break a few of my own rules here. Or at least bend them a little.

Therefore, change of plans. Thank God, we're also in the era where no one calls anymore anyway. Since texting is the new wave of communication, I decide to take the chicken way out and text him. If he never replies, then I know it's the wrong person and I don't have to hear a human voice tell me I have the wrong number. I can just read it and go on my merry pissed off way. I get Gerdie's attention and snap a photo of him, looking very perched and fluffy. I type in the message.

Me: I thought that if we decide to get to know each other we should make sure our loved ones get along. Otherwise we should cut our losses now.

And with Gerdie's smiling face, well, I *think* he's smiling, I press send.

Then I throw my phone across the room, landing in a pile of clothes.

Getting myself more comfortable in my bed, I tell myself I'm really tired and if he messages back I'll see it in the morning. I don't really care that much anyway. Five, four, three, two, and I jump off the bed and snag my phone, flipping it over with superhuman speed and check to see if I got a message.

No message.

I look to see if my text has been read yet, and it hasn't. Dang. It's cool, maybe he's flying. Or home and sleeping. Or...

Ding. My phone goes off and I freak out, tossing it like a hot potato.

"Shit!" The sound startled me. I just stare at it lying on the floor.

"Ding. Shit. Ding. Shit. Ding."

"Gerdie, I get it." I shake it off and lean off the bed, reaching for my phone. I keep it covered and readjust myself. I take a deep breath and while holding said breath, I flip it over.

"FUCK!" I swear loudly, seeing a stupid notification that my phone has an app update.

"Fuck. Shit. Ding. Fuck. Shit. Ding…"

"GERDI—"

Another ding interrupts. I glare at it and it's then I see a text and a photo attachment to my reply. My finger, which is shaking like a pansy, slides my phone open to see a photo of a fluffy brown-haired dog. Below the message reads:

369-555-2549: I showed Ellie your photo. She's not normally into birds, but she has a good feeling about Gerdie. She knows they may not hit it off, but she's willing to try. Maybe if you sent a photo revealing what's under those feathers, it would help.

My smile hitting my ears almost hurts as I shake my head. Of course, Chase and his wit and his sneaky little codes. I save his contact info and begin texting him back when another one pops up.

Bates Motel: Ellie takes that back. She wants to see everything. A full frontal is preferred. Pup-pup-puplease.

Oh my God! How corny is he? Playing his game, I reply.

Me: Gerdie normally doesn't show the goods on the first date. How about just a headshot?

I type it, and shame on me, I place the phone in between my legs so as I get Gerdie who is in the middle of my bed, I also get a side shot of my inner thigh. I press send and regret it the second it goes through. What the hell is wrong with me? I do *not* send cheesy text messages. I drop my phone and cover my face with my hands and sigh, when the ding echoes around my room. I pick it up and almost choke. On my phone, is a picture of the cutest dog, lying on a naked chest. And of course, the dog is leaning to the side so I get a great view, giving away that he's completely naked. His message reads:

Bates Motel: Deal, I'll match you with two headshots ;)

Oh my God. This guy. "He is so full of himself," I mumble as I open the picture fully and use my fingers to zoom in. *Two heads is right.* God, I miss him and his gorgeous energizer cock. I wish we were still wrapped up in my hotel room licking and biting. I sigh as I save the photo, the ding coming through again.

Bates Motel: I kinda miss you, Katie Beller.

Fuck. My heart squeezes, with a flutter in its wake. I don't put thought into my reply, I just type and send.

Me: I kinda miss you too, Chase Green.

Bates Motel: Thank you for giving me a chance.

Ugggghhhh what's *WRONG* with me? His message is just a message. Why do I feel like I want to laugh and cry at the same time? Why is this guy making me feel? He's like a wrecking ball, taking me out, one emotion at a time. In the end, I'll be a mess. He *will* hurt me and I know that. Statistics know that. Society knows that. But why am I falling for it? Why do I get that giddy feeling from his words?

I do what I do best and take the chicken way out and not respond. A few minutes pass before my phone dings again.

Bates Motel: Good night, Katie Beller.

Me: Good night, Chase Green like the color.

chapter
EIGHT

I walk into the bar, seeing the typical Tuesday night crowd. Dressed in my normal ripped at the knee jeans and a Punk tank top with a sweet iron on face of Pee-wee Herman that reads *I know you are but what am I*, I walk past the bar of familiar faces and smile. I missed this place.

"Beller!" The loud calling of my name draws my attention to Dex at the end of the bar.

I lift my hand, but his less than happy face causes my model wave to die and fall back at my waist. Geez, what's his problem?

"What's up, Dex? Thought you'd be happier to see me—"

"In my office. Now." He tosses the towel on the bar and walks ahead of me. The last time I felt this way was in high school when I was being led out of my class by the principal because Suzanne, the cunt, Miller told on me for accidently setting the toilet paper roll on fire in the girls' bathroom.

I follow Dex into the back office and…

"Shut the door."

Yes, sir.

He sits behind his worn desk, and I take a seat on the other end, plopping my Converse on top.

"What can I help you with? You know last time you demanded I come to your office, we, ya know?" I wink, poking fun at our past little work fling. He doesn't look happy, so I quickly decide I'll poke fun another time. "Okay, what's up? Why are you so grouchy? You still mad you had to cover my shifts?"

He tosses a book at me from across the desk, and it doesn't take too long to recognize the cover.

Awkward.

"Why, Dex, I didn't know you knew how to read." I smile, playing it off.

"Cut the shit, Kat. When were you gonna tell me about this?"

"Uh, never. Why? I didn't think it was a big deal."

"Katie, you wrote a book that's now a NYT best seller."

"Ehhh, I mean, it's not like people are *really* reading it. What's the big deal?" I give him the universal "pfft" hand gesture, re-crossing my legs.

Pressing his elbows against his desk, Dex sighs heavily, leaning forward. "Why would you hide this from me? I thought we were solid."

I lock eyes with him and his eyes… They kind of look hurt. Does he actually feel offended I hid this from him?

"Dex, it's not that big of a deal. I just didn't want anyone to know. I had no idea which direction the book would go. What if it failed and I told everyone, and then we had picketers outside the bar every night trying to stab me for giving bad advice?"

He looks at me in that way he does sometimes when he doesn't realize I'm watching. "I would protect you. But that's not the fucking point. There are already lines of people looking for you."

Oh shit. "Wait, what? Like violent people?" I knew it. People just can't handle the truth.

"No, babe, people who want to meet you, autographs, photos, that shit. You're like a goddamn staple to begin with in this bar and now you come out that you're some famous writer holding the leading torch on fucking love and shit."

I laugh. I mean, I *did* play with a lot of fire when I was younger. KTP, they would call me, Katie the Pyro. Not the point.

"Oh, come on. I'm sure you're just exaggerating."

"Kat, knowing you're back tonight, I had to hire an extra set of bouncers. It's been like a madhouse. Thanks for the extra business, not that the regulars are happy about it, but you need to stay low. Maybe just feel it out. If it gets too much tonight, tell me. I'll cover you."

What? Dude, no way. I'm working tonight. I've missed serving booze like people miss those Housewives shows. It's what I do and love. "No, it's cool, I'm gonna work."

Dex gets up, walking around the desk. Sitting on top, he leans over, grabbing my thigh.

"You sure? I'll cover you. Just don't want to stab a motherfucker for touching my girl tonight."

Seriously what's *wrong* with this guy tonight?

"Awe, Dexy poo, are you getting all sappy on me tonight?"

He squeezes my thigh, and I yelp, throwing my legs off his desk. "Fuck no. But it's either you be careful or I just fire your ass." Back to the Dex I know and love. We both stand.

"Got it, captain." I salute him, and he spanks me on the ass, causing me to jump and squeak as we walk out of his office laughing.

"Belcher! I heard you're famous!" Freddy yells from seven seats down as I walk behind the bar.

"Only in the book of world records, Fred," I tell him as I fire up the cash register. Working in a bar, you tend to not pick up the best habits. Mine was being able to belch the longest and loudest. It's just a talent very few are born with. And since I was one of the blessed, I chose to share it often. You don't get your last name changed from Beller to Belcher for any mediocre reason.

"I saw your picture on that Friendsbook site. You sure are a pretty thing in a dress, Belcher," Fred replies, gulping down his draft beer.

So needless to say, not too many people ever see me in anything but my jeans and tank tops. One year at Halloween I dressed up like a cheerleader, which forced me into a miniskirt, but I also added my own little touch to it, which made me a serial killer cheerleader. I looked bloody. And awesome.

"Oh boy, the secret's out. I own a dress. Better call my publicist and have her burn down the Internet before anyone sees!" I joke, counting the singles in the drawer.

"So, then it is true!" Randy yells from the end of the bar, dropping her purse under the counter. I sigh.

Oops.

"I mean, define true? I could just be the decoy. No one would ever know." I shrug my shoulders, sliding the ones back in and pulling out the fives.

"Oh, bull. You wrote that shit. I read it. Like in one sitting and I don't read anything but Cosmo and porn. That story was *bomb*, girl." She walks up to me and hugs me from the back. "I loved it. It was so you. I could hear your voice the entire story."

"Does she mention me at all in the book?"

We both turn to Fred, who now has beer foam hanging off his beard. We both laugh, as Randy pulls away from me.

"Oh, she might have. She does meet this handsome man. His scruffy beard used to make her pretty little privates tingle while he suctions his mouth to her lippity lips." She ends on a pop. I roll my eyes, while she bursts into laughter, all while Fred spits out his beer.

"Hey, you are *not* getting a free round for that, so don't blame the choking on the bar."

Fred gives me a look. One that says *how dare you accuse me of trying to get free drinks*, and then *well, can I just get half of my cup filled?*

Out of nowhere Dex is behind me, his chest brushing against my back. "You okay?" he asks softly.

I turn my head and smile. "Yeah, all good. I've been out here five minutes and I'm still alive."

He backs up and walks away, yelling at the beer runner to finish filling the coolers.

Randy and I catch eyes and she gives me the "what was that all about" look as I shrug my shoulders, replying with a silent, who the fuck knows.

The night picks up really fast. Dex wasn't lying when he said the bar had a whole new crowd. It was absolutely insane. I had all the normal Tuesday regulars yelling in my ear, "*why didn't you tell us?*" "*Is it true?*" "*Are they going to make a movie?*" I was slipped a total of seventeen numbers, and that's just the number before I stopped counting. I don't know what all of a sudden made me more appealing. It's not like I got a make-over or won the lottery. Yeah, I have a few more bucks in the bank, but that money is going to something special. Like a bird kingdom for Gerdie. But it's like people who never saw me before are seeing me now. It's actually really fucking annoying.

"Hey, Katie, saw your photo on Facebook. You looked great."

I lay four bud lights on the bar and turn to my right to see Paul, a semi-regular, offering me a weird smile.

"Yep, thanks, what can I get ya, Paul?"

"Anything. Surprise me. And get two shots. One for you."

I know where this is going, he's going to ask me for my number. But I'll break it to him after I take his free shot. I pour him a whiskey neat, because even though he wants me to *surprise* him, I know that's what he drinks every single damn time. I pour us two chilled shots of tequila, and when I place them on the bar, he makes his move. Grabbing for my hand and holding it, all while he offers me that weird ass smile again. "You really look great, Katie, maybe after work—"

"Paul, get your fucking hands off her. You're dating

someone. I know it and I'm sure your new lady friend wouldn't find it cute if you're asking another girl out."

Shame washes over Paul's face, as I try not to laugh. Dex picks up the two tequila shots, handing me one.

"Thanks for the shots, though, Paul," he says and clinks his glass with mine, and we both throw our heads back and swallow.

Seriously. This has been my night.

When it's not Paul, it's someone else. When it's not a male, it's a female. *"How did Abby know in the end it would work out?"* *"How did she learn to create all those profiles?"* *"Is Abby you?"* The amount of times I had to explain that I've never myself catfished anyone was *insane.* I don't even use Facebook, people!

Okay, so how did I know so much about it then? You can't write a whole book about a girl who creates fake profiles to find love and *not* use social media. Well, yes, the fuck you can. You don't need to use the devil's device to get it. People talk about it day and night. Well, actually they don't talk, they tweet. They post. They comment with smiley faces, sad faces, and hearts. Don't even get me started on those poop emojis.

But that's how we communicate today. And that's what's so fucking wrong with us. People come in this bar and they come to meet people and drink, but seventy-five percent of the time they have their noses stuck in their phones. They tell the person next to them how their crazy friend from high school is getting married, their neighbors are out to dinner at this new Asian place, and their oh so cute coworker's stepsister's adopted niece had a baby, got married, farted, died! Who needs to fucking talk to anyone anymore when you have a site that ruins it for everyone!

I refuse to be that victim to social media. I enjoy an old-fashioned conversation. Hence, why I love the bar. I get to talk to people all night long. Face to face. And the drunker they get, the better the stories I receive. That's the real 'social.'

I know. I can go on.

Back to the bar.

It definitely was a smart plan that Dex hired more staff. Once it passed midnight the bar got a little rowdy. Not that it doesn't normally, but nothing we *normally* can't handle. The extra heads at the bar had us one in, one out, and Randy and I could barely keep up with orders. That and every single person who wanted to stop me and have a life chat.

When it was finally closing time, I wanted to crawl on top of the sticky bar and take a nap. I had a few more shots in me than the approved amount, and from the scowl Dex kept giving me all night, I'm sure I'll hear about it later. But hey, those are free shots for me, and money for the bar. I consider that a win-win for everyone.

Once all is squeaky-clean I grab my purse from under the register and wave goodbye to everyone.

"Hey," Dex calls out, trying to catch up to me while I leave.

"Hey, what's up?"

"You want me to walk you home?"

I give him the crazy eye. Walk me home? "No, I'm fine. Thanks."

"You sure? It's been a long night and you look wiped."

"Yeah, because it was a mad house. What's up with you?"

He's been acting off the whole night. Dex and I had our fling, which lasted almost a year. But that's all it ever amounted to. We tried to do the whole feelings bullshit, but it just wasn't working. We were both broken in some sort of poetic way and decided that if we wanted to keep the great friendship part that we had, maybe we had to wave the white flag on the relationship part. It was mutual and from that moment forward we've been friends. Close friends. Possibly with a little slip into the back office here and there. But tonight, he seems off.

"Nothing, just want to make sure you get home okay. You're a celebrity now. Don't want my best bartender getting snatched." He puts his hands in his pockets, his big form stepping from foot to foot.

"Awe, well, aren't you sweet." I go and lightly punch him in the chest. "But, I'm good. For real. I'm sure I look scary enough after tonight that I'll frighten people more than I'll appeal to them."

"I doubt that, Beller."

Okay, *weirdo* Dex. I think he's the one who's wiped out. Leave for two weeks and my hard-ass boss gets all soft on me.

"I'll see you tomorrow," I say, giving him my model wave and head toward my apartment. As I walk home, I do the one thing I've been trying to hold off on doing, which was easy since we were swamped, and that's to check my phone. I will be totally okay if he didn't message me. It's actually not even a big deal. No sweat.

I pull my phone out of my purse and slide on the screen. I don't have one message. I have *seven*. My heart summersaults in my chest. Speed punching in my password and fucking it up three times, I go and lock myself out of my phone.

"FUCK! You have to be *kidding* me!" Of all the times! I've never had anxiety. Because why would I? I'm an easygoing, go with the flow kinda chick. But right now? I have just diagnosed myself with the worst case. My heart is no longer doing summersaults, it's banging on my chest. Seven messages!

What could he say in seven messages?

Get a hold of yourself man.

It's five minutes.

I take a deep breath and continue walking home. It'll go by fast. I'll be reading his love/hate texts in no time. A few more minutes and I look back at my phone. "Oh, come on!" It hasn't even been a full minute! The universe is against me. It's mad because I'm putting a stop to hookups. I'm being punished.

I complain the whole way home, and by the time I make it to my building the five minutes have passed and I'm entering in my password and bingo. I'm in.

I start with the first one that looks like it came through around eight o'clock tonight. It's a photo of Ellie. The message reads:

Bates Motel: Ellie wants to know what Gerdie is up to. She's horny.

I laugh to myself as I slide my key in my door. I scroll to the next text that came at just before nine. It's another picture of Ellie who seems to be sleeping on her pink flower pillow. The message reads:

Bates Motel: She decided she had a headache and went to bed.

At a quarter to eleven, I received a photo of a slice of pizza, the message reading:

Bates Motel: Wish you were here.

The next two to follow are pictures of the disappearing pizza. The sixth one is of Chase's finger pointing to his bare chest reading:

Bates Motel: Full belly.

I roll my eyes with a smile at the fact that his hand is

pointing to his abs and not his actual belly. The last one, which came in about ten minutes ago, is of him reading my book. The message reads:

> **Bates Motel: It's okay. I'll just help Ellie figure out a way to find a companion. I know a girl who wrote a book about it.**

It makes me smile that he has a copy of my book. By the time I get through all the messages, I'm in my apartment, have discarded my purse, and am lying on my bed. I decide to be bold, and instead of texting back, I call.

The phone rings twice before he answers.

"Katie Beller." His voice is deep and hoarse. Like he's been sleeping. *Shit! I totally forgot what time it is.*

"Oh, I'm sorry I woke you. I forgot what time it is. I'll let you go."

"Don't you dare hang up on me, Katie Beller."

Summersaults.

"I just got all your texts. How's Ellie doing?" I ask, kicking off my shoes.

"She's not great. Really wanted to talk to Gerdie. Missed him. At one point she thought to maybe stalk his Facebook page hoping for an update. But he doesn't seem to have one."

I laugh. "Gerdie doesn't believe in social media. It's killing the world of real conversations."

"Ahh, yes. Social media is ruining the world, one love story at a time. Abby proves it in chapter ten when she experiments with her fake date, Henry."

I still can't believe he's read my book.

"I'm still not sure how you read that. Did you have your fan club read it out loud for you, during a *model* shoot?" I tease, but then want to claw the image out of my head of him and his *fan club.*

"Nope, I read it all by myself while taking a shit every morning after leaving your room. I didn't want you to know I pooped, so I always waited."

"Oh my God! Okay, TMI, Green."

I hear him yawning into the phone.

I look at my clock glowing on the nightstand, and it's almost three in the morning. "Seriously, sorry, I forgot how late it is. I'll let you go."

"Please. Don't. I want to talk to you."

More summersaults.

My heart is soon on its way to the Olympics if he keeps this up.

I kick my socks off, getting comfortable. "Okay, so what would you like to talk about?"

"You. Anything you," he responds.

I'm not sure what he wants to know. My life is about as exciting as watching paint dry. I keep it basic. Little details about the bar. My favorite color.

I make him fork up some information as well, and I'm shocked at how willing he is to open up to me more on his personal life. I learn he has two younger sisters, which he seems to love deeply. His parents, who sounded like the perfect family, both live in Duluth, Minnesota, which is twenty minutes away from his place. He still attends Sunday brunch when he's in town and his mom still sometimes does his laundry.

He explains in more detail about his hockey career. He's played hockey his whole life. And it's his passion. Since they just wrapped up pre-season training, the team is heading on tour for promos soon and he's going to be traveling right up until he breaks for the next signing tour. Listening to him talk about the sport, I can sense the change in his voice. His excitement for it. Passion. I get the feeling the modeling gig isn't as glorious as it seems. I guess being man-handled by women all over the universe can get old.

We both go back and forth sharing stories of Ellie and Gerdie. When the clock hits five in the morning we decide to call it quits. "Well, make sure to get some sleep so you don't zombie out and get whipped in the face by a puck at practice," I joke, now yawning myself.

"I will. Make sure to give Gerdie a long, wet kiss for Ellie. She misses him, you know."

"Well, I think Gerdie might miss her too." We're both met with silence, the sound of our soft breathing humming through the phone.

"Well, good night, Katie Beller."

"Nighty night, Chase Green like the color."

Fucking summersaults.

Fucking Chase Green.

Fuck.

chapter NINE

I've been home under a week and my simple life has turned into a whirlwind. Work isn't about serving people the 'talky juice' so they spill *their* beans anymore. It's turned into more questions than answers. More suggestions than opinions. People don't want to sit there and just talk. They want to diagnose love with me.

It's absolutely miserable!

I wrote a book about a girl who wanted to prove a point. And in the end, she did. She showed that love is not about the outside person. It's about the inside person. A girl who faked who she was and watched all these people fall for her. Abby, *who is not me,* found men on Facebook. Gave them the virtual words any man would want to hear while they stared at the cliché fake photo she posted. Then, Abby went out and met these guys in person. Pretending to be a stranger, just in the way, a simple girl asking if that seat was taken, or just simply a human asking to have a conversation. Every time, those men turned her down. And every time it proved Abby was right. Men nowadays wanted the looks. Not the brains, *or* the insides. It was a sickness in society no one was willing to cure. It was the reason why Abby was destined to always be single.

Again, disclaimer, I was *not* Abby.

I wasn't worried about *being* Abby. I was worried about the single population of women out there throwing the wrong vibes out into the lion's den just to get a bite. I didn't want to be the love whisperer and offer sessions in the back room and tell every single woman who walked through those bar doors how to handle love. I just wanted someone to realize they were worth more than just a pickup line. More than a free drink, a pointless game of flirting, darts, and a one-night stand.

But people just wanted to analyze. In life, it's natural to take sides. Everyone does it. People were on one side or the other. They agreed or they didn't. It was when Chrissy fucking Baker walked into the bar that really set the lines.

"Oh, look who it is, The *Doctor Phil* of Ohio," the Witch of the West says walking up with her butt buddy Stacey. Lucky for me, they take the two open stools in front of the bar. Right in front of my section.

"Wow, you two look great! I'm sorry, though, I didn't know it was eighties night. I would've dressed up for it," I comment back, grabbing for the beer spout and pouring a draft.

Both girls look at one another clueless and back at me. "What are you talking about?"

Clearly, I'll keep the explanation to myself.

"Nothing. What can I get you, girls?"

"I'll take a Cosmo."

"I'll take a lemon drop martini."

They both spit their fancy orders at me like they're on the set of a *Sex in the City* episode. Not that we don't serve that fufu shit, but if you read the sign outside, we're a dive bar and as I know how to *make* martinis, you're just in the wrong place for those.

"Super, coming right up," I chirp, walking away, grabbing for the cheapest vodka we have.

"So, Katie, do tell, how *did* you pull this one off?"

I turn my head, pouring the vodka into the shaker. "Pull what off?"

Both giggling, Chrissy sticks out her shoulders, responding, "This whole book thing? I mean, come on, no one believes *you* actually wrote it, do they? You're clearly some sort of decoy for a bigger author trying to keep in the dark."

I turn away, clenching my fingers around the vodka bottle. My eyes close, taking a deep breath, before I slap my fake smile on my face and face them again. "Can't say I know what you mean?" I return, finishing and bringing both drinks in front of them, tempted to knock them over into their laps.

"It's just that… You're not really a, how do we say… a dateable person. I don't mean to say it in a mean way, but come on. You don't date. *No one* has seen you with a guy. And if so, nothing they would take serious. So, there's no way you could write a book on it."

Her evil eyes meet mine. I do my best to show nonchalance, but her words struck home. I'm not one to deny or make excuses for my track record. Or lack of. It's life, obviously. But when someone throws it in your face, then tries to then stomp on the dirty already in your eyes, you tend to kind of... well, slip.

"Oh, I agree. I have absolutely no track record with love. But when I was making all this money I had no idea what to do with, I was also having a ton of animal sex with a book model. Charlie Bates? Not sure you know the name, I barely did, but shit, he sure knows how to make music with my labia. I'm talkin', like humming and buzzing all over that shit until your insides start vibrating. Any who. Yeah. Love? What's love? Nowadays I only know about vibrating vaginas." I smile widely and turn to Stacey. "But, Stacey, you and Brent probably know about vibrating vaginas, right?" I offer her my biggest wink and turn, walking down the bar. I don't turn to witness the questions or the blowout. I walk all the way down the bar, past the eyeing Dex and past Randy, who I let know I'm taking a break, and as cool as a cucumber go back to the office and hide until I stop shaking.

chapter TEN

By the time I make it home I'm half dead. For the past week, it's been the same song and dance. I work. I black out until I get home, then I pretend I'm not hurrying into my bed to check my phone and see all the messages from Chase.

It's been the same every night since our first call. I send him the teenage "are you awake" text and he calls me. I answer on a whisper, because I'm a school girl, and he replies purring my name.

I don't know whether all the personal talks we've had should freak me out or comfort me. I can't say I have ever had a guy who wanted to hear the sap and gore of my childhood and upbringing. But he pushes and I slowly tell him. He never seems to pull away, and with that I tell him more.

I wasn't raised as your typical Brady bunch child if that isn't obvious. My mom and dad died in a car accident when I was super young and I was left with my aunt and uncle. They were definitely what you call stellar step-in parents, minus the stellar part. Meaning I basically grew up on my own. I didn't have the mom I'm sure Stacey Wright had, which braided her hair, while telling her all about the birds and the bees, or Chrissy Baker's parents who fed her diet pills and told her exactly how to snag a husband, hook, line and sinker.

I went to high school and kept to myself. I graduated with flying colors and those flying grades landed me in a pile of nothing. Mainly because my new stepparents couldn't afford college. Mind you, the money they got from my parents' insurance settlement, I saw nothing of. But that's life and the system.

The adults always win.

Luckily, I was able to get a job and attempt to pay for college on my own. But that only lasted so long when work intertwined with school and I couldn't do both. I had at that point moved out of the relative hell hole and lived on my own. I chose to lose my education and pay for rent, then live in hell and get a nine-to-five desk job.

Tonight, our conversation started off different. I was on edge after the fiasco with Chrissy and Stacey. It made me doubt what Chase and I have built, and I just didn't want to be a blind victim. I worried they were right. There was no way I could know anything about love, or be anyone's somebody.

"Hello, Katie Beller, you're a bit late tonight." Chase's deep voice rings through my needy ears, sucking up his vocal sound likes it's a forbidden fruit.

"Sorry, it was a late night. Tons of drunks, drama, and

bad karaoke," I reply, falling into my bed. I've gotten rid of my work attire minus my black-laced boy shorts and a tank top. I rest my head on my pillow, clutching my phone to my ear. "Please do enlighten me on what happened in the life of Chase Green today."

His chuckle is like a buzzing sensation I constantly want to press against my clit for release.

"Ahh, well, it was very uneventful. Being in Canada for hockey, I spent the entire day at practice, then had team photos and interviews. Then I was forced to attend a horrible steak dinner that consisted of cold mashed potatoes and by the time I knew it I was begging to go back to my room, which I'm now at, wanting to order pizza but refuse because my guilt would literally kill me if I did it without a specific little firecracker in my room to share it with me."

And this is why Stacey and Chrissy shouldn't matter.

I sigh into my pillow.

"I had a bad night," I admit, which is unusual for me.

"I'm sorry to hear that. Wanna talk about it?"

As much as I want to swoon at the gentlemanly effort, I don't. "No. It was nothing. Just a bad night I want to erase, is all."

I hear him shuffling, possibly getting adjusted in his hotel room bed.

"Katie? I was thinking…" He pauses, his breath humming through the phone.

"I'm glad you can think, Green," I reply smiling, leaning more into my pillow. I don't need to see him to know his smile is broadening across his face.

"You know me so well, Katie Beller. But I think we should know each other a little bit better."

Hmmm, now he has me intrigued. The horrible night is slowly being pushed into the back of my mind, while I ponder his intentions. "Okay, Green, spit it out. What's up your sleeve?"

"Well, first off, I want to tell you something."

Uh-oh.

"I miss you."

Uh-*ohhh*.

"And I was thinking... That maybe we should FaceTime..."

"FaceTime?" I bust out laughing. "You want to FaceTime?"

"Yeah. I want to see your face. Your smile. Dammit, Katie, I miss you and I'm not afraid to admit it. I want to see your sexy as fuck eyes as they laugh or get defensive. I'm going through withdrawal."

I don't know what I do first. Clench my legs together or gasp. I'm a lady always. Duh, I have a vag, but I have never been a swooner. It's just not my style. But holy shit.

"You want to FaceTime..."

"Yes. If you don't, it's fine. I mean—"

"Let's do it."

"Yeah?" He sounds surprised I'm agreeing.

"Sure, why not. But beware, Green, I've been slaving over a bunch of drunks all night. I might not be as appealing as you remember."

"Doubt that."

Before I have a chance to change my mind, my phone starts buzzing, Chase's incoming FaceTime call coming through. I click accept and a few beeps later, his beautiful face appears on my phone. I semi panic, because I would have liked to take a preview of what I actually look like, maybe pinch my cheeks to get some rouge before he sees me. His face lights up my screen and instantly I notice his bare chest. Great. So not only do I probably look like shit, I'm now drooling.

"God, you're sexy," he comments immediately, his voice hoarse.

I throw my hands into my hair, trying to give it some volume. Or style. I catch a glimpse of myself in the corner and groan. "Sexy as a dead person. God, I look horrid. You can hang up any time now. I won't be offended."

"Hell no. You're a sight for the eyes, Katie Beller." He smiles, causing me to return the gesture.

We fall silent, allowing the compliment to wash through me. "Well, thanks, you're not so bad yourself."

"We should've been doing this from day one. I want to beat myself up for not suggesting this sooner. I've missed your face."

And damn, I have missed his. Just seeing his content smile, his laid back posture. Talking on the phone hasn't dulled the ache I get every time I speak to him. I look at him, forgetting just how beautiful he truly is. His smile, his eyes, his seriously sexy chest. It makes me feel that he's a dream to me, and this isn't real.

"I have to admit something, though."

"What's that?" I ask.

"I just feel so vulnerable, sitting here with no shirt on. I'm watching your hungry little eyes eating me up. I know I'm more than just a piece of meat, but unless you want me to put a shirt on, I think to make me feel on the same level as you, you should take yours off too."

I stifle a laugh. "You're kidding me, right?"

"No, actually. You're intimidating me. Like a wild tiger, staring at her piece of meat, ready to pounce."

Shaking my head, my eyes slip from his, to his chest. He does have a sexy muscled—

"See! You're doing it again. Take yours off or I'm going to be forced to put mine back on."

This is ridiculous. His mischievous pout causes me to warm down below. It's not like he hasn't seen my chest before anyway. And I'm still wearing a bra.

"Fine, Green. Shirt for shirt." I take my phone and leverage it on my bed post, then lift my tank top, bringing it over my head.

"Jesus, you're a sight," he groans.

I toss my tank on the floor, bringing myself back into a lying position. "So what do you want to talk about? Now that we're on the same level?"

"Fuck, I want to talk about taking our pants off next. You're seriously so fucking sexy. And I'm so thankful for video chat."

I watch him lose focus on my eyes, drifting to my chest. I can see one hand holding the phone just above his navel while his other hand is out of sight. "Whatcha doin' over there, Green?" I poke, knowing his missing hand appears to be in his pants.

"Fuck, I'm trying to break the sad news to my dick that it's not going to have physical action with you tonight."

I blush instantly, watching his shoulder move, knowing it's in result of his hand motion. I squeeze my legs together to hide my own arousal from his words.

"No way, open your legs back up. I was pretending I was with you, snaking my hand up your thighs."

Oh God. I want to follow suit and use my hands for good, but where my phone is sitting he has a full view of me. My eyes dilate at the vision of him in my room, using those large hands to hunt up my thigh, feeling just how warm and wet I'm becoming.

"Babe, you can't look at me like that," he groans, his shoulder movement picking up speed. How wrong of me would it be to lower my hand and dig it into my underwear?

"I just think that if you get to pleasure yourself, so should I." Where in the ever-loving fuck did *that* come from?

"I'll take my pants off if you take yours off," he says, his breathing picking up.

I debate it for mere seconds before I take both hands and lock them around the hem of my underwear, slowly bringing them down my legs. Once they're off, I toss them to the side. I can't believe I'm doing this. But on the hind side, I do get to watch Chase work his gorgeous cock.

"Now, this is the problem here, I only get a partial view. I should probably move my phone up—"

"Fuck no, don't you move. Hold on."

I watch him sit up, getting a glorious view of his tightening abs. He grabs a pillow, taking his phone and adjusting it. Lying back down, I moan at my visual.

"Okay, even Steven. God, babe, you look fucking beautiful like that." And I can say the same for him. From my view, I have his toned thighs, leading up to his groin and his hard cock, standing tall and thick against his stomach.

He brings his hand back around himself. We seem to be in a standstill on what to do next. This is definitely new territory for me. I mean, as for the whole party of one, yeah, but phone, or in this case video sex, is a newbie for me.

"Not so sure how well this is gonna go, Green. I'm normally alone when mastering my self-pleasure." I hear him groan, his grip tighter around his shaft.

"Trust me, you can just lie perfectly still and I would blow in under thirty seconds. The image of you pleasuring yourself right now is going to make me come in my hands before we even get started." His hand begins to move, slowly stroking himself, and it allows me to loosen up, because watching him stroke his engorged cock turns me the fuck on. I can't stop wishing I were his hand working that silky monster.

"Babe, your eyes look hungry," he jokes, moving his hand up, his thumb brushing over the tip of him. I fight not to lick my own lips but even remembering that thing inside me sets my mouth watering. I know by the way he's stroking himself, he's trying to tease me. Maybe get me to relax. But with the slow burn in my lower belly I begin to play his game.

"You have no idea how hungry I am," I tease, and my hands proceed to lower to my sex. I'm still feeling a bit shy, but his deep voice breaks me.

"Don't stop now, baby. I want to see those hands over that pussy, touching it like I wish I were. I wish I were sucking and biting and thrusting my finger into that beautiful tight cunt of yours." His words are so hot, the tightness in my stomach builds.

I take my hand and do what I'm told, sliding it down my stomach, past my navel. I reach the dip in my pelvis, until my fingers are brushing against my already saturated lips.

"Fuck, you're so sexy. Open your legs wider. Let me see heaven."

I open my legs and with a bold move, I take my fingers and spread my lips open for him. His groan ignites that slow burn in my stomach.

"Jesus, I can see how wet you are. Baby, rub that little clit of yours, stroke yourself as if I were there playing with your beautiful pussy."

Like a good little girl, I use my fingers to rub at my lips, smearing the wetness. I close my eyes, enjoying the friction I'm causing. I hear his heavy breathing and small grunts I know I'm causing, which gives me courage, and I take my finger and insert it inside.

"Oh, fuck yeah, I wish that were my cock stroking you in and out. Fuck..."

I can tell he's working himself faster. That spark is beginning to ignite and I'm not sure how long I can last. I insert another finger and moan, the fantasy of my fingers being replaced by his cock, his mouth over my nipple and his lips on mine.

"God, this feels so good. I wish this were you. Soaking your fingers, spreading me open and fucking me raw."

We're working ourselves faster, the sounds of us both so close. I lift my free hand and squeeze my breast, pinching my nipple in the process. I can hear the slapping sounds of Chase as he frantically beats off.

"God, fuck, you're fucking beautiful. Fuck, fuck, fuck..."

Like clockwork, I clench around my own fingers, moaning out my orgasm. I lay my head back, silently screaming my release. I hear Chase grunt and open my eyes to watch him explode up his stomach. We're still slowly stroking ourselves until the high wears off and the shyness kicks back in. I stop rubbing and pull out, the urge to cover myself strong.

"That was... wow. I must say, Katie Beller, I have a new fondness for FaceTime."

I chuckle, reaching for my robe and beginning to wrap it around me.

"Babe, don't hang up. I gotta get a towel." He disappears, assuming to the bathroom, before quickly returning and taking up the screen.

"Now, I have one question to ask you."

"What's that?" I shyly smile, nervous of what's going to come out of his mouth next.

"How much battery life do you have left? Because we're doing that again."

chapter ELEVEN

The bar is slammed. Not shocked, though. It's Thursday, and as my black tank top states, it's *#ThirstyThursday*. So, it's gonna be a long night.

People love reasons to drink. Manic Monday, Tequila Tuesday, Wine Wednesday… I simply love any reason to serve them. I'm sure there are people out there who get satisfaction out of landing big contracts, closing deals, matching their bra and underwear. I get satisfaction out of making people happy with my excellent bartending skills. I didn't plan on this being my life. I did at one point want more for myself. But life just sucks sometimes. I used to have a teacher in high school tell me all the time how life wasn't fair. And things won't always be handed to me. I know she was just referring to the cliff notes I always took from Jenny Buckner in English class, but in a way, she was right. No one handed me anything in that respect, and life was completely unfair.

I landed at Anchor bar on a whim. I was at school and struggling. I knew I had to find a way and fast to get some cash or I wasn't going to be able to pay for my upcoming semester. I had about seven dollars in my pocket, even less in my bank account, and a shit-ton of regrets.

I walked in, sat at the bar, and placed my seven dollars on top, telling the bartender to serve me until I ran out of money. The bartender looked at me strange, then even stranger seeing I only had seven bucks, knowing it would barely get me a beer. A draft beer was placed in front of me, and I drank the last of my money away. By the third beer, I knew the bartender was feeling sorry for me. That, or he also couldn't count and we were going to have an issue once it was time to settle the bill. By the fourth he asked me my name and my story. By the fifth he offered me a job.

That was almost seven years ago, and I never left. Dex didn't care that I had no experience. He said he could tell I had everything else it took to be good behind the bar. We didn't hook up right away. The sexual tension was there, that's for sure, but for the first year, we just worked side by side. He insisted on training me personally, so we kept the same hours. Of course, I was a natural, so it didn't take long, but our hours never changed. Our schedules would always align. And I guess when you spend so much time with one another, a hot badass, tattooed bartender, and, well myself, things happen. It first happened in his office, while closing up one night. We both had a few too many shots, and while we were counting cash in the back, one thing led to another and I was sprawled over his desk while he fucked the shit out of me.

I know. Vulgar. But that was Dex. He didn't do things slow, or gentle. He was a biker, after all, so he was rough around the edges and all that jazz. I didn't mind, though. I wasn't looking for flowers and cuddly endearments. I liked what we had. It was simple. We didn't talk about our feelings, or future. We just worked, kept each other sated, and that was that. It was when we tried taking that simplicity and making it complex that ruined us. Our fights at work got ugly and it was quit my job or take the sex out of the equation, because we weren't working as a couple.

I serve up four drafts and another round of tequila shots for the group of guys who have settled camp in front of me the last couple of hours. They've been very generous with offering me shots, and I kindly accept. I know Dex isn't happy about it, because he's practically growling at me from the end of the bar. I turn, lifting my shot glass, and raise it to him with a smile. He's been such a grump since I've been home, and I'm going to pin it as he really needs to get laid.

That shot does it, and he comes storming my way.

"Whoa, slow down, Dex—"

"In my office. Now." He grabs at my arm, making it hard to keep up with him. "Randy, cover the bar for a sec, yeah?"

We pass Randy, who's giving me the *"what the fuck"* look, and I just shrug.

Door shut, he spins me, pressing my back to the closed door.

"Geez, Dex, what's your problem? It was just a shot." I breathe.

"This isn't about the damn shot. You're different. Something's going on with you."

"Like what? For real, I'm cool. Maybe it's *you*. Maybe you

should go get laid. You look like you need it."

"Unlike you?" I'm not sure if that is a question or a statement.

"Excuse me?"

"I know your look when you're sated. When you're riding the pleasure train. You've been fucking someone. I can tell."

My eyes widen at his boldness. His body takes a step closer. "You with someone, Kat?" His eyes are intense, as he waits for an answer he looks like he doesn't want to hear. I think about Chase. And all the video masturbating we have done the past couple of days. He has brought me to the highest, most powerful orgasms, and it's me doing the heavy lifting. It's his words, his requests, and his manly grunts of lust and pleasure that boil my arousal to a heated explosion of sensations.

"Dex, not that it's any of your business, but no, I haven't."

Because technically...

"You with someone?"

Another question I can't really answer. Am I? I can't really answer. *Yeah, I'm secretly with a model and we FaceTime and have virtual masturbating sessions like virtual goddamn rabbits.* Kinda sounds strange. But take out the pleasure piece, and I couldn't even say what we are. We definitely aren't a couple. We really like each other. I would say I'd be harboring on like and *really* fucking like at this point, but I won't let myself acknowledge those weird feelings, because this might be all we have. There are no plans for the future. I haven't even signed on for the next installment for the book tour. But if I don't, I don't know when I would see Chase. His schedule is so busy, and I'm needed at the bar. I'm not sure that leaves time for a relationship outside of what we currently have.

When I look into Chase's eyes, I see more than just a fling. More than just an adventurous time with a girl who would never fit in his real life. But when we disconnect and reality sets in, that thought wades. The age-old theory will always sit on the tip of my mind. People want what they can't have. And Chase can surely have me. But can he still be happy in public? What if I'm a double cliché, it all being *about* the chase—no pun intended there. The need to taste test something that's so wrong for you, but oh so good.

"No, Dex, I'm not. Seriously, I don't need this harassment from you." I lift my hands and push off him.

He willingly backs away, trying to read my expression. A few more seconds of our stare down, when he releases his visual hold on me.

"Sorry. You just seem different lately. Don't know why."

"Well, I'm still me. All boring parts of me," I reply, shrugging my shoulders and smiling. That last shot may have put me over the buzz limit.

"I care about you. Just wanna be there for you, yeah?"

I smile at him strangely. "Yeah, Dex, I know, same here." I step forward, wrapping my arms around his thick waist. I give him a hug, squeezing extra tightly, until he gives in, squeezing me back. "Thanks for always looking out for me, Dexie," I joke, using the nickname I know he hates. He presses his arms around me tighter, and I feel his lips on the top of my head as he kisses my scalp.

Pulling away, he reaches for the door. "Okay. Get back out there. I'm not paying you to dick around."

I laugh, skipping out as he smacks my ass. I pass by Randy, who still has that look on her face, and if I wasn't feeling a little tequila high, I would have the same.

"Jesus Christ," Dex barks behind me as I trip and drop all the empty bottles I was carrying to the garbage.

Jesus Christ is right. I don't know how I got to this place, but somehow, I'm hammered. I told myself to lay off the freebie shots, but then I would be a rude bartender, and no one wants a rude bartender. It was after I was egged on by my college frat boy fan club to jump on the bar and pour tequila like a luge into their mouths. I made it to the third one before Dex ripped me from the bar, kicking the guys out. I thought it was super rude, but his speech on getting us shut down for alcohol poisoning outweighed my good bartender theory. He also said if I ever let another person take a shot out of my belly button he would fire me on the spot. I only did it after Randy did, but I didn't see her getting chewed out.

The bar is finally closed and I'm trying to help clean, but it seems like I'm making more of a mess than cleaning.

"Sit the fuck down, Kat," Dex orders as I stare at the mess. Maybe if I stare at it long enough I can teleport the bottles back onto my tray—

"Sit!" the angry bear roars, and I snap out of it and jump onto the bar. I miss it and slip. Thankfully, Dex, being so close, catches me.

"I should seriously fire you right now."

"But you won't because you love me," I slur, wrapping my arms around his thick neck. His eyes cut into mine. As he walks us to the seating area I'm sure so he can dump me there.

"You're sitting here until I'm done, then I'll take your fucked-up ass home."

"Thanks, Dex." I smile, feeling my back pocket buzz.

"Dex, is that my butt buzzing or are you just happy to see me."

Shaking his head at me, the annoyed grunt is evidence of how he feels right now. I reach for my pocket and grab for my phone. Chase's name pops up, a FaceTime request calling through.

"Oh, goodie," I chirp.

I swipe right to accept the call and wait with one eye open before I see Chase's sexy face appear on my screen.

"Hey, you. Still at work?" The warmth of his smile heats me down below.

"Yep, just got done." I'm in full smile mode, teeth and all. I probably look like an idiot.

Taking notice of my surroundings, he says, "Um, are you—"

"Kat, you can't take this call later, babe?"

"Are you... Is someone carrying you?" Chase asks, confused. Maybe looking a little mad.

"Yup, it's just Dex. It's okay. He's carrying me home." I'm drunk, so I forget to finish the whole, *gonna drop me off and leave me* part of the sentence.

His brows knit together, his kind smile slowly fading.

"Is this the same guy who you let suck booze from your belly button?"

I laugh. "No." *Wait...* "What?"

Chase blows out a sigh, his expression annoyed. "Yeah, the video that was posted on your fan page. Looked like you had an eventful night at work." I don't miss the anger in his tone.

"Wait, my fan page?"

"Jesus, Katie, how drunk are you? Yeah, you have a fan page. Someone posted a video of you tonight at your work." He's annoyed.

I'm shocked. I have a fan page?

"You know what, you look busy, and I'll let you go."

"Good idea," Dex mumbles.

I jab him with my elbow.

"Wait, Chase, I'm not!"

"I'll talk to you later." And then he's gone.

Dex doesn't do much talking to me after that. And when I attempt to try calling Chase back he doesn't answer. Dex drops me off at home and I don't even have to bother telling him he can't come in. Being angry with me for some reason, he barely stops the bike as I jump off. I make a mental note to apologize for getting drunk tomorrow and make it up to my apartment, let myself in, into my room, and pass out on my closet floor trying to pull my pants off.

chapter TWELVE

I've always considered myself an old soul. Wise in many ways. I enjoy a stout or a nice glass of whiskey over wine or a fufu Cosmo. I enjoy a good debate over life's mysteries over the latest show of Housewives. I don't lose my composure and I certainly don't get drunk and act like a fool.

But last night? What the fuck?

I can't even give myself a reasonable excuse for what happened last night.

Last night was not me.

Ever.

I drill holes into my brain, trying to dig up any reason on why I got so drunk. I don't want to make excuses, but I was just happy. That sounds fucking sappy, I know. But I was. Chase has been putting this warmth in my life ever since he landed in it. Not just the warmth down below but in general. My days have been brighter with his calls, our talks, our insanely hot FaceTime sessions. And it feels so goddamn liberating. There, I said it.

He's making me feel wanted. Needed. As if this gigantic weight is being lifted off me. I was less in cruise control of life and more living in the now.

The problem with living in the now, *right now*, is that I think Chase hates me. And right now, I feel horrible.

Per my call log, I tried calling him back.

A billion fucking times.

Oops.

I wanted to try again for the billion and one, but I decided to crawl off the floor and shower before I did so. I thought about putting Gerdie on my shoulder to ease the blow if he tells me he's done with me or in the other case realizes that Ellie needs him, so he can't get rid of me.

The fourth ring sounds and I'm convinced it's going to drop, when the connecting sign lights up. My heart instantly picks up, and I debate on hanging up. But then that beautiful face that I dream about day and night pops up.

"Hey," I say softly, not sure what I'm walking in to.

"What do you want, Katie?" he replies, sounding tired.

The first name only hurts. Taking a big gulp, I tuck my tail between my legs. "Listen, I'm sorry about last night."

"You don't owe me any apology."

I kind of agree.

"But I do. I know when you called it looked bad. But it's not how it was. Dex is my boss. He was just trying to help me."

"I don't need an explanation."

"But apparently you do because you seem to be mad at me." And to be honest I'm not sure he has the right to be. Yeah, it looked like more was going on when Dex had me in his arms, but let's address the fact here that Chase and I are nothing. We've never said what we are to one another. Yeah, there has been that high school banter and wedding planning for Gerdie and Ellie. But at the end of the day we are just us.

"Look, I just called last night because I saw the video and before it cut off it looked like you had fallen off the bar."

It did?

"I guess I didn't realize what kind of bar you worked at."

Whoa, wait a minute.

"What's *that* supposed to mean?" I watch him throw his hands roughly through his hair.

"That's not what I meant."

"Fuck it wasn't. What, do you have a problem with where I work? Unhappy it's not the Ritz? I work at a bar, Chase. Dive bar actually."

"That's not what I meant, Katie."

"Then what *did* you mean? Because it sounded pretty much like you were judging where I work. Listen, I told you from the start. I'm not someone you go for. You should have listened to me from the get-go." I'm picking up the volume of my voice. I refuse to acknowledge that he isn't wearing a shirt and his hair is sticking up in that sexy, I just rolled out of bed style.

"Would you stop putting words in my mouth?"

"No, Chase, I'm not putting words in your mouth, I'm stating facts. And I guess you're finally realizing I'm not for you."

"Goddammit, Katie, you are—"

Something behind him cuts him off, as he twists on his couch.

"Hey, babe, I used the key—"

"I gotta go."

And he disconnects.

What the fuck?

Chase hung up on me.

He never called me back to explain.

And who the fuck walked into his place?

I'm currently the walking statistic I wrote about in my book, because I mope around my house waiting for him to call me back. The problem is, he doesn't.

My mood plummets, and even when I order enough Chinese food for my entire building it still doesn't spark an ounce of happiness out of me. Two pounds of Lo Mein noodles and a marathon of *Dexter* later, and I just want to grab a random stranger walking down the street and wrap them in saran wrap and stab the fucking shit out of them!

Okay.

Back to sanity.

I need to get out of my apartment, but it's my day off, so I can't go to the bar. Nor do I really feel like facing Dex. End result might be *me* wrapped up in the saran wrap. I take another shower, since I smell like soy sauce, and do laundry. I clean Gerdie's cage and organize my Converse shoes by color. Black, black, black, blac—

The sound of my phone buzzing has me throwing myself

out of my closet, tripping over my laundry basket.

"Fuck," I grunt hitting the floor, scraping my knees in the process. Getting back up, I make it to my nightstand and grab my phone.

Kristen's name fills the screen.

Disappointment etched all over my face, I release the breath I was holding captive and answer.

"Hey, girl." I head back into my closet.

"Hey. How you feeling?"

"Like a million bucks, that's been trampled on and burned."

"So, you feel like beaten ash?" she asks, trying to figure out my animism.

"Sure, that. What's up?" I sit Indian style, deciding to change up the order of the shoes, oldest to newest.

"Well, I saw the video last night. Wanted to make sure you're nursing that hangover I bet you have."

"Pfft. No hangover a life-size order of Lo Mein won't cure," I say, taking my shoe rack and dumping all the pairs into my lap. This way I can go by the feel. Some shoes have been with me longer. Lasted through a lot. They mean more to me than the newer ones that I'm still on the fence about—

"Okay, so then what's up with you and Dex? I thought you two were history?"

That gets my full attention. "What do you mean, Dex? Nothing's going on. That was ages ago."

She laughs in the phone, and I hear a loud noise in the background. Most likely my video, because sadly I can hear my own voice singing *Pour Some Sugar On It*.

How embarrassing.

"Well, the video says otherwise."

"What do you mean, says *otherwise*?"

"Katie, you leap into Dex's arms, which he kinda did not look happy about and with a lemon squeezed between your lips, you force the lemon into his mouth."

I fucking did not.

"Don't worry. I took it down. The one of you almost falling too. Not that it's bad press. People like to see the real sides of authors, but there are always mixed sides. It's better to keep your personal life more to a minimum."

This also strikes up another important question for me. "And *when* did I get a fan site?"

"You're welcome. I knew you wouldn't do it. You need one. It's how you drive traffic to your books."

"I don't need traffic," I argue.

"Yes, you do. Speaking of, you haven't confirmed for the remainder of the tour."

Ugh. She threw the ball.

I knew she'd wait for me to come to her, but now that damn ball is in my court to decide whether to sign or not. If I sign the contract for the remainder of the author tour, it commits me to two more signings and the final awards conference. I don't know if it's a good idea to take off work. Even though Dex might just fire me, so I'll be completely free to go.

That and I'm not sure I have a reason to go anymore, anyways. I wasn't in it for the fame or the money, so I don't care about the signing or selling books. But Chase.

The one word that rings in my ears like a blow horn, giving me a reason to say yes to her.

"I don't know. It's just a lot to commit to. I'd have to work it out with Dex, and—"

"Oh, Dex, will say yes. He's in love with you, he doesn't

know how to say no to you."

"He is not!" He's not.

"Whatever you say. How about Charlie Bates?"

At that I choke on air. "*What*? Why?"

"I don't know, he messaged me personally, not his PR, asking me to keep the seating structure the same. He would make up any charges for the accommodations. Just was weird to me. But then I thought about how you two interacted."

I bring out my best acting skills, rolling my eyes, scrunching my eyebrows, and give her an award-winning "Pfft." "Dude, nothing. That guy? No way."

"Uh-huh."

"Dude, for real. Something's wrong with that guy. I swear he has Tourette's or something."

Okay, now I'm sounding just dumb.

"Whatever you say. But if you are. Just be careful."

"Dude, totally not."

"Fine."

"Fine!"

Can I stop acting so guilty?

"Fine. Can you just hurry up and make a decision? Your attendance is highly sought after, so I would hope you say yes to it."

I need to really stop acting like this weirdo person I don't recognize. I tell Kristen I need just a few more days, and I promise I'll give her an answer by Friday. I get off the phone and abort my shoe closet makeover.

I wish I had it in me to just pick up the phone and call Chase, but I don't. There is this thing embedded in me that tells me not to. Don't be that girl who pretends not to see the signs. And there *are* signs. I can't let go the comment about work. I've never hidden who I was, or where I worked. That's who I am. Do I wish sometimes my life may have turned out differently? Sure. Everyone does. I wanted to live on a yacht with the whole *My Little Pony* Squad. I wanted to rent a cottage in the clouds with the *Care Bears.* Do you see me doing any of those right now? No. But I'm okay with that. I'm choosing how my life's turning out and that's good enough for me. I love the bar. I love the people I work with. All in hopes I'm not fired, of course. But Chase sounded unsure. I heard it in his voice. And as much as I want to play naïve, our phone call didn't just magically get disconnected. He hung up on me. And it was due to whomever walked into his place.

The anger builds all over again.

I'm not calling him.

Asshole.

Fuck insecurities.

Fuck this stupid shoe closet.

chapter

THIRTEEN

I t's been two days.

Since the shoe closet incident.

I refuse to point out the real reason why my mood has been a little dark. He never called. And I'm okay with that. *No, I'm not.* Yes, I am. There was going to come a time where life intervened in our little fantasy world. That rabbit hole of Chase Green was going to catch up to me sooner or later and I would have been spat out. It's better it happens now before I get too attached.

Because what I am now is *not* attached.

I'm attached.

I hate men.

Maybe Stacey is right. There can't be any way I could understand why love is so flawed. Maybe because I have never gotten close enough to it to really know.

I don't have to work tonight, but I have to make things right with Dex sooner or later. I walk into Anchor, it being a Sunday night, so it's pretty tame. A live band plays for open mic night and a few patrons are sitting at tables. I don't see Randy, which means she's also off, but I do see Dex. He is casually leaning against the back of the bar, his arms crossed over his chest, listening to the band.

"Hey, stranger," I chirp, sitting on the bar stool. He doesn't expect me, so he looks shocked at first. Once he's able to compose himself, he turns away from me.

"What do you want, Beller?"

"Oh, I'm Beller now?" I tease. He turns my way and his eyes don't look very playful. *Got it.* "Okay, sorry. I just wanted to come by and apologize for the other night."

Still staring at me, I can tell he's trying to figure me out. The alien in front of him that has taken over my body, actually apologizing for something. In return, I offer him my sad puppy eyes, knowing he can't say no to that.

A few more seconds.

Okay, maybe a few more after that.

There it is. Resolution. I see it. He knows it.

He slowly unwraps his arms and walks toward me, leaning over the bar, so his face is close to mine. "If you ever get drunk like that again in my bar while you're on the clock, you're fired."

I don't speak. I've never been a 'yes, man,' so I nod my head. His eyes tell me he accepts my apology, but he looks like he's searching for more.

"Who's the guy from the call?"

"Huh?"

"The pretty boy. Is that him?"

Him equals Chase. But I'm going to play dumb. It's safer. "Not sure who you're—"

"Kat, are you fucking that guy? Are you with someone?"

Way to just lay it all out there.

I don't want to lie to Dex. He has been there for me since the moment we met. Put away all the bad shit when we attempted, crashed and burned as a couple, he truly is a great guy. And that's why I only semi lie.

"No, Dex, I'm not dating or fucking him. He's just a friend."

And that's not totally a lie. I'm not fucking him. At the moment he may or may not be a friend. That is still out for debate. Just then the band finishes, the applauses breaking our moment. Dex pulls way, knowing he has to settle with the band, and that leaves me with a scapegoat.

"So, does this mean I still have a job?" I ask, standing myself. He turns to me. That look that tells me he always wants to say more.

"You know your schedule. Don't fuckin' be late."

Ahhh, always the hard-ass. I offer him my smile that he tries to grunt at, but I know he loves, and head out. I may suck at love, or whatever it's called. But at least I still have a job.

I work a double on Monday. Tracy, the day shift bartender, called in sick, and Dex told me this was my payback. I pretended to whine and moan, but I was already out the door before we hung up. I had been in my house for almost three days, and if I sulked any more, asked my damn bird for advice or tested out that damn online magic eight ball, I was going to commit my own damn self to the 'you are pathetic, read your own book' asylum.

Tuesdays are always pretty busy, so the night went by fast. By the time I get home, my feet are killing me and I just want to pass out on my floor while pulling my jeans off.

"I knew I couldn't trust you, newer shoes. On long days it's the older ones who always stick by me." Mumbling, I throw my 'newer' Converse at the back of my closet. I pick up the second shoe to chuck it when I hear the buzzing. I freeze mid toss to hear it again. I drop my back to the ground and stretch so I can see my clock on the nightstand.

Two in the morning.

Our normal chat time.

My heartrate spikes, and I panic. My brain is screaming for me to answer my phone while my body lies in my closet frozen in time. It takes a good mental beating for me to snap out of it and shift up and run for my phone.

It's then I see it.

Bates Motel FaceTime calling.

Shit.

I panic.

Do I answer? Ignore? *Yes, you answer!* Outrageous.

Shit!

I go against my battling brain and swipe right, accepting the call. And once I do, I remember what I probably look like.

SHIT!

"Hi, Katie Beller." My name rolls gently off his tongue.

"Hey." My nerves are practically choking me, and it's apparent in my voice.

"Is it okay that I called this late?"

I take in his appearance, and as I always prefer, he's shirtless. Inspecting his surroundings, he's in another hotel room, the bedding not familiar to his own.

"Yeah, sure. Unless you're calling to get hostile with me. In that case you can just send a text. It seems hipper nowadays to break things off in text messages." Shut up, Katie.

His eyes widen with confusion. "Shit, do *you* want that?"

Now *I'm* confused. "Chase, you haven't called me in over three days. You told me you were less than pleased with my work establishment, then hung up on me. What else would I think?"

His eyes look wounded. His free hand threads through his hair. His lids are briefly closing. "I'm sorry about that." His eyes reopen and I see something in them. Conflict? Uncertainty?

"Hey, listen, it's fine. If you want out of whatever this is, it's fine—"

"Katie, stop." He sits up, bringing his phone closer, allowing me to see every beautiful feature, including the stress etched on his face. "Katie…" Saying my name again, and every second he doesn't finish that goddamn sentence, I lose those seconds off my life.

"I miss you, Katie Beller. Like fucking hell."

My breath stalls.

"I'm so sorry for our fight. I said some shitty things. I'm shitty."

"You're not shitty, Chase." It's rare I use his first name.

"No, I am. What I said about your work. I didn't mean it. I would love you—I mean, I would love any place you worked at. I wouldn't care. I just want to continue to still be a part of your little world."

My heart starts racing. The emotions I've been pretending don't exist are suddenly working their way up my throat. I feel as if I'm being pulled in two different directions. My heart wants one thing while my brain is fighting it. And my brain isn't giving up very easily.

"I have to ask." *God, I fear the answer.* "The last time we spoke. A woman. You hung up on me. Who was—"

"My sister. Just my sister."

Relief washes over me. I was worried he was going to tell me worse. His expression looks worse off, though. Maybe all this isn't to win me back or to create a future between us. Maybe it's just to ease his conscience. Dammit!

"What do you want from me, Chase?" It's a simple question but allows for an array of deeper answers. I would take the simple response. Accept the short route out of this. But I also need to know.

"I want you, Katie Beller."

"But why? Why me, Chase?" My voice cracks, the intake of breath almost choking me.

"Because you do something to me. When I'm not getting to look into those spelled eyes, I'm unsettled. When I can't hear your voice, it offsets me. When I can't watch you chew on your lip when you're close to losing it, I lose everything. Sleep, focus, care for anything." He pauses just enough to catch his own breath. "Please don't get in your head about us. I'm sorry I didn't call. I'm an ass. Fuck, I was fucking jealous of that guy carrying you. I acted like a dick. But I can't take it back. And I'm so damn sorry."

Being on FaceTime doesn't allow you to hide your emotions. I can't mask the tears welling up behind my eyelids.

"Say something, please."

I slowly inhale air into my lungs. I'm strung tight in a trap of emotions I'm not used to. I've been living the motto that the only thing in life that matters, the only steps I take that are important, are the ones I do myself. But with Chase. I see this vision. This future. That he may be in it. And that scares the fuck out of me. I have this heart that's been dead or just seriously broken for most of my life coming alive and wanting to beat the hell out of my chest just at the thought of him. And *that* seriously freaks the shit out of me even more.

But hearing him confess, his pleas for us to *be* an us. To be something. That does something to me too. Gives me hope? Fills that empty dark place I've secretly wished to have filled? I always thought I missed my chance at this. And maybe I haven't.

Sometimes with Chase it feels like I can't breathe. He suffocates me with all the emotions he causes me to feel. Sadly, I question, is this the "aka" love that all those people talk about? Or is this the real thing? Is this why it hurts and feels so strong? If I don't open up to Chase, will I be missing my chance?

There may always be that doubt about us and how different we are. I will always be who I am. And he will be him. But maybe life has something up its sleeve for us. Opposites attract and all that shit. I just don't want to miss my chance. And by being so scared of the 'what might bes' with Chase, I might do that.

I just need to take that goddamn leap.

Jump off that cliff, in serious hopes that Chase and his words catch me along the way.

"I miss you too, Chase Green like the color," I reply just above a whisper.

I'm not weak by any means, but there will always be

something Chase Green does to me. "Weak in the knees" by SWV is sadly playing in my head during this serious moment, but fuck it. He makes me feel like nothing I have ever experienced, and that song was seriously awesome in the nineties. I offer him a reassuring smile and the relief on his face is evident. His fingers lift, as he touches his screen.

"Thank you for not giving up on me."

I blush, as if I can feel the warmth of his fingers caressing my cheek. "You don't have to thank me," I say, feeling suddenly shy.

"I do. Because if I messed this up, then I wouldn't have been able to forgive myself." He sits up straighter, his shoulders going up and down with each deep breath. "Not being able to see you, hear you. God, I want nothing more than to touch those lips for real. Not just this FaceTime bullshit. I need you. All of you." His words mimic exactly what's swirling in my head. It's been so long since Chicago. "Tell me you're signing up for the next event in Denver. Because if you tell me no, I'll fucking kidnap you and force you to—"

"I'm going to sign up for the rest of the tour," I blurt out. I hadn't made up my mind. Kristen has been blasting my phone with creative emojis wanting an answer, but I still wasn't sure.

But right now.

Listening to him.

I am.

"You're coming."

"Well, not at this moment. But on the rest of the tour, yes."

His eyes light with that special Chase Green Mischievous. "If you were here with me right now, I'd make you come so hard you'd lose feeling in your legs."

At that I laugh. I imagine he probably could succeed at

that. I love the way his smile reaches his eyes. He looks happy. Far from the man in the beginning of our phone call. God, I missed our chats. These intimate moments, where we felt free to be ourselves. I snuggle into my bed, bringing my knees to my chest.

"Well, that sounds like a challenge, Green. But just my legs? Sounds half ass if you ask me." My skin breaks out in a feverish layer of goosebumps at the darkness his eyes overtake. My hands rise to touch my neck of their own accord. My fingers brush at my neckline, knowing this is one of his favorite spots.

"You're evil. You know my dick is hard as stone right now." He maneuvers so he's using only one hand to hold his phone.

My imagination is working overtime on where his other hand just disappeared to. I bring my hand in between my breastbone, sliding it down my belly button, just to the lining of my underwear.

"Do you think it's comparable to how wet I am?" I know I've won this one when I notice his arm movement. He's stroking himself. "I wish you were here so I could show you. Have your fingers deep inside me. Soaking them." I close my eyes and dip my fingers inside my panties. Lo and behold, I'm actually drenched. I hum as I begin to pleasure myself, the mental image of his beautiful, thick fingers on my mind.

"You're killing me, baby." His voice is hoarse and I can tell he's working himself harder. "Show me your pussy. I want to see what you're doing to yourself."

Without care, I flip the phone so it views outward and he gets an eyeful of my hand working myself in a lustful frenzy.

"Fucking beautiful. I want to be there sucking on you, my tongue inside you, my finger so deep, you're fighting for air, the pleasure overbearing. Yeah. Faster. Fuck, fuck…"

I begin to clench, my thighs fighting not to close. I moan Chase's name loudly as I explode all over my finger. I hear Chase's brutal grunt and know he's right behind me.

Feeling sated and perfect, I almost don't open my eyes. I flip the phone view back on myself and pop one lazy eye open.

"That was fun."

"We need to do this in the flesh and soon."

Agreed.

Chase starts into a light conversation about his day, telling me about some important scouting for an NHL hockey team. If he catches the eye of some big-time scouts, there's a chance he could be drafted to the big times, and all his problems would go away.

I yawn, asking him what problems he's referring to, and his response is generic, telling me the one where we are a hundred miles apart.

I feel like I blink and when I open my eyes again, I notice my phone is resting on my chest. I look at the time and it's almost five in the morning. I pick up my phone, but Chase is gone.

"Oh, shit." I must have fallen asleep on the phone. I notice I have a missed text message.

Bates Motel: Thank you for showing me this amazing happiness I never knew existed. Sweet dreams, Katie Beller.

I clutch my phone to my chest, as I turn to my side and snuggle into my pillow.

No, thank you, Chase Green, for showing me how to live again.

chapter FOURTEEN

The Westin Hotel, Denver Colorado—Two weeks later.

I climb out of the cab, offering the man a hefty tip. His impeccable speeding skills got us to the hotel seven minutes early. He helps me with my bag, and I head into the Westin hotel in downtown Denver. The hotel isn't historical like Chicago's, but more modern and chic.

Anxiousness floods through my body as I check in. Excitement. Nervousness. A vibration of all sorts of shit, knowing that in just minutes, I get to see Chase. In the flesh.

I lift my phone from my bag and send him a quick text that I've arrived. He replies instantly, telling me he's coming for me. A layer of goose bumps flutter over my skin at the thought of his hands on me, in me. The flush in my cheeks has me looking around, making sure no one's staring at me. I hurry and check in, and make my way to the elevator when I see him.

In all his manly glory. When our eyes meet, goose bumps cover my entire body just at the way he's staring at me. Swallowing me with his gaze. My blushed smile spreads across my face and we both step forward into action, heading to one another—

"Oh my God! I didn't think you were coming until tomorrow!" I stop suddenly when Kristen appears in front of me.

Shit! "Heeey!"

She comes in and hugs me while I look over her shoulder at Chase.

Sorry, I mouth and pull away.

"So, what happened? Did I mess up your days? Shit, I'm sorry, I would've picked you up from the airport."

"No, no, it's fine. I just thought to, um, surprise you. Be a good client and come early."

"Oh! Okay." She's looking at me quizzically. "What's up with you? You look funny."

Probably because I'm trying to smile but resemble more of a constipated person. But I'm super nervous. I suck at playing it cool, and Chase is walking up behind us.

"Me? *Pfft*, nothing. I'm just glad to be here." Oh God, don't come up to us—

"Hello, ladies," Chase speaks, startling Kristen. She whips to her side, taking him in.

Another look of confusion on her face.

"Mr. Bates. Hello... I... I wasn't expecting you until tomorrow. Sorry, was your room all set up?" She lifts her hand, which is holding a bunch of papers, sifting through the bundle. "Yeah, I have you arriving tomorrow. Man, I'm off my game. First Katie, now..." She looks at him. And fuck. Turns to look at me. Don't let it click. Don't let it click—

Fuck.

It clicks.

"Hmmm... Interesting. Well, I hope the hotel was able to accommodate the two of you."

I'm just nodding like an idiot, my head resembling a broken bobble head. Chase is standing there with his hands in his pockets and that damn sexy smile on his face.

Kristen turns her attention fully on me. "Well, since you're here, wanna go catch some dinner? There's a really good sushi place downtown."

Chase doesn't move his head, but his eyes are going back and forth.

"Yeah, um. I'm kinda tired. Gonna just order some pizza. Bring my bags up and what not." Oh my God, I'm not even holding any bags, since I left them with the concierge.

"Hmmm..." Is all she says. She looks at Chase, back at me. "So, I assume then you're just going to head up now?" This cannot be going any worse right now. Kristen is clearly trying to call me out. Not sure why. This all could be a very strange coincidence.

"Yeah, super tired. Traveling is exhausting." Says the person whose flight was under two hours.

"Hmm... Mr. Bates, how about you? You hungry?" Now she's just starting trouble.

I gape at Chase, wondering how he's going to get out of it.

"Just ate, sorry. Thanks for the offer, though. I was just headed... to the gym... huge workout comin' on."

I'm going to kill him.

The look on Kristen's face pretty much says, thanks for the TMI, and shakes her head. "Well, alright then. Why don't you go take that nap. Drinks later then. No excuses." She waves to Chase and turns, taking off down the long hotel corridor.

The moment the door shuts behind us, I'm up in Chase's arms, my back slamming against the wall. My legs wrap around his lean waist and his lips are on mine.

"God, I've missed you," he moans, devouring my mouth, delighting me with the sweet taste of mint on his tongue. His grip is lethal, squeezing my ass through my yoga pants as he presses his already hard cock into me. "Feel that? That guy's been like that since the second I met you. You make me hard as hell all the damn time." He prolongs our kiss, taking my lips fully, his tongue mingling with my own.

This feels like heaven and hell mixed in one. We can't seem to get at each other fast enough. Chase increases the pressure of his grip, grinding himself into me. We both moan at the contact.

"You always taste so sweet." He releases my mouth, working his way to my bottom lip.

"The red bull vodka I had on the flight should take credit for that. Why are our clothes still on?" I moan, going straight for his belt buckle. His phone vibrates in his front pocket, which is a nice add-on to our hot make-out session. I grab for it, pulling it out.

"Hmmm, not a bad add-on." I turn the screen over.

"Sterling Marketing wants to get in on this action," I say, wiggling his phone between us.

Working his hands up my ribcage, he suddenly stops, reaching for the phone. "Give that to me."

The call ends and starts ringing again. Same caller.

"Your marketing company sure is eager to talk to you. Want me to answer and tell them you're busy?" I joke, pretending to answer the call.

Chase's demeanor changes, grabbing for his phone. "Don't."

"Why, you're not into threesomes?" Totally kidding since I'm definitely a one-on-one kinda girl.

"Katie, give me the phone." Again, call missed and a third time, the phone vibrates. He catches me off guard, snatching the phone from my hands. Tossing the phone, his hands are back on me, cupping my breast through my thin T-shirt, squeezing. His thumb and index finger take latch of my nipple and pinch.

Phone quickly forgotten, my mouth is back on his. "Clothes, Chase, now." I need nakedness, sex, lots and lots of orgasms.

His hands become ruthless, fondling my chest while he sucks on my lower lip, kisses my chin, my neckline, his hips pushing into mine.

"So eager, aren't we?" He chuckles into my neck, his lips wet and inviting on my heated skin. Maneuvering his hands, he reaches for the hem of my pants and dives in. His fingers travel down in between my thighs, pushing my underwear to the side. He groans, discovering how wet I already am. Using two fingers, he smears my juices around my sex. "Damn, baby, you're fucking soaking." And he's pushing two fingers inside.

I forget just how good it felt to have him touch me. Mimicking his fingers with my own does his fingers no justice.

"More, please," I moan, dropping my head back against the wall. His warm mouth is back on me, kissing me feverishly. He maintains a slow but aggressive pace as he continues to finger fuck me. I'm quickly losing my grip on my orgasm. Chase can feel my insides gripping him, so he pulls out slowly. Taking a moment to grab my vision, he slides back in. Each time pushing deeper. It's when I feel his knuckles at the opening of my sex that my body trembles with need.

"Fuck, yes, more."

"Such a little beggar you are." He laughs, but grants my wish. His fingers less calculated and greedier, he works me faster, harder, taking my mouth, his tongue colliding with mine. Each thrust of his fingers is matched with his groin rubbing into me. The feel of how hard he is makes me want him, crave him with an animalistic urge.

"Fuck, Chase, I'm gonna... Fuck, ahhh..." And with him slamming roughly into me I come all over his hand, my walls capturing his fingers in a death grip.

Chase eases up on our kiss, slowly pressing small wet pecks around my lips, down my chin, and across my collarbone. As I catch my breath, I pull my head up, my eyes on his.

"Holy shit, that was awesome."

Chase busts out laughing.

"That was just a preview of what I have planned for you." He pulls his fingers out of my pants, lifting them to his mouth. He's *not* going to do that. Before I can swat his hand away, or die of embarrassment, he sticks his fingers, covered in my juices, into his mouth.

"Fucking perfect," he says as he licks them clean, making

a popping sound as he pulls them out. "It's like getting dessert before dinner."

I cover my face. "Ew, Green, you watch too much porn. That's not really a thing." I mean, I don't *think* it's a thing. My long résumé of sexual partners agrees.

He pulls us off the wall, walking us toward the bed. "Well, it's a thing for me. You've been teasing me with that sweet little pink pussy of yours. And ever since that first night, I've been thinking about how sweet it is. And how you've been taunting me on FaceTime. I might just take some to go, for whenever you're not around."

Ew! How can you take juices to go?

"That was just an appetizer for me, though. It's time for the main meal." He tosses me on the bed.

"Clothes off, beautiful," he requests as he does the same, lifting his shirt up and over his head. He doesn't break eye contact as I sit up and pull my shirt off. He tosses his onto the floor. As I shimmy out of my pants, he unbuckles his. I pull my thong down with mine, leaving me bare, but still, he doesn't take his eyes off me.

Damn, he's good.

Reaching in his back pocket, he places a condom wrapper in between his teeth.

Then he drops his pants.

Don't look. Don't look. Don't... shit.

I look.

His dick is fucking gorgeous. I'm not sure a dick is supposed to be beautiful. It's a dick, but by golly his is fucking pretty. I want to pet it and brush its hair. I *definitely* want to suck on it a little bit.

What the fuck did I just say?

"You said you wanted to suck on it."

What!

"Oh God, I said that out loud?"

"Sure did. You have your eye on the prize, I see," he pokes fun, stepping out of his pants. Walking to me, he climbs on the bed and straddles me. His model cock in perfect view, he rips the foil package open and places it on the tip of his dick. I can't help but watch him as he slides it down his shaft, wishing that were my hand stroking him. I can tell the way I'm ogling him is turning him on. Once fully in place, his hand slowly works its way back up and down again.

"Did you want me to leave you alone or am I gonna get to join in?" I tease, watching him gently stroke himself.

"Oh, you're gonna join in, all right." He chuckles, leaning forward, taking my mouth. His lips graze mine, as his knees inch my thighs open. "You're the main attraction." He releases my lips and whispers in my ear. Positioning himself perfectly, he pushes inside me.

I think both our eyes close, lost in the sensation of us. Our bodies suck each other whole. Our hands grip one another, wanting to be savages and wild, but our touch is unhurried, gentle. Chase's slowness brings my hands into his hair, pressing for more closeness. Every time he pulls out, I urge him back in. I don't want to acknowledge what's happening, but this is not like the rest. This isn't just sex. It has meaning. Emotion. Unspoken words.

He brings himself out and again slides back, the perfection of his cock triggering my eyelids to shut. With closed eyes I grab his hair, bringing his head down. His lips hit mine and it's like perfection exploding. Our tongues connect and the electricity sparks, breaking whatever silent moment we were sharing to end. The temptation, the urge for one another breaks through, and we begin to tear at one another. His movements become more aggressive. His hands claim every part of my body, his tongue claiming me.

My groans of pleasure mingle with his as we fuck, make love, connect in a way that's new for me. Who knows what it's like for him, but I feel it. An unfamiliar territory we just entered. I last two more powerful thrusts before I lose control and clench, letting my orgasm rip through me. Chase isn't far behind, because he thrusts roughly once, twice and on the third, he cums inside me.

We're both breathing heavily, trying to catch our breath. We're sweaty and naked. I try and conjure up something humorous to say, because I'm afraid this just got awkward. Before I have a chance to speak, Chance leans up, catching my eyes.

"I missed you."

Three words.

Simple. But so much pow.

"I… I missed you too."

He pulls his hands away from my waist and wraps them into my hair. "No, I really missed you. Not just this." He brings his eyes to our still connected bodies. "I missed *you*." His eyes back to mine, his look soft but with a thousand-pound weight of meaning to them. "Would you laugh at me if I confessed I was nervous to see you?"

"Pfft, I doubt that," I reply.

"Swear it. I paced the hotel lobby for almost thirty minutes trying to think of something cool to say to you when I saw you."

I stare up at him until I realize he's not joking. Then I

bust out laughing. "And what speech exactly did you come up with?" I ask.

He bends down, offering me a quick peck. "Well, I didn't get very far. It started with, Hello, you look super-hot and I'm going to eat you raw. Can I help carry your bags?"

Oh my God!

I squeal in a fit of laughter.

"Why are you laughing? Would you have allowed me to carry your things if I said that?" he asks, starting to tickle my ribs.

"Stop!" I yelp, struggling to catch my breath between fits. "Seriously, yes, I would have not only let you carry my bags, but I would have let you feast on me all night long."

He stops instantly.

I open my eyes, catching him intensely staring down at me.

"Now what?" I ask, trying to control my breathing.

"You just make me the kind of happy that I don't know how to explain." He's looking me over, making sure his words sink in. "I know you think it's because of your thunder cat ways in bed, but it's more."

At that I roll my eyes. He chuckles, pressing another kiss to my lips.

"You're something I can't explain, Katie. I know you'll fight me and say how opposite we are. But to me, we're the same."

I'm not sure what similarities we carry, but the look in his eyes says he's going to tell me.

"Anything that's happening in my life, good or bad, the first thing I do is think about you. Because you're the one I want to share it with."

A small intake of breath has me surprised at his confession. I don't have to think hard before realizing the same conclusion. I reach up, cupping his smooth-shaven cheek. "I would have to agree with you on that. You're my go-to too, Green. I think you have been for a long time now."

He crushes his mouth onto mine. Immediately, he's parting my lips with his tongue.

"Tell me more," he hums, pulling away and kissing down my chin.

"Tell you what?" I sigh, stretching my neck to give him better access.

"Tell me all the things you like about me. Besides my glorious cock. I'm feeling needy and need you to make me feel wanted." I prepare to whack him in the head, but he licks down my neck, taking a small nip out of my skin. I drop my hand and moan, arching my body into him.

"You have great tongue skills," I say, my eyes shut, lips slightly parted.

"This is an obvious statement. Doesn't count. Try again." He bends lower, wrapping his wet lips around my nipple. Using his *skilled* tongue, he begins a swirling motion around my flesh.

"I love your hands," I reply and instantly yelp as he bites down on my nipple.

"Doesn't count. I already know you're obsessed with my physical attributes. Give me something from here." He lifts his hand, placing it over my heart. He raises his head, catching the sudden nervousness in my eyes. "Tell me the first thing that comes to mind from here."

I don't know what he wants me to say. Confess all my wants, dreams, desires for this man? That would be opening myself up for disappointment and hurt, if this wasn't really what this was. And if I'm not the protective bear over my own heart, who will be?

"Give me something. Let me know I'm not just a piece of meat to you."

I laugh. This is silly. I'm being silly. There's nothing wrong with a few friendly praises between lovers. "All right. Well…" I stall. Just spit it out, Katie. "I like the way you smile at me. It makes me feel… pretty." Oh my God, that sounded so corny!

"Because you're beautiful. And you make me happy. And I have never smiled with such intent the way I do with you."

Okay his, comment was *way* deeper. There's a tornado of butterflies forming in my stomach. He's still staring down at me, his eyes filled with meaning. Intent.

"I also lied. I want more than just one."

I slowly nod. My mind is racing with a million things I want to admit. How my life has been so much happier since he's come into it. How his kindness has made me feel worth something. I want to admit that my heart feels like it's beating for the first time since losing my parents. Maybe the bear in me is holding me back from giving my heart the full package. Maybe I need to step aside and let whatever this is fully in.

"You make me feel alive. And I haven't felt that way in a very long time." I feel his body go rigid the moment the words leave my lips.

Idiot.

I couldn't have said something more basic like I enjoy your laugh or some shit?

"You don't have to reply—"

Chase covers my mouth with his large hand. "Shut up, Katie. Don't you dare take that back." He slowly brings his hand away, dipping down to kiss me. Pulling away, he says, "I started living again the day I fell into your room. What I had before. It wasn't happiness. It wasn't real. I know this is crazy. Us, it's all crazy. But I've known something for some time now, and I just need to get it off my chest."

Oh, fuck.

"Katie, I'm…"

BANG! BANG! BANG!

What the…

BANG! BANG! BANG!

"Open up, Katie!"

Oh shit!

"Shit, it's Kristen."

Chase frowns, and I panic as I toss him off me. He catches himself just before falling off the bed, and we both start scrambling for our clothes.

"I can't find my pants," Chase says, looking around the room.

"Fuck! Well, just leave without 'em, hurry!" I throw my shirt over my head and snatch my pants off the floor.

"Seriously, Bates, get out." I jump in front of the mirror to see how disheveled I look. "Fuck." Yeah, I look like a guilty little hussy who was just getting it on.

"We have a problem."

I whip around to face Chase, wondering why he's even still in my room, when I notice him standing by the closed connecting door.

"No…" I breathe.

"We never went and unlocked it from the other side."

"Oh my God."

"Katie! Open up, man!"

Shit!

"Get in the closet."

"What?"

"Get in the closet! Right now."

"You have to be kidding—"

I don't have time to argue. I'm already pushing him inside and shutting the door on his pretty little face. I swear if he makes a peep, I'm going to murder him.

"Katie—"

I whip the hotel door open and smile way too brightly. "Hey! What's up?"

"Uhh, nothing. What took you so long?"

I allow her to enter my room, my heart about to beat out of my chest when she stops directly in front of the closet.

"Sorry, I was, trying to do a workout video."

"A workout video? Yeah, right. Do you even know what working out is?" She stands there, her hands gripping her hips.

I give her my infamous *Pffft* face and start jogging in place. "Pfft. Yes, of course! See? Fitness is a new thing. Gotta stay fit and all."

She glares at me, looking uncomfortable at my sweet workout move. "First off, you look like a monkey trying to climb an invisible tree. Please stop. Second, you do realize that your infamous *I'm lying* motto is Pfft."

I gasp at her very accurate accusation.

"I'm *insulted.*"

"I'm sure. Your room smells weird…"

"My shoes. Old pair."

"I was going to say more like—"

"Sweat! I'm sweating. I need to shower."

I wish she'd stop giving me the crazy eye. "Great, sooo…"

Shaking her head, she says, "Whatever you say, workout time's over. Let's grab food. I barely ever get to see you, so you're coming out with me. Then we're going dancing."

Dancing? I hate dancing. And my stomach is in knots right now with what Kristen just interrupted. The last thing I want to do right now is eat.

"Okay, so go get in the shower. I'll wait for you."

Fuck!

Why must my friend have the worst timing ever?

"You know what. I don't need to shower. Let's just go." I walk toward the door, grabbing her arm and dragging her with me.

"But you just said you smell?"

"Yeah, well... For some people it's a turn on. Going to play my cards right tonight. Now let's go."

chapter FIFTEEN

So maybe my stomach wasn't in *that* big of a knotted mess, because after Kristen insisted I borrow some clothes, since she realized I was still in a tank and yoga pants, she took me to this amazing Mexican place and I just polished off an unimaginable number of tacos. After I got over the initial panic that I left Chase in my room, partially naked, I came to the realization that he was a big boy and could take care of himself. Then I began stuffing my face.

Kristen kept the conversation off me and her suspicions, thankfully, and allowed me to stuff my face while she complained about the tour. I guess I never put too much thought into what goes into these signings, but the background work sounds absolutely horrible. Ticky-tacky requests, needy authors, no-shows, and all the safety guidelines needed for everyone involved. I would have never known that seven people passed out of dehydration at the last signing, four authors bailed last minute, and security had to break up three fights due to long line issues. And that was just on day one!

Feisty little gang of attendees.

We're currently walking into Flame nightclub, a dance club on the east side of town. Kristen insisted since I was a day early and we didn't have to be up till later tomorrow, it was time to drink. And drinking is what she plans to do.

"Two rounds of tequila and two vodka tonics," she orders, swinging her back against the bar to admire the hoppin' dance floor. "Man, I bet there's a bunch of eligible ass out there."

I spare her a look as she licks her lips. "Jesus, how long has it been?" I gape, feeling bad for my poor friend. Or for the victim she clasps her needy claws into later.

"Oh, don't give me that wait it out for love crap. I love you, but I need ass now. I can't care less what they say that leads me to getting some. Plus, I've been swamped with work. No time to date."

"Who says you need to date to get laid?" Wow, do *I* sound like a walking hypocrite.

"Well, yeah, too busy for that too."

Looking back at the dance floor, I feel her head turn, now giving me the look over.

"And what about you? You're clearly getting it."

I turn, and she's looking at me in that curious, but aggressive 'spill or else' kinda way.

"Who, me? No. Sex? Like with who? Like what even is that?" Shut up, Katie.

"Then it's a good thing you and I came out tonight. We can both get some no name tail."

Yeah.

Right.

"Oh, yeah, what about that guy? He seems to know his way around the dance floor." She points, and I take a good look at the dude who is recreating *A night at the Roxbury* when a large group enters the club. "He doesn't look like he's wearing a ring—"

"You've got to be kidding..." I trail off as I watch a few authors who I recognize, some readers, and the one and only.

"What are you... oh, yeah, this is a prime spot for events. Close to the hotel. Focus on the dance floor. I mean, look at him move. Do you think I should just go up to him?"

I really can't focus on that train wreck on the dance floor when my traitorous eyes won't stop staring at Chase. He's changed since ditching him in my closet. Now dressed in a pair of dark fitted jeans, and a white henley shirt that looks as if it was made just for him, his hair perfectly in place, it doesn't take long for him to feel my eyes on him and he turns, catching me gawking. As soon as I see that slow smile creep up his sexy as fuck face, I whip my head away. Then groan, because my current view is now the hot mess on the dance floor.

"Your drinks. That'll be twenty-one even."

Kristen insists on paying for this round, and we let her prospect do his thing while we tend to more important matters. Kristen lifts up her shot, and I follow suit.

"To you being super awesome and killing it at the signing."

I roll my eyes, because I'm not sure I'm killing it. There are way bigger authors here than me, not to mention ones who have way better free shit on their tables.

"Don't even give me your bullshit. Just say *thank you, Kristen* and take the shot with me."

I smile, shoving down the bullshit I was totally going to reply with.

"Thank you, Kristen." I beam my pearly whites at her, and we both throw back the shot. I place my empty glass on the bar, as I grab for my drink. Just as I place the straw into my mouth, I feel him. I don't want to admit how creepy it is how my body reacts even when I can't psychically see him, but I know he's near me. I'm sucking in as much liquid as possible, when his deep voice washes over me, sending a blizzard of goose bumps over my skin.

"Hello, ladies. Fancy meeting you here." Fancy my ass.

Kristen turns first, while I pretend he's not there. Still sipping or chugging my drink, I wave down the bartender to come back. And to hurry.

"Oh, hey, Charlie. Hanging with some of the authors tonight, I see?"

At that I turn.

Still sucking on my straw like it's my job, I stare at Chase, waiting for him to respond. Not that I should care. He can hang out with whoever he wants to. Even though I did see the pretty brunette two tables down walk in with him.

"Yeah, trying to get to know everyone. Plus, I didn't want to stay holed up in the closet all night long."

Kristen looks confused.

I choke on my drink.

"Okay then. Well, have fun. Just ignore Katie and me tonight. We're planning on making horrible decisions. Whatever you do, no mention of this once we're all back on the clock." Kristen turns back to the bar and grabs for her drink while Chase's eyebrows lift in curiosity.

"Is that so, Ms. Swan?" he questions, throwing down the

gauntlet. I don't know what to say because he's standing there, with his hands shoved in his jeans pockets, his eyes unblinking, waiting for a confirmation or denial. I'm busy choking on my own words, so I shrug my shoulders instead. Before I get the full visual of his frown, Kristen saves me. She nudges me, and I turn as another tequila shot is shoved in my hands.

And since I'm a total pussy, instead of using my words to explain to Chase that I wasn't planning to find a random warm body to lie with, I fill my mouth with tequila in its place.

"Wow, well, then you two ladies enjoy. I'm going to get to know Amber a bit more. Or is it Kelly? These pen names. But I hear she writes"—he bends forward as we both lean into him—"erotica. Bet she has an imagination a man can appreciate." He pulls away, winks at us, and walks straight into the damn dance floor.

My mouth falls to the floor, as we both gape at his tight ass sway as he disappears into the crowd.

"That Amber is one lucky bitch. I wouldn't mind adding Charlie Bates to my bucket list."

"Tell me about it…" Wait, *what*? I turn, smacking her in the arm.

"Hey!"

Mine.

Shit.

"I mean, *ew*! No way. You can do *waaay* better. He probably has some sort of disease. Model disease. Yeah, model disease. Stay clear." Shut up. Right now.

150

That little weasel. He wasn't kidding when he said he was going to test out Amber. Because he hasn't left the goddamn dance floor! My jealousy spikes with every song that comes on and that smile he's carrying doesn't leave his stupid face. He looks like he's enjoying her. And she can dance. Like really dance. The way her hips move back and forth, her hands all whipping her hair around, I mean, how does someone learn how to do that obnoxious dance? And why the ever-loving fuck is Chase enjoying it?

I thought he was just trying to get under my skin when he made that comment. I mean, so I didn't confirm I wasn't going to hook up with a random tonight, but he had to know I wouldn't. But did he? I continue to stand at the bar, getting myself all worked up over his actions. He hasn't even looked over my way once since he walked away. Doesn't he even care what I'm thinking? What if I was at the bar sucking face with a dude? Would he even care?

It's like he's tempting me to do something about it. With every hip grab, he's daring me to come and claim him. *Which* I will not do. Who does he think I am? A lying dog who will comply with his threats? Two can play at this game of who really wants who, bullshit.

I slam my drink on the bar, startling Kristen. "Let's dance," I state, starting toward the dance floor.

"Uh, I thought you don't dance," I hear her state the truth as she catches up to me.

I push my way through the crowd, finding a group of guys in the middle of the dance floor. Perfectly aligned next to Chase.

Fucker.

"You guys wanna dance?" I yell over the loud music,

offering my sweetest smile. I'm a little drunk and have no game, so not sure what that smile really comes off as. Either way it works, because we get a few hell yeahs from the crowd, and Kristen is grabbed by the waist by a cute guy. Tall, dark hair. Just up her alley. The guy I addressed takes claim on me. He isn't really my type, no blazing green eyes, perfect dirty-blond hair. He doesn't look at me the way that makes my knees beg to buckle. But the second I get a quick glimpse of Chase in my side vision, I realize this guy will do just fine.

I grab his hand and pull him to me. Kristen is right when I say I don't dance. Mainly because I don't know how to, so this game of who can make who jealous more, quickly starts blowing up in my face, since I look like I'm having a seizure over trying to get hot and heavy on the dance floor. The guy grabs at my hips and "Whoa!" I squeal as he whips me around, throwing my butt into his groin.

"Don't worry, I'll do all the moves for us," he yells into my ear and starts a slow, but inappropriate, as they call it, bump-ing and grinding into my ass. I've suddenly forgotten about Chase and our game, because I'm momentarily mortified at what's happening. Homeboy is swaying me back and forth like a rag doll, sounds leaving his mouth, causing the tequila to churn in my stomach. I look over at Kristen for help, but she seems to be enjoying herself and the grinding. *Shit.* Before I allow this dude to get off on dry humping my ass, I pull away and excuse myself, claiming major bathroom break.

I finally get my turn, since chicks' bathroom has only one stall, and shut the door, thankful for the privacy. I don't get the opportunity to lock it, because it's suddenly pushed open. When I turn to give hell to whoever doesn't know how to wait their damn turn, I realize that person is Chase, as he pushes himself into the bathroom and shuts the door.

Then locks it.

"Seriously, what's your deal with women's bathrooms?" I snap, trying not to stare at his mouth, his tight shirt, his eyes. Those damn fucking eyes. He doesn't answer me, but prowls in my direction until he has me backed up against the wall.

"Are we done plaything this game?"

I have no idea what he's talking about.

"Not sure what you mean."

He brings up his warm hands and, placing them on my hips, he drags them down until he hits the bottom of my skirt. "You know exactly what game I'm talking about."

Admit nothing.

"No idea what you're talking about." I close my eyes as his palms hit my bare legs, squeezing my thighs as he brings his hands back up my legs.

"The game where you pretend you're here tonight to get lucky and make me jealous. The game where I pretend I want someone else until we both finally admit we only want each other." His hands reach the lining of my panties, capturing the thin strap around his fingers, and begins tugging them down my legs.

"Chase, wha-what are you doing?" My voice is thick with need, and as soon as I get my shit together, I'm going to push him off me.

Which doesn't look to be anytime soon.

Somehow, I willingly step out of my panties and watch with hooded lids as he sticks my thong into his pocket. He steps forward, leaving zero space between us.

"Will it help if I went first?" he says, his breath a warm delight against my cheeks.

I nod.

He leans in, his lips grazing mine. "Right now, I'm insane with jealousy at the way that fucker handled you. I wanted to break each finger that touched you."

Okay. That was *so* hot.

He grazes his lips to the corner of my mouth, offering me just a tease. "I think it's time I stake my claim." One brush of his lips to mine. "You're mine, Katie." Another kiss, this one more pressure. "And no one else's."

Okay. He's got me.

My hands are up and locking into his hair. His hands are around my hips, lifting me up. My legs wrap around his waist and our lips collide into one another.

Both sets of hands grabbing, pulling, ripping to get to one another. My skirt is up and over my hips, my hands frantically tearing at his pants.

"We shouldn't be doing this here," I pant, getting his zipper down and releasing his large erection. The feel of how hard and smooth he is in my palm overrides the wrongness of what we're doing. Chase pushes his jeans down and grabs for his cock. He places it exactly where it's begging to be, and without further thought pushes inside me.

"Oh God," I moan, pulling at Chase's hair as he frantically thrusts in and out of me. He's not taking his time, nor is he being gentle. He's not trying to woo me; he's making a statement.

"Mine," he grunts, taking my breath away with each brutal kiss he offers me. I can't control the swirling wave of possession also building in my chest. The electric current in my core. I press my fingernails deeper into his skin, bringing him closer to me.

A firework of sensations blasts to every one of my nerve

endings and my orgasm detonates through me. Chase is right behind me, pushing one last time, before I feel his hot release inside me.

Panting, I say, "I can't believe we just had sex in a public bathroom."

Chase is trying to catch his breath, splaying wet kisses down my neck.

"It was a must do," he replies, quickly kissing my lips and allowing my legs to drop. He pulls out, and I wobble, trying to get my bearings. I feel the wetness sliding down my thigh and groan.

"Oh my God, we really did just have sex in a public bathroom. With a line outside!" While I'm completely mortified, Chase doesn't seem affected. He laughs and grabs for the paper towel dispenser, ripping off a few sheets and helping me clean up. "And why are you just laughing?"

Of course, banging on the door cuts his answer short. His non-answer, that is. I jump into action, pushing his hands away and cleaning myself up. I look in the mirror and "fuck." I look like I just got fucked in a public bathroom. Chase laughs again, and I'm fighting to keep from punching him clear out.

"You know we could have waited till we got home to do this. Acting like horny teenagers isn't normally my thing," I say, pulling my skirt down and fixing my hair.

Chase looks perfect as always, not a hair out of place. He washes his hands and turns to me, an approving smile on his face. "It was apparent I made a point. Which, by the way, you just orgasmed. I did also. Now when you go out there and if that douche from *A Night at the Roxbury* tries to come near you, he will smell me all over you."

My mouth falls open just as his smile grows wider. "You... You..."

The banging on the door startles me again, and it's when Kristen's voice seeps through the door that I go into complete panic mode. "Jesus! It's like she has a radar anytime I'm around you!"

"Katie, are you in there? Everything okay?"

Shit!

"Better let your friend know everything's okay," he says, ducking as I lift my hand to smack him.

"Katie?"

I push Chase into the stall and slam the door. "Don't come out." And I do one last hopeless adjustment of my outfit and hair, then open the door.

"Hey, what... are you okay?"

"Yeah, fine. Those tacos, though... *Man.* You do not want to go in there," I stress and pull her shoulder to lead her away from the bathroom.

"But I swear I heard... Were you moaning in there?"

God, yes.

"No! I was watching a video while pooping. Things kids post nowadays." I don't make eye contact. It's just not necessary. I drag her back to the bar and insist the next round be on me.

And the round after that.

And after that.

chapter SIXTEEN

There is an entire marching band inside my head, beating on my brain. And they are horrible. No real beat or rhythm. Just bang, bang, pow, kick on my head, causing a splitting feeling to rip through my frontal lobe.

I groan as I flip onto my side, realizing I'm partially lying on a warm body. Oh God. Please be someone I know. Please be… I open one eye to a body, thank God, I recognize. Chase is sleeping, his mouth slightly parted as his chest rises and falls.

Shit. How did I get home last night? I close my eye because the light is making the banging worse and I rest my head on his chest. *Did I walk? Did Kristen come with me? Did…*

"Good morning."

Rats. I take in a deep breath and reopen my eye. "Hi," I

respond nervously. I would have never thought in a million years I would ever forget a night of passion with Chase Green, but this fine morning, I cannot, for the life of me, remember the end of my night.

"How you feeling?"

Yeah, I feel like that's a trick question.

"Good, and you?" Gonna reverse psychology this.

"I feel fine, but that's because I didn't drink the bar out of tequila last night."

I groan again, embarrassed, and shut my eyes. "Tell me I didn't do anything embarrassing."

He stalls.

Shit, he stalls!

"Well, define embarrassing?"

Oh God. I'm never drinking again.

I lift my head. Give him a good once-over and hope I'm playing my cards right. "Did you at least enjoy the mind-blowing sex we had when we got home last night?" I can only assume because I'm naked.

"By mind-blowing, you mean, you undressing yourself and passing out on top of me while licking my chest like a lollipop?"

I gasp.

He's lying.

He better be lying.

Oh God, he doesn't look like he's lying.

"You're lying, right?"

"No. Can't say that I am. But that was all before you tried to do a sexy dance for me on the bed, managing to fall off it twice."

I give him the *no, I didn't* look.

He just wiggles his eyebrows, giving me the *oh, yes, you did* look in return.

What's wrong with me? Since when do I get blacked out drunk and make an idiot out of myself? *Well, a lot so...* Shut up, consciousness.

"It's okay. I thought it was cute. You were very determined."

I know he's trying to hold in his laughter. I dig my nails into his bare chest as his laughter explodes. He flips me onto my back. With my hands now captured and being lifted above my head, I have no choice but to look up at Chase. His eyes still hold that sleepy look, his hair a sexy mess. "Stop laughing at me." I pout, still managing to wiggle my hips, waking up his lower parts.

"I'm not. I think you're cute."

"Cute! Great. Little sisters, close friends, and bunnies are cute," I reply with a pout.

"You're beautiful."

Okay, I'll take that. Going a little overboard, but it shuts me up. He bends down, meeting my lips for an extra juicy morning kiss. His tongue dives into my mouth, stealing my breath. It doesn't take long before his palms are caressing their way down my arm and latching onto my naked breast. His touch on my flesh awakens every part of me. His mouth numbing the pounding in my head and the hardness resting against my hip, offering me the best morning wake up.

"So, explain to me these romance books."

I ignore him at first, thinking he's not talking to me, until I realize he is and stop trying to maul his face.

"Tell you what? I know nothing about them." I wrap my hands around his neck, pulling him back down. He gives in, kissing me with vengeance until we both need air and starts again.

"No, I mean how women write romance. Is how they write it, how it feels in real life? Like when I kiss you, do your toes curl and butterflies flutter in your taut tummy?" He smiles, fighting the laughter.

"Where are you getting your information, Green? That sounds more like indigestion."

He kisses me quickly and says, "I was curious, so I read some of the books that I'm on the cover of. The way you women describe sex, with words like hard member or flesh and folds. Is that what you call your pussy in real life?"

I don't know how to react right now. First off, he just admitted to reading romance novels. He also just said the word member and folds in the same sentence. "Are you drunk, Chase?" I have to ask.

"For you," he responds, nipping at my bottom lip. "I'm being serious. I read a book once, where the male really did a number on the girl. Talked some real raunchy shit. Is that what you want? Lots of spankings and dirty talk?"

At that I bust out laughing. The mental picture of Chase getting all porn lipped on me.

"No, I'm not into domination and shit." Seriously, what books is he reading?

"Are you sure? Because I feel like I should know these things. Your likes, dislikes. Now that I think of it, you should probably know mine as well." More quick kisses and a dip to my nipples before he starts firing off question after question.

"Okay, so question number one. Do you like being tortured in bed?"

Jesus, starting them blunt. "No! God, what do you take

me for?"

He smiles, approving of my answer. "Okay, good. I'm not sure how good I would be at torturing. Next question. Are you into using weird objects and shit in bed? Hate to admit I read this, but…" He pauses. "The dude used a lot of cucumbers."

"You're ridiculous, you know that, right?"

"Possibly, but I need to know how to please you. Because in the end of these books, they always get the girl. Just covering all my bases."

And as cliché as those books are, I'm going to add on to it. Because my heart just melted.

He wants to get the girl.

Sigh.

"You know, you read some pretty strange romance books. I'm not into weapons, kink, domination, I don't own a spreader bar, which may be a shame from what I've heard, and I don't like to be tied up and whipped until I'm on the verge of blackness to get off. I'm, if you haven't noticed, a simple girl."

Staring down at me, he replies, "You are anything but simple, Katie Beller."

I might have to pay a fee when I check out because my heart is melting all over this bed! I'm feeling embarrassed by his comment, needing to bring the attention off me.

"Well, those books are nonsense anyways. All filled with insta-love and froufrou bullshit."

"And what is insta-love?"

"Pfft, you know those stories where the couple meets and instantly they're in love and can't be apart? People eat that shit up, but it's not real. Love doesn't work like that."

His eyes become quiet, but intense. "So, you don't believe in the whole love at first sight theory?"

"No. I believe in lust at first sight, sure. But people confuse lust with love. They go jumping into these serious relationships, and when that dies, the love masked by lust crashes down on a theory, leaving one or both parties hurting. People need to take their time figuring out what love is. Not this overnight bullshit."

I kind of just went on a tangent, and Chase is looking at me like I said something to hurt him. His playful smile has dulled a tad, no longer reaching his eyes.

"What? Do *you* believe in it?" I ask, trying to figure out what just changed in him.

"I believe that when you know you know. And that people don't have to know each other for eons of time to form that deepness of feelings for one another."

I guffaw. "Are you serious, Green? Where did you get that from? You've been reading *way* too many romance books." I chuckle, looking at him, but he's not sharing the humor. "What? What's wrong? Are you bothered by what I said?"

He looks troubled. In battle with wanting to say more than what he does.

The phone starts ringing, but we both ignore it as I watch the fight die, a mask covering his prior face of emotions. "No, of course not," he replies, but I sense a lack of truth in his response.

"You can't believe in love at first sight," I repeat myself just as the phone stops ringing, then quickly picks back up.

"And why can't I?" he asks, snippier than I was expecting. "Would it be so terrible to believe in it? To think two people can have such a strong connection without having the eons of time together?" The phone continues to ring, and I can tell it's grating on Chase's patience. I haven't seen this side of him, but he's aggravated. That's a fact.

"Chase, I was just saying…"

The last ring does it for him and he picks up the phone and speaks, "For Christ's sake, hello?… Oh, yeah, hey. No, um… She's right here. I was just… I lost my key and needed to call room service. Yeah, here she is." He stops talking and hands me the phone.

My mouth drops, praying the person on the other line is not who I think it is. Chase nods and mouths, it is, and I take the phone.

"Hello?"

"Do I want to know?" Kristen's bright and bubbly voice flows through.

No, she surely does not.

"Nothing to report. I think he's doing a walk of shame. Smells like cheap perfume." I look at Chase and wiggle my eyebrows, but he sadly doesn't join in on the fun. He gets up and grabs for his clothes and begins dressing.

"Huh, I wonder if Amber got her claws in him. Might wanna drill her later for details," she says then starts yelling at her assistant about a missing banner.

I sit up in bed, watching Chase dress while Kristen starts going on about the schedule for today. The entire time Chase refuses to look at me. I toss a pillow at him, trying to get his attention, but he simply turns, whispering he's gotta get going, and then walks through the connecting door. And to my surprise, shuts it.

What the fuck?

Readers wait for no one. And apparently neither does Chase Green. I got off the phone with Kristen and got ready, thinking Chase would grab me to walk down, but to my surprise he was already gone. Not that I couldn't go down by myself, but it was kind of our thing. Hold hands in the elevator until it opens and then release, walking away as if we were just two strangers.

But today I was holding hands with no one. I walk to the ballroom and there's already a line down the block and into the next state. I look over at Chase's table, and he is already talking to someone, not even acknowledging me when I walk in.

Was he really that upset with me over the whole insta-love thing? Could he actually be mad at me because I didn't believe in all that fairytale bullshit? I want to storm over there and tell him to get his head out of his ass, and that love is never instant and it takes time and work to find the right one. Those books are make-believe. Romance at its fake best. Why would he be mad at me for just stating the truth? *Because maybe he feels something stronger for you.* I look back over at him just as he lifts his head. Our eyes meet. The corners of his lips rise in a small smile and he goes back to his fan. What am I missing here? He says he wants to get the girl in the end. Am I the girl? He believes it's possible to have such strong connections in moments of meeting someone that could equate to insta-love. Am I that someone? *No.* Okay, I actually chuckle out loud. Clearly, I'm not *that* girl.

I don't get much more time to debate because my line is growing and I need to get to work. I spend the entire day hugging, signing books, and hearing stories of how readers gobbled up my book. It never does get old hearing the praises, even though you're still not sure how you got here.

The day is finally coming to an end and I'm able to take some time to sit and reminisce about the day. One reader in particular stood out. Her name was Emily. She was shy and waited patiently in line. When it was finally her turn, she came up and asked if she could hug me, and of course I said absolutely. I signed her book, and she told me how much she enjoyed my story. She then handed me a handmade wooden box. Confused at first at the strange gift, it wasn't until she explained the reasoning for it that my heart swelled.

Emily went on to explain it was a wish box made from an old oak tree from her childhood. When she was growing up, there was the most beautiful oak tree in her backyard. The tree was a place for her to hide when she needed to be alone, where she took her books to read, a place where she went to wish. She wished for everything under the sun when she was little. From a pink bike, to wishing her parents wouldn't fight so much. She wished Derek from science would talk to her and that her mother would get better once she fell ill.

Soon after she graduated high school, life took its course and her mother lost her life to cancer. She spent hours upon hours under that special wish tree, praying her mother finally found peace. That her father would be okay without her mom. That she would find reasoning in why life took her mother so young. This tree, it was a place where she felt solace.

It wasn't until she was in college that her father began struggling with the payments on the house and was forced to sell. A local contractor eager to buy up the land and surrounding area to build modern townhouses offered her father a price he couldn't refuse and before she could argue, her childhood home was sold, along with her special tree. She spent days making calls, trying to find out who was in charge of the construction, but with no luck. The demolition was set to happen.

She couldn't see her tree be destroyed. All the memories and wishes she had made under that tree. She still had so many open wishes out there to come true. So, when the day of the demolition began, she did the only thing she could and chained herself to the tree. The construction crew yelled and demanded she get the hell away from the tree. They would call the cops. Have her arrested. But she didn't care. She would have done anything to save her tree.

It was when the contractor finally showed that her life changed forever. A tall man by the name of Charles Hanson came storming up to her, demanding she remove herself from that tree. She was costing him money by holding up his crew. He made it to her and the moment their eyes collided, it was love. He leaned into her, asking if she was all right. Yelled at his entire crew to back away from the tree and shut down all production for the day.

Emily and Charles married a year later and she showed me pictures of their two beautiful children.

She explained to me that Charles loved her so much that he did everything in his power to save that tree. He reworked his plans around the tree so his love would have her wish tree. It wasn't until just last year that the tree caught a bug. Charles tried his best to save the tree, but it was too late and the city was forced to cut it down. It was a sad moment for her. Remembering all the times she spent under that tree, wishing, finding peace, loving life.

Her husband did what he could to save pieces of her tree, and she spent her free time carving out special boxes from what her Charles salvaged.

It was then I looked down at my special box in a different light. Emily finally explained to me that she had made the box especially for me. She said my book at times made her very sad. She hoped that in my own life I had found love. She told me she spent half her life wishing to find love. And the day Charles walked into her life, she knew her wish had come true.

She wanted that for me.

I couldn't even fathom that someone thought so much about my life. Of course, I cried. To know there are such selfless people in this world made my heart swell. I wanted to wrap her up and take her home with me so her kindness would spread to everyone and everything in my life.

Sadly, she told me she had to be home to get dinner ready for her kids and Charles, and I had to unlatch myself from her. We exchanged information because I insisted we keep in touch, and she was on her way.

Her words stuck with me while I wrapped up the day and also while working with Amy, my assistant, on restocking my paperbacks. And when I stole glances at Chase, it made me think of what I would wish for.

"How'd you do today?"

I lift my head from straightening a pile of bookmarks to find Kristen jamming away on her phone. "It was hectic, but good hectic. You?"

Not even missing a beat, she continues to fire off a message. "Girl, why didn't I go to school to be a teacher or something?"

"That good?"

"Fire after fire. I had an author get drunk and vomit under her table. This was *after* she spent most of the day secretly handing out shots to readers. Now her publicist is in an up-roar on why I pulled her. Two authors who just *had* to have their tables next to one another because they were inseparable got into it and now aren't talking. Demanded one or the other be moved. *Mid signing!* And *now* it's been brought to my at-tention that one of the author's models was basically having a threesome in the bathroom."

Of course, my eyes widen and shoot to Chase. *He wouldn't—*

"Oh, he wouldn't. Chase is actually one of the decent models here. It's that whore, Winston Mills. If you see him walking around, grab him and tell his skank ass he's gone. Go figure, the author is also hiding him from me."

I don't realize I'm holding my breath until it becomes ap-parent for me to breathe again. Chase must feel me staring at him because he turns, catching my stalkerish eyes. I want to pull away, but once those eyes latch onto mine, it's almost impossible. Chase Green just has this way with me. A force I don't know how to break. I continue to stare back at him, wishing I could walk across the hall and wrap myself in his arms. Tell him I'm sorry for being so selfish. I wish I could grow a large set of balls and tell him how I really feel about him. The way my body gravitates to him, his touch, his words. I wish… I wish… It's then it clicks. I wish to be something to Chase. That's what my wish would be. Chase is staring at me, curious about why I look like a light bulb just went off in my head, but I'm too busy thinking about how the second this signing is over, I'm going to do what I've never done before. I'm going to open up to him and be honest about how I feel.

"You have a reader. I'll catch up with you later. Horrible outdated movie and room service later? I can't say I need to drink after last night."

I snap out of my epiphany to look to my right at a man standing in my line. I would agree to that shit. I nod, knowing all too well I plan on blowing her off. Because I have a date with Chase and the confessional later. She scurries off while I turn to my line.

"Hi there, how are you?"

The gentleman, tall and broody, doesn't respond. He stands there looking at me while holding my book.

"I'm Bailey, nice to meet you." I proceed to stick out my hand, but he doesn't take the bait. "Don't be nervous. I'm just as nervous as you are. Did you want me to sign your book?" I smile, grabbing for my pen.

The man finally steps forward, but instead of handing me the paperback he tosses it onto my table, knocking off books and disorganizing the bookmarks. I hear Amy squeal as a bunch of books fall over into her lap, and I jump back, completely caught off guard at his outlandish move.

"Hey, that wasn't very—"

"Not nice? You know what's *not nice*? This trash you wrote!" He finally speaks, his voice deep and menacing. He takes a predatory step toward me, while I take one back, knocking into my table. He's seeping with anger, and it's quickly unsettling for me. "This shit fucked with my wife. Your bullshit and lies you fed her."

"Sir, I doubt my book—"

"She left me. Your bullshit book caused her to leave me. That bitch told me she was better than me." He lifts his arm, swiping all the books off the table. Amy screams as I stumble over my two feet. I turn to get out of his personal space, but he's too quick. His thick fingers latch around my neck as he begins to squeeze.

"You think you can ruin lives for money, bitch?"

His grip tightens. My legs begin to kick as my hands frantically try to rip his hands off my neck. I barely hear the commotion in the background as the air restriction takes effect. I try pleading with him to let me go, but no words escape. My hands get heavier and shear panic sets in. I'm seconds away from losing this battle.

I'm giving it one last ditch effort to release myself, when in an instant, I'm thrown to the ground. Everything happens so fast, as hands grab for me, while I turn to see the man on the ground next to me, Chase on top of him, giving punch after punch.

Dizziness is stopping me from crawling over to Chase to make him stop. Loud voices are everywhere as people run to see the commotion. Amy is on her knees next to me, trying to assess how bad I'm hurt. "Oh my God, Bailey, are you okay?"

"Chase, get him to stop," I groan, my voice hoarse.

Amy doesn't register, since I called him by his given name. I lift myself up, grabbing for my throbbing neck. I wince at the pain, but get to my feet. The rush of blood to my brain causes me to sway. I try to get to Chase just when security shows up, ripping him off my assailant. His chest is heaving and before he even composes himself, his wild eyes meet mine.

It's the frantic look in his eyes that finally causes me to acknowledge what just happened. The shock quickly wearing off, my lower lip begins to quiver. I break away to look at the man who's still fighting the restraints of the security officers, his angry gaze glued to mine.

Before I fully break down, Chase is lifting me into his arms.

"Chase," I whisper, as I lay my head into the nook of his neck, and he bulldozers through the curious crowd to get us away from my attacker and out of wandering eyes' view. Opening up the door to the storage room used for storing all excess paperback boxes, Chase sits on a pile, cradling me in his arms.

"Baby, are you okay? Let me see your face." His voice is soft, but there's a slight stutter to it. I pull away, and he begins inspecting my neck. A hiss travels up his throat, as he grazes his finger around my skin. "He's fucking dead."

I don't want to talk about that man. I want to snuggle deeper into the safety of his embrace.

"Shhh, it's okay. I got you. Don't cry, baby," he coos to me, bringing his hands around me, cocooning my body to his.

I hadn't realized I even started crying, but now that I've started I can't seem to stop. With each sob, I inhale his comforting scent. His warmth surrounds me and in time I begin to settle.

"Katie?"

I lift my head, turning my sore neck toward Kristen standing a few feet away from us, two uniformed officers with her. "Hey, sorry. Something in my eye."

Kristen huffs at me, eliminating the space between us. "Oh, stop. This is serious. Are you okay?" She bends down to get a better look at me. Remembering I'm in Chase's lap, I begin to squirm off, but his hold only tightens. Okay then. Not going anywhere.

"Yeah. A little shaken up. Gonna have to find a fashion liking to scarves, I think, but other than that I'll be okay."

Another eye roll, but somewhere in there is sympathy. "Katie, if you can be serious for like two seconds, these officers would like to ask you some questions."

I nod and try prying myself out of Chase's arms. He's hesitant to let me go, and Kristen visually notices it. She offers me a quick *what's this all about* look, but I ignore her, trying to slap Chase's hands off me.

"Down, boy, she'll be right back." Kristen stands and grabs for my hand as I climb to my feet.

I turn to give Chase a reassuring smile that I'm fine to meet with the law to give my statement.

After spending a solid thirty minutes answering questions I really couldn't answer, they sent me on my way. No, I didn't know the man previously. No, I didn't know his wife. No, I didn't do anything to antagonize the lunatic for him to attack me.

Chase stood by my side the entire time, his anger building with each ridiculous question they asked me. He eventually told them I'd had enough and needed to rest, pulling me away. Amy told me not to worry about my table mess and she would get it all cleaned up before tomorrow, so Chase led me back to my room, which I was thankful for. As tough as I was acting right now, going back to the crime scene this soon may have cracked my hard shell more than I would have liked.

Opening up my hotel room, I saunter in, throwing my purse on the bed. "Man, so looks like I can scratch being attacked by a psychopath off my bucket list." I turn, and Chase is on me instantly. Lifting me in his arms and laying my back softly on the mattress.

"No jokes."

"Since when did you become no fun?" I reply, not wanting to rehash this.

"When I saw some fucking asshole attack you." He brushes a piece of hair away from my face. His fingers brush against my bruised skin and his eyebrows scrunch with anger.

"I'm fine. Seriously."

His eyes dip to my neck. "You're not fine. You're hurt. I can still feel you shaking."

"Chase," I say his name, wanting to correct him, but I can also still feel the small tremors my body is creating over the attack.

"No one's going to think less of the big bad Katie for feeling upset. Scared. That should happen to no one."

I'm not liking that he won't let it go. It scared me, yes. But I just want to drop it.

"Katie, talk to me."

"What do you want me to say? Yeah, it was messed up. He scared me. He just went off about how I was the one who made his wife leave him. Like as if. He clearly was a total jerk and his wife probably should have left him way before now." Just as I didn't want, I can feel myself getting worked up. I didn't make that woman leave her husband. I'm not the cause of his distress.

"You did nothing wrong, Katie."

Like he needs to tell me that. "I know I didn't," I reply, getting angry.

"Then why are you getting upset?"

"Because. He attacked me. He blamed me for his failures. And then fine, what *if* it's my fault? What am I even doing here anyway? This isn't me. This book thing is not—"

Chase's lips halt any further rant. He touches my mouth with his, kissing me gently. Once he feels me relax he pulls away. Bastard.

"That's all I get? I'll keep ranting if you're gonna stop." He doesn't offer me more of his luscious lips, but even his sexy chuckle is a reward. He brings his hands to my face, cupping my cheeks.

"Don't discredit how talented you are because of someone else's downfall. If that woman left her husband after reading the book, it was because you gave her courage to. And after seeing the way he treated you, I think you did a good thing for that woman. I read your book. It has meaning. Even I took something away from it."

I offer him my cute—okay, not really so cute shy smile. "Oh, yeah, and what insight did I offer you, Green?"

He stares into my eyes, his beautiful irises glowing back at me. "You taught me there is real love out there. And to never settle. Because one day, I would find exactly what my life was missing."

Okay.

Holy fuck.

He hasn't looked away from me since he began speaking and the meaning in his words is threatening to smack the wind right out of me.

"I'm… I'm sorry about this morning. I didn't mean what I said," I spit out.

He smiles tenderly back at me in return, brushing his thumb along my cheek. "You don't have to apologize, Katie. You say what you believe, and I envy that about you."

I'm not sure insulting him on having feelings is being envious. "Yeah, but I shut down anything you were saying. And possibly telling me." I draw in a big gulp of air and take a leap of faith in us. "And, well, it had me thinking all day. I don't… I mean, I *do* believe in love at first sight. If it's like having emotions that are so strong, it's almost a painful feeling you can't dissect. The confusion of how something so crazy can be happening with someone you've barely met. When your life just seems brighter. Happier. Hope—"

I welcome his lips, wrapping my arms around his neck. He kisses me with intent, his tongue diving into my mouth and stealing my breath. We kiss for what seems like ages before we eventually break apart. My vision is blurred, but that's what his kisses usually do to me. He pulls back, his eyes intense with want.

"Katie," he says my name on a hoarse whisper. I open my mouth to reply, but he places a single finger over my lips. "Just wait. Let me say something."

I nod, now curious, but allowing him the floor. It takes him a bit to gather himself, but then he speaks.

"That feeling? When you're unsure if it's good or bad? The pain of seeing someone so amazing that you don't know if she's real or not? I felt that. For you." He takes a moment to allow his words to settle then continues. "The bafflement at how someone can fall into your life so quickly and you want nothing but to offer her everything? Katie, you've become the brightness in my life. Your beauty, your strength. Your big heart. Before I met you, I could agree with you on not believing in instant love. What fool would? But the moment I fell into your room, that changed for me." He pauses to make sure I'm still with him. My mouth is slightly parted, a little in shock, and partially struggling to breathe.

"I know you're anti-love. And I'm not telling you this to

pressure you. But I need to get it out. Because each second that passes that I hold in how I feel, is like drowning with the truth. I *am* in love with you, Katie Beller. I have been since the day we met."

There's no hiding the gasp that leaves my mouth. "You... you what?" I heard him wrong. I had to.

His laugh resonances as he speaks, "Katie Beller, I'm madly in love with you. You and all your crazy."

Okay, shit. I heard him right.

"I-I..." I have a sudden stuttering problem. My throat feels thicker than normal and my chest is too tight. "I... shit." I think he broke me! Chase Green just admitted he is in love with me. ME! All the wishes and hopes. Dreams and aspirations that have flooded my mind since the moment Chase Green fell into my door, all come crashing at me at once, and I say the one thing that concludes all those wants. "I love you. I've felt it for a while. But I was too scared to acknowledge it. I was afraid you'd hurt me. But shit. I do love you too. *Shit!*" I end on a squeal as Chase scares me by jumping off me, now standing on top of the bed over me.

"What are you doing?" I ask, seriously confused. I thought we were having a moment there.

"I'm celebrating. Katie Beller just admitted she loved me!" He laughs and starts howling, all while jumping on the bed. My body bounces in between his jumps and I can't help but laugh along with him.

"Have you gone mad?"

"Yes. Fucking yes. Mad*ly* in love." He stops instantly, startling me again, then drops down to straddle me. "Fuck, I love you. I've been wanting to say that forever." He dips down, kissing me, his smile evident on my lips. "I have to undress you now," he says between nips and licks. I have no objections, and we work in unison to tear at one another's clothes, until we're flesh against flesh.

"We slipped up yesterday. But I'm not sure I can go back to having anything between us. You okay with that?"

Thankfully I'm on the pill, but if I wasn't it wouldn't stop me from telling him yes. I nod and watch as his irises disappear into the blackness. I love that look on him. The need. The lust. The love. He presses my thighs open with his knee, and I open for him willingly. He places his lips to mine and slowly pushes inside. It's more meaningful than any other time he's entered me. His movements are unhurried as he pulls out and guides himself back home. His fingers tangle into my hair, lips back on mine. With each kiss, each slow thrust, he strips me of my walls.

"You're so beautiful like this," he breathes, spreading kisses up the lining of my chin. He brings a hand down to coddle my breast. The sensation causes my body to arch, the slowness of each thrust making my needy sex pulsate. I moan as he takes my nipple into his grip and softly pinches my hard bud. The low tension in my belly tells me I'm not going to last much longer.

"Chase," I beg, unsure of what I need. But he does. He knows exactly how to play my body like the perfect violin. The sounds of my arousal are in perfect harmony with each thrust, each pinch, each slow kiss he offers.

"I love you, Katie." His soft words sift into my ears, into my heart. And I can feel them in my soul. The truth of his admission, the feel of his body taking me to a place only he's taken me. It's all too much. A single tear falls from my eyelid as I give in and every nerve ending in my body explodes with ecstasy. I moan out my release, my nails digging into his muscled back. And soon after Chase is following me in his own release.

His weight covers my body, our heated skin, both covered in a sheer layer of sweat. He lifts his hand to wipe away my tear, and I close my eyes, embarrassed at my out of control emotions.

"Why are you crying?" he asks.

"I don't know. It's just… this is a lot for me. I… I've never said that to anyone before." My admission shocks him. It's apparent in the way he inhales, his eyes widen. "I know, it's a silly thing to get emotional about."

He shakes his head. "It's not. And I can't even begin to explain how happy that makes me… well, not that you've never said it. But I'm the lucky bastard who won your heart." His smile is wicked and so damn sexy. I can't help but match him. He drops a quick kiss on my lips then goes to cleaning us up. Once done, he wraps us both in the comforter, resting my head on his chest.

"Will you tell me about your life? Growing up, anything?" he asks, combing his fingers through my hair.

I think about my life and all the sadness attached to it. "There's nothing really to tell. I grew up in a small town in Ohio. My parents died when I was in high school. I went through the whole stepparent bullshit until I was old enough to be on my own. Attempted college, but it didn't work out. Around the same time, I found the bar and never left."

"What made you so down on love? So against it?"

He sure is going guns blazing with the questions.

I shrug my shoulders and speak. "I guess I just saw how happy my parents were. They had that forever love. That love most people spend their entire lives searching for. I grew up wanting what they had. But then they died. And it made me realize nothing's forever."

"I'm sorry, I didn't know your parents were gone."

More shrugging. "It's fine. It happened a long time ago. When they died, the feeling of strong love that I felt died with them. I was never treated the way my parents treated me. It made me hard on the inside, and the more of life that passed, I just realized love was not what I thought it was. I watched people claim to love, but cheat. Do horrible things to their spouses, the stories, the deceit. It was nothing compared to what I watched my parents share. And I promised myself I wouldn't be a victim of this broken love."

His lips brush my head, offering me a consoling kiss. It feels strange to open up like this, since it's the first time I've actually shared that. I don't talk much about my parents, because no matter the time that passes, it still hurts.

"Well, can I say I'm glad you opened your door that night and forced me into your room, because otherwise I wouldn't have been able to save you from this broken love you speak of." He places his hands under my armpits, dragging me up his body so our noses are brushing. "You can call me super Chase. And if you ask nicely, I'll even wear a cape for you." He laughs as I smack him in the chest. He doesn't skip a beat and kisses me senselessly. I'm feeling bold and climb up, straddling him, placing my palms on his rock-hard pecks.

"My turn with the twenty questions. Why aren't you in the NHL? From everything I hear about you, you're really good at hockey. Why you hanging out with crazy authors, risking your reputation instead of the NHL?"

Okay, maybe wrong question to start with. The spark in

his eyes dulls and it's obvious I've hit a sore subject. "Hey, I'm sorry. You don't have—"

"No, it's fine. It's…" He stalls, taking in a deep breath before finishing. "It's complicated."

"Complicated how? I'm sure you're awesome. Everyone should be banging down your door."

"Well, it's not that easy. I started in the minors. Signed a contract with an agent. It's his job to get me there. And, well, there have been some roadblocks."

That doesn't sound good, but I'm still shocked why someone as eager and passionate as Chase wouldn't fight through those. "Well, you should tell them to get you signed or you're going to get another agent. You're not getting any younger, buddie," I joke, wiggling my hips.

"I'm trying. I'm in the works with a lawyer. But right now, things are kinda messed up. Let's just say I got myself in a bind I don't know how to get out of without sabotaging my entire hockey career. And all I want is to play. So, I have to tread lightly right now."

My eyes don't hide my concern for him. If he's in trouble, then I hope he's getting the proper guidance he needs. He's confessed since the beginning about people taking advantage of him for who he is. He lifts his finger to caress my eyebrow.

"Sounds messy. Do you need me to kick anyone's ass? Give me a name and number. I'll take care of it."

He smiles gently, working his hand down my face to cup my cheek. "Thanks, but this is something I have to handle. And as soon as I get it worked out things are going to be good again."

His words worry me. "Are you okay, Chase?"

"I am with you." He wraps his hand around my neck,

bringing me down to meet his lips. I could never get tired of kissing him. We kiss until the air in our lungs expires, and he offers a nice slap to my bare ass cheek. "Now. I say we order a sick amount of pizza and you reenact some of those sex scenes in your book."

I shake my head, laughing. "Stop reading my book, Green."

"Stop being so wonderful."

chapter
SEVENTEEN

I don't know how I ever woke up before Chase Green. I don't know how anyone wakes up without a human alarm clock bringing my dead to the world body awake with a glorious orgasm. I was dead in a dream, when a warm hand made its way down my stomach and past my navel, caressing my skin, all the way down to my core. I debated at first on smacking his hand away because I was so tired. And hungry. The pizza was ordered last night but barely touched. Our bodies, on the other hand, no piece of skin was left *un*touched.

His thick finger ventures in between my sex and even half asleep he makes me wet. He enters me and with his warm breath hitting the back of my neck, his tongue gently sucks on my earlobe, a morning moan flows from my lips.

"Good morning," he whispers softly, pushing his finger

deeper inside me.

I lay my head back, allowing him better access to my bare shoulder, his teeth gently grazing the surface of my skin.

"Feels like it," I reply slowly, working my hips with the movements of his hand. The hardness of his dick pressed against my ass cheeks makes me crave more than just his finger.

"Oh, well, then we better make that good morning an explosive morning." He works his finger faster, his mouth back on my flesh. He sucks to a point; I fear he's going to leave a mark.

"Chase," I moan out my warning to watch it.

But he doesn't let down. His thrusts quicken and his free hand wraps around a chunk of my hair, gently pulling my head further back, allowing him access to my lips. His mouth is on mine and the moment our tongues collide, I explode. He doesn't release me. He kisses me all the way through my release, until my body becomes lax in his hold. I feel his lips forming a smile and when I open my eyes, his shiny greens are staring back at mine.

"Now *that's* an explosive morning." He grins, pulling his finger out.

I roll to my other side so we're facing one another, and he brings his strong arms around me, hugging me to his chest.

"Let's play hooky today."

"Kristen would kill us. Well, she'd kill you. She loves me too much."

Chase chuckles, kissing the top of my head. I love his small gestures.

"Wouldn't you save me? Without me your mornings would suffer."

I press a kiss to his bare chest. "Well, I've seen her angry, so I'd have to just accept the fact that I was back to waking myself up. I would miss you, though. *Oh*—"

Chase startles me, flipping me so I'm flat on my back, his amazing body covering mine. "Say it ain't so. You would save me."

I fight to keep a serious face as I reply, "I really can't confirm I would."

His eyes light up and I secretly get excited at what he's going to do if I don't comply.

"You love me. You'd save me."

"Yeah, but it's still so fresh. I'll get over it. *Shit!*" I start to scream when he begins to tickle me. "Chase, stop!" I cry.

"Not until you admit you would save me... and tell me that you love me."

"No." Wrong answer. He goes at it even more aggressively and I'm choking on my own laughter and pleas for him to stop.

"All you have to do is say it, and I'll stop. Maybe even reward you."

I refuse to give in. I shake my head because I'm laughing too hard to speak. That's when he goes for the kill and starts squeezing my inner thigh.

"Oh my God! Stop! Fine! You win! I'd save you!"

"And?"

"I love you."

"Again."

"I love you," I repeat.

He stops tickling. Thank God because I was seconds away from pissing myself.

"I love you too. And when I get my shit together, I want

us to figure out our lives. I can't do long distance with you, Katie."

Wow. He just went deep on us. He can't do long distance. But what does that mean? "Chase…"

"Don't overthink it. I'm not asking you to leave your life. I'd come to you. Shit, I'd move across continents for you. If you'd have me."

Jesus Christ.

"Chase," I say his name, this time on a whisper.

"I know. It's a crazy statement. This is crazy. *We're crazy.* But I love you. And that's all I care about right now."

He sure is right. This *is* crazy. He can't possibly be thinking straight. "Chase, what about your career? Your life back in Minnesota?" There's no hiding the smidge of stress that flashes in his eyes.

"Do you trust me?"

"I don't know. I'd have to think about—Okay! Okay! I do," I finish, needing him to stop fucking tickling me. "I trust you."

"Good. So just trust that I have some major changes in the future. I just need to work them out and then us? We're going to take this thing a whole step further. Then further after that."

I seriously love Chase Green right now.

"How about we put all this talk on hold and you use that pretty thing you have growing up my stomach and put it in that warm place waiting just for him. *Then* you can continue to show me just how much you love me." My boldness causes a grin so wide, I feel another jolt of his hard cock on my stomach. He kisses me roughly, and I accept his challenge. He's inside me within seconds and bringing me back to another screaming orgasm.

"How are we going to break it to Ellie and Gerdie?" he asks, grunting with each push. He's so large and hitting so deep I can barely respond.

"Maybe they can share a room," I moan, digging my nails into his tight ass.

"Fuck, that means you've considered us living together." He pulls out and slams back into me. Shit. I didn't even realize the intensity of my reply.

"For the weekend then maybe—"

Chase slams his mouth to mine, stopping me from finishing my sentence. "You can't take it back now, Beller. You see us playing house together. Now I'm holding you to it."

I can't respond because he's like a stallion slamming home over and over again, until my eyes cross and I'm threatening to bite my own lip off while my body explodes with sensations only Chase can provoke out of me.

"Fuck, I can stay inside you forever. I love you…" He trails off as his orgasm blasts through him, his hot seed releasing inside me.

"God, you're hot. Last chance to play hooky." We're in the elevator on our way down to the ballroom. He's holding my hand, as he always does, but maneuvering our connected hands to rub my ass.

"Stop, no. Again. I said I'd save you in the heat of the moment."

He bends down, kissing the top of my head. I mentally sigh. Then realize I vocally sigh, when I hear Chase's chuckle.

"I love your sighs. So innocent behind your badass persona."

I give him my mean stare down, but that face. That smile. Those eyes. They melt me. We hear the elevator ding, letting us know we've made it to the ground floor.

"Letting this sexy hand go is the hardest thing I do every morning." He lifts my hand and kisses the top of my skin.

I can't help but smile. I'm in love. And I admitted it. I should probably pull my book off the shelves because I can't relate to any of this love broken babble anymore. Chase Green saved me.

"Thank you," I say, not really sure what it means. But it needed to be said.

He leans forward, covering my mouth with his. "I love you, Katie Beller."

Trying to fight these new happy emotions that have taken over my body, I inhale a breath for strength and reply, "I love you too, Chase Green."

The opening doors break up our moment and it's like slow motion as our hands break away. Back to the author and model, business as usual. The only thing that doesn't change are the big smiles we both carry.

Chase walks as close to me as he can, saying it's a substitute for not being able to hold my hand. I blush like a damn school kid, because I'm sure we look like idiots.

Before turning the corner, we see Kristen hustling over to us.

"Shit, we're not late, are we?"

Chase looks down at his watch. "Right on time actually."

"Charlie! There you are. I've been calling your room." Kristen halts right in front of us and stops to catch her breath.

"Yeah, sorry, I was… in the gym all morning."

"Well, your agent has been in an uproar looking for you. She said she's been trying to contact you for days with no answer."

I look at Chase, and he's gone stone-still.

"What do you mean looking for me?" His usual casual tone is off.

"She paged me first thing this morning. She's in the hotel."

It's then I watch his face pale.

"Hey, you okay?"

"Mr. Bates, she's very upset. You assured me all the paper-work was taken care of. She's claiming she didn't sign off on this part of the signing."

Chase isn't moving or responding.

"Chase, what's going on?" I'm staring at him, but he's just standing there in a blank fog.

"Mr. Bates—"

"There you are! Babe, I've been looking everywhere for you!"

We all turn to see a beautiful blonde. Legs for hours, curves in all the right places approaching us. I begin to feel unsure of what's about to happen.

Chase quickly turns to me. "You said you trust me. Please just trust me right now, okay?"

"What? What do you—"

I'm cut off when the woman jumps into Chase's arms.

What. The. Fuck.

"Babe is your phone turned off?"

Babe.

Babe.

Babe.

I take a step away from Chase. He senses my withdrawal. He drops the woman and turns to me, but his attention is taken away by this woman.

"Rebecca. What are you doing here?"

He knows her.

Of course he does. It's his agent.

People call people babes all the time in California.

"I missed you. I wanted to surprise you."

Agents shouldn't miss their clients.

Fuck.

My stomach starts to turn.

Kristen grabs my arm. "Uh, Bailey, we need to get you to your table."

I should probably leave, but as they say, it's like watching a train wreck, unable to pull away. But this train wreck is my life, and I have a sick feeling soon to be my wrecked heart. I take a shaky step forward to address his agent.

"Excuse me. Hi, I'm Bailey. Author. You must be Charlie's agent?"

Please be his agent.

"Yeah, his PR agent, but most importantly, his girlfriend," she replies with beaming confidence.

There's no way to hide the gasp as her words fill the air. *His girlfriend.* She said the one thing I begged not to hear. He couldn't have lied to me and fed me bullshit just to end up playing me in the end.

I'm in shock.

I can't stop staring at her as she smiles cheerfully back at me.

"Katie." Chase tries to grab my hand, but I slap him off me.

"Okay then." I begin blinking away the tears that I am shamefully about to shed. "Excuse me," I choke out to our audience.

Once my legs start to work again, I run to the bathroom. I hear my name being called, but the door shuts behind me. As soon as I'm in the stall, I lean forward and throw up. Once, twice, a third time, before my stomach stops convulsing. I reach up, trying to grab for my ears that won't stop ringing, but my stomach convulses again, throwing up for a fourth time.

"Katie, you all right?" I hear Kristen, her voice etched with worry.

"Fine." I grab for some toilet paper, dabbing at my mouth, using the back of my hand to wipe the tears from my eyes.

"Are you sure? What just happened out there didn't look fine."

God, her acknowledging it means this isn't a bad fucking dream. *Girlfriend.* He has a girlfriend. My stomach threatens to heave again.

"Honey, what's going on? I thought you weren't getting involved with Charlie Bates."

And God, I wished I never did. Every single moment we've ever shared flashes through my mind, the pain crushing at my skull. The lies. His lies. *I love you, Katie Beller.* I grab at my head, closing my eyes.

"Katie, are you going to talk to me?" I hear her voice closer, the gentle knock on the stall door.

"Seriously, it was nothing," I reply, my voice choked. I hold my breath, trying to keep in the ball of emotions raging inside my throat wanting to release.

"Katie, I'm not the bad guy here. Talk to me."

No, the bad guy is standing outside this bathroom. Next to his girlfriend. A struggled gasp leaves my mouth and I lose the fight and the tears come in waves. I cry, hunched forward, holding my stomach.

I hear Kristen making a call. "Yeah, I need security to the east side of the hotel. We need to clear the hallway. Yes, of everybody. No one stays. That's right. I pay enough money to this hotel. That's right. Thank you. I want a call when it's clear. Thank you."

She knocks again. "Honey, let me in."

I just want her to go away. I refuse to let anyone, even my best friend see me broken. So ashamed at what a fool I have become.

"Oh, fuck it," she says and without opening the door, Kristen starts crawling under the stall door.

"Oh God, that's disgusting, Kristen," I groan, wiping at my soaked face.

"Yeah, well, the things you do for friendship."

I move over, allowing her to slide all the way underneath. She finally stands and grabs for me. I hug her back and lose to another round of emotional sobs.

chapter
EIGHTEEN

Everyone lies. It's almost human nature. How much you drank last night, the amount of sex partners you've had, whether it be more or less. How great your life is, great job, bad job, it can almost be a sickness for some.

I never found a liking for liars. It wasn't something I had to do in my life. I was who I was. I didn't have to make up a story to make myself look cooler or more accepted. I guess that may also be why I'm me. Alone. Simple. Working at a bar, living off of others' façade lives.

Kristen had the entire east wing of the hotel cleared out to allow me to exit the bathroom with my dignity. Chase was nowhere to be found, nor was his girlfriend. Kristen knew it before I even said it. I wasn't staying a second longer on the tour. I couldn't. She offered to pack up my room and got me quickly into a cab to the airport. She suggested I stay and rip him a new one, but I couldn't. I couldn't look him in the eyes after last night and this morning and keep it together long enough for him to even attempt to explain.

Because there was nothing he could say that would change the truth. He's been lying to me since day one. Since the moment we met. The conversation rings in my ear the entire way to the airport about the first time I asked him about a girl-friend, and he told me it was complicated. How complicated does having one have to be? Complicated as in, she was in the dark about his modeling escapades? And how pathetic was I? I fell for it. I fell fast and hard into this web of lies. He had me linked to all the words, endearments, the late-night talks, the passion. It was all for nothing. Because he never took us serious. Was his love even real?

I broke down in the cab, and once again on the flight. I spent half the flight sobbing in the tightly fitted bathroom. When we finally landed, I was exhausted and numb. I didn't bother turning my phone back on. I knew he would at least call. How could he not? I'm sure he needed half his shit out of my room.

Or maybe he didn't. I'm sure he also wanted to just forget what just happened. I'm sure he had a lot of explaining to do with his *girlfriend*. And that didn't involve trying to explain to me.

I'm shocked, in my condition, I make it home in one piece. When I walk into my apartment, the silence of my small home saddens me even more. I lower my head, taking in breath after breath. I used to love the quietness of my life. But now, being here makes me feel so empty.

I numbly drag my aching legs into my room. I let Gerdie

know I'm home, opening his cage and brushing his beak with kisses. "Hey, baby, Mamma's home early, isn't that awesome?" I croak, trying not to lose it in front of my bird.

"Awesome. That's awesome."

"It is awesome, Gerdie."

Not.

I wake up feeling groggy, unaware of my surroundings. For a quick moment, I forgot I'm in my own bed, until the memories from the last twenty-four hours blast through me, my gut aching all over again. I must have passed out without putting Gerdie in his cage, because he's perched on top of my head.

"Gerdie, a little room, buddie." I swat him away, and he flies, perching himself on my dresser. I lift my legs, dropping them on the ground. I debate on lying back down, but I have to pee and I have the worst taste in my mouth. I get up and relieve myself and brush my teeth. I head to the kitchen, debating on drinking half the bottle of tequila sitting on top of my fridge for breakfast.

My stomach, uneasy as it is, I sadly pass. I make a pot of coffee, straight black, like my mood. I take a squat on my couch. Sipping the dark liquid, I stare at the object on my coffee table. My phone.

Should I turn it on?

Or should I toss it out my window?

The bigger question is if I can handle what comes through once I turn it on.

I know I promised Kristen I would call her once I got

home, so I know she has to be worried. At least I need to turn it on to call her, then I can change my number or just lose my phone altogether. I barely used it before this disastrous glitch in my life. I'll be fine without one. I lean forward, grabbing for it and holding the on button until the phone begins to light up.

Once my home screen pops up, my phone starts vibrating. I toss it on the table, as if it's going to reach out and bite me. I watch it ping and ping. Notifications, one after another, pop up. My hands shiver, afraid of what I'll see when I read through the notifications.

One deep breath and I reach for it. I have fourteen voicemails from Chase. Five from Kristen, and a shit-ton of text messages. *I can't do this.* I can't hear his voice or listen to his excuse. I quickly unlock my phone and shoot a text to Kristen, telling her I'm home and sorry I didn't call last night. I'll call her soon, and then I toss the phone. As much as my curiosity wants to hear what he has to say, it won't fix what he did.

I get up, ditching my coffee, and grab for the bottle of tequila.

I head back to my room, planning on drinking away the curiosity and sleeping off the regret.

It's close to nine at night when I stroll into the bar.

Dex spots me instantly, shocked to see me. "Thought you weren't supposed to be back until next Wednesday?"

I shrug my shoulders. Walking up to the bar, I say, "Plans changed. Why, aren't you happy to see me?" My smile doesn't reach my eyes.

"No, it's fine. You okay? You look… off."

I sit down, losing my smile completely. "What is it with you always asking me if I'm all right?" I snap unintentionally.

He watches me a bit longer, getting the hint. He drops it. "Got it. So why are you here? You ain't workin."

"Nope, but I want to drink." I ended up putting a sweet dent into the tequila bottle. I passed out on my floor crying to Gerdie, then woke up to darkness and the silence in my place strangling me. My head was pounding, and I knew I couldn't stay in the quiet any longer. So, I headed to the bar.

I just needed a place where I can feel like my old self. To pretend I haven't turned into everything I never wanted to be. I never understood cheating. People who wanted more than what they already had. And working at a bar, I saw a ton of it. People think that being at a dive bar means they can show up and no one will recognize them. It's the perfect place to have a secret affair and sit in the corner, outside of their ritzy normal establishments and woo it with a woman who's not their girl-friend *or* their wife.

Are they *that* unhappy that they have to stray? Is mar-riage *that* hard? Or are men *that* selfish and don't know in this century how to stay faithful? My parents loved each other. They showed it in every single way, to a point where my gross face was threatening to become permanent I wore it so often. My dad always had flowers in his hand, and my mom was always smiling, finding ways to make my dad happy. I used to think when I was little that *that's* what I wanted. I wanted that forever love my parents had. But then they died and I realized nothing was forever.

That was the starting factor for why I always strayed away

from love. Or, maybe it wasn't, but after the death of my parents, that love I felt died with them. The love they showed to me wasn't carried on through my extended family. My bright imagination and optimism slowly faded and as life got harder, so did my heart. When you're little, I guess you're taught that love is essential. It's all-around. The one thing in life that is free, my dad would always say. When I would overhear my parents talking about money and bills, my dad always told my mom we would never have to worry because as long as love was still free they would get through anything.

Maybe it's a good thing they aren't around anymore because I'm not sure how long they would have survived knowing how much love costs nowadays.

"Another." I slam my hand on the bar for the third time, and again, Dex puts another shot of tequila in front of me. I haven't said much since I sat down. Which is for the better. I just want to sit here and remember a time when I wasn't so stupid.

Because that's exactly what I am. What happened to built-in girl intuition? That bullshit that says women always know when a man is cheating or unfaithful. I hear it all the time at the bar. How one girlfriend is telling her sobbing friend at the bar to stick to her gut. Her man is definitely not being faithful. She knew her man was cheating. She practically caught him. But she was so in love, she sold herself short, willing to turn a blind eye to it.

I swore I would never be that girl.

I also swore I would never get suckered by fake love.

"Another." I slam my hand on the bar more aggressively this time.

"You wanna drink yourself stupid, fine. But not until you

tell me what's fucking up with you."

I lift my head, making eye contact with Dex. His dark eyes seep into mine. He's always made my skin tingle. No matter our status. He's never judged me or wanted anything from me but me. And that's why I don't back down when I demand he serve me. "Pour me a fucking shot, Dex."

He continues to stare at me, waiting for me to back down, but I refuse. I won't be confessing what a mess I've secretly become. I came here tonight to bury those feelings and unwanted pains with tequila and then press my reset button. This is just going to be a glitch in my—

Giggling from the corner of the bar distracts me and I lose concentration on my internal speech. I look behind me and see a couple. *The couple*, holding hands and practically brushing noses. My eyes narrow, as I watch the man scrape his fingers up her arm, his wedding band noticeable in the dim light. The woman, *not* his wife, giggles once more, and the sound is like nails on a chalkboard for me.

"You gonna talk?"

I shake my head and turn away from the couple. "No, I'm not. I'm going to sit here. Just serve me, Dex." Both hands are flat on the bar. I need him to know I mean business. I won't be fucking pushed—

Again. That fucking giggling. I whip my head back to the couple, witnessing them in a lip-lock of betrayal and lies.

"That's fucking it." I push off the stool and get up. Storming over, startling them both, I slam my hands on the table.

"Jesus, lady, what's your problem?" The cheater asshole husband hisses at me.

"What my *problem* is, you cheating fucking asshole, is that I'm sick of seeing you and your home wrecking girlfriend in my bar!"

"Excuse me?" the man barks, throwing himself out of his seat. "You better step away—"

"Or what? Gonna lose your business? Good! Get the fuck out of here! Go home to your *wife!*" I step forward, leaning over the table, poking him square in the chest. "I'm sure she would love to know what you've been up to!"

His lady tramp comes at me, but before I have a chance to pull her fucking hair out for participating in such a horrible act, Dex is behind me. His arms wrapping around my waist, he lifts me up, dragging me away from the table.

"Put me down! You fucking cheater!" I'm fighting in his grip, trying to still yell at the table. Before I know it, Dex is slamming the office door behind him.

"Calm the fuck down." His warm breath hitting the back of my earlobe, I struggle to suck air into my lungs, having trouble catching my breath. I just want to go back out there and rip that guy's balls off for being a liar and a cheater and making his wife feel like she might be something special to him. And making her feel like she finally had a chance at being loved.

Without realizing it, my shoulders begin to shake. I've begun to cry with Dex's strong arms wrapped around me. His hold tightens, his lips pressing to the top of my head. He pulls away, his thumb brushing against the fading bruise on my neck. His voice is low and feral.

"Who the fuck hurt you, Kat?"

At his words, I stiffen. In a blink, my emotions swap, and anger takes over. I break out of his hold, whipping around to face him.

"No one hurt me. Because no one has the power to," I

state, hanging on to my own words, praying I believe my own lies. But I can't. Because someone did hurt me. I finally took a chance and let go of everything I believed in and fell into the hands of a man who fucking ruined me. I should've never let him in. And now I hate myself for it.

Dex is watching me. His eyes darken if that's even possible. Back in the day when we went at it, our fights got pretty intense. We're both passionate people in our own fucked up way, so when we fought, it got bad. But those fights would always end up in a heated entanglement of our bodies, scraping at one another to get naked and fuck out all our anger. It was super-hot, but super unhealthy.

The look Dex has in his eyes for me right now is dark. And heated. If I threw myself in his arms right now and asked him to fuck me against this desk, he would. My chest is heaving, in and out. I'm angry. And hurt. I don't want to feel the way I do anymore. And I know Dex can make it go away.

I throw myself at him, our lips slamming together. My hands go up his chest, pulling at his shirt, as his hands wrap around my ass, lifting me up. He turns, dropping me onto the desk, and as our tongues collide in a feverish kiss, my hands work at the zipper of his jeans, while his dig into my scalp, pulling at my hair.

I just need a release. I need to feel something. I need to forget about Chase fucking Green and every single memory he's scarred into me.

Chase fucking Green.

My hands release from Dex's zipper and I pull away. "I can't do this."

Dex is less adamant of stopping what I now regret I started. But with a little more force, he pulls away. "Fuck," he growls, throwing his hands into his hair.

I can't make eye contact, ashamed at myself. "I'm sorry. I shouldn't have done that."

"Don't fucking apologize." The anger is noticeable in his tone.

"But I should. I don't know what I was thinking."

He turns his angry eyes on me, and I make the mistake of looking at him. He wants to say something. Yell at me mainly. Fuck me against the table, until we're both screaming. A small part of him wants to hold me. A side of the big bad Dex I get to see on rare occasions.

But he does nothing. He burns me with his stare, until I break away.

"I'm sorry," I repeat, but he puts his hand up to stop me.

"Fucking don't." And then he turns on his heels, throwing the office door crashing into the wall, and disappears.

Fuck me.

Fuck everyone.

chapter NINETEEN

Watching someone self-destruct is a lot easier and noticeable when you're on the other side of it. When *you're* not the one self-destructing. Denial is a real thing. Because no one admits fault to anything. Claiming they can take care of themselves and don't need help. I used to put myself in other people's shoes who were hurting. Love broken and unable to see light out of the hole love kicked them down into. I always said I'd be the one who'd thrive. Be resourceful. I'd build a homemade fucking ladder and climb my ass out of that hole. I'd find love and kick its ass, then move on. I wasn't a dweller.

I was a motherfucking conquerer.

I was also a fraud.

Being all badass in my head was so much easier. It was

easier to mentally tell myself to get out of bed. Stop calling into work, possibly shower. And I seriously fucking stunk. I was no strong hotshot who was indestructible. I was the fucking advocate for weak idiots who let a four-letter word hold them down and constantly jab the humiliation in their face.

But then again, I repeat to myself over and over that I wasn't even in love. No way. I swear on it.

Love takes time. Takes patience. Takes work. Three things Chase and I never had. This tour would have ended and our time would have been up. We never had time to grow into something more than the small little fantasy world we created for ourselves. And even that was a fantasy.

I've been out of work for almost two weeks. I know Dex wants to strangle me, but I know he'll get over it. Because as selfish as I am, I know something Kristen said is true. In some sort of way Dex does love me. And that makes me feel even worse for what I did. I ended up renting a car and driving seven hours up to New York, to my parents' graves. I lay in the soft grass at the cemetery, trying to remember the last memory I had of my parents. I was a sophomore in high school and I had just been asked to prom. And when I got asked, that meant I needed a dress. It was the first dance I had been asked to and my mom was over the moon. Maybe even more than I was. So, we searched and searched and when we found the perfect dress, the worry on my mom's face as she looked at the price tag killed me. She hid it well, and as I insisted we find something cheaper, she masked her worry with a smile and insisted we buy it.

The guilt the entire time that dress hung in my closet was almost unbearable. The guilt while I eavesdropped on my parents' discussion when my dad said we couldn't afford it. My mother's pleas to let me keep the dress. She just wanted me to be happy. To feel beautiful. My dad looked into my mother's eyes, and knowing he could never say no to her, he said okay. They would work it out and adjust funds to afford the dress. I watched my mother's sweet smile spread across her face as she cupped my father's cheek, offering him the most loving kiss. And at that moment, I felt the love my parents had for me. They loved each other like no other. And I hoped one day to make them proud, finding a love just like theirs.

I wore that dress the night of prom. We took photos at my parents' house with my date, Justin, and then we all traveled to his house so we could take more with his. My mom and dad both kissed me on the cheek, my mom fighting off tears. My dad hugged me, telling me to have fun and to behave. I blushed and shooed them off, trying to look cool in front of my date.

As they walked to the car and my father helped my mother into her seat, I broke away from Justin and ran up to the car, giving my dad one last hug and turning to my mom, telling her thank you. And that I truly felt beautiful.

My parents died in a car accident on their way home that night. A drunk driver who had fallen asleep at the wheel. Reports confirmed my mom died at the hospital, my dad on impact. I wasn't surprised my mom slowly slipped away shortly after hearing about my dad. It just made sense. She loved me, but she loved my dad more. And she needed to be with him. I was notified by my biology teacher and driven to the hospital by a police officer. I arrived three minutes after my mom passed.

I wipe away the tears I've shed at the memory, remembering the days after. The confusion. The pain. The anger at that damn dress I had to have. It was white and sparkly, and I felt beautiful in it. I remember tearing it to shreds. Yelling, screaming, sobbing if I just didn't go to that dance. It was also the last time I had ever dressed in anything above my fancy ripped jeans and tanks.

I adjust the flowers I brought nicely on top of the green grass and press my fingers to my lips. I kiss my skin and brush the remanence alongside my parents' name.

"I miss you both so much," I whisper, the wind picking up, blowing my hair into my face. "I'm sorry I haven't made you proud. Found what you two had. I just don't think this world will ever be able to compare the love you two had. I thought one day I would." I wipe more wetness from my cheeks. "But maybe you just set the expectations too high."

The winds pick up more, the clouds rolling in quickly. It takes mere seconds for the sky to open up and the rain to pour down. It drenches me from head to toe and everywhere in between, making it impossible to distinguish which tears belong to the angry clouds and which are my own. I give my parents' headstones one last glimpse and head home. I know I need to get my shit together. The world isn't going to stop because of my pity party. Maybe this battle has been my own fault. Trying to find and compare a love that was just not out there. I need to get over it. Time heals all, and I got nothing but time.

chapter TWENTY

Seeing the small Cleveland skyline makes me happy to be home. I feel lighter and less angry. I miss Gerdie like nobody's business, and I even stopped at some flea market on the way back, picking up some homemade bird treats.

I pull up into my apartment complex and some sort of commotion is happening in the front lawn. I park and get out, grabbing my bag and goodies for Gerdie. The closer I get the more I recognize Kristen standing on the front stoop, having it out with my landlord.

"Hey? What are you doing—"

"Jesus Christ, Beller! Where the hell have you been?" Kristen pushes away from my landlord, who looks annoyed but relieved. Meeting me, she grabs me and squeezes me into a bear hug. Well, a mini bear hug since she's five foot four and like a whopping hundred pounds probably wet.

"I went to visit my parents. I needed some time off."

She pulls away, investigating me. "You went home?"

"I wouldn't call it home anymore, but yeah. I just needed a break. Time to think."

"Katie, I've been worried sick about you. I've been calling you. I've left you a billion messages. Your damn answering machine is full again, and Dex, God that guy needs to get laid or slipped some ecstasy. He's one crabby asshole."

Oh, man, I bet Dex *loved* getting hounded by Kristen. They met a few times before, never really hitting it off. She didn't care for Dex's biker attitude. Even less for Dex's friend Tank, who showed her all the ways a body could be bent then never called her again.

"I'm sorry. I didn't bring my phone with."

Sighing, she grabs for some of the things in my hands. "Katie, that's what phones are *for*. Seriously. I was about to call the cops if your landlord here didn't let me into your apartment. I thought you were dead or something."

My eyes widen. "Geez, morbid much?" I say, holding in my laugh, but her no joke expression tells me she isn't going to be laughing with me. "For real, sorry. I just needed a time-out. I'm totally good now. Come on." I guide her back up the steps and sidestep my angry landlord. I get us settled in my apartment and while she runs back to her car to grab her bags, I go to coo Gerdie. I tell him about all the other pretty birds I saw on my journey and that as much as I searched I didn't see a match for him, so he was stuck with me. If I was going to be a spinster for the remainder of my days, so was he. Fresh water and his yummy homemade bird treat later, I meet Kristen in the living room. She's opened a bottle of whiskey and placed two glasses on the coffee table. I take a seat, tucking my feet under my butt.

She pours us each a two-fingered glass and hands one to me.

"So, you gonna fill me in on what the heck has been going on?"

I take a good swig of the amber liquid, allowing me some time to figure out how to approach this. "Nothing really. Just work and vacation. Got to see some great—"

"I'm being serious, Katie. I want the truth for real this time."

And if anyone deserves the truth it's her. "I'm in love with Chase Green. And he is not mine to be in love with."

Her eyes widen at my confession.

"I know. I, Katie Beller, have a heart after all."

"I'm not going to act like I'm surprised. But seeing as you two are on a real name basis, I will just assume it was serious?" She looks at me with sad eyes. I only nod. "Can I ask when this started?"

Another sip. "Day four of the first tour."

She swears, taking a drink of her whiskey. "Shit, that soon?"

I nod.

"Was he ever inappropriate? Is there something I should know that concerns you or the tour?"

"No, of course not. He was a complete gentleman... And it was mutual. Nothing he did was without my thumbs-up." We fall silent for a moment, both sipping on our drinks.

"The club?" she asks.

"Yep," I reply.

She nods again. "And I assume he wasn't just in your

room calling for a new key at seven in the morning either that one time."

I shake my head. "Definitely doing more than getting a new key."

"Got it." More silence. More sipping.

"And the girlfriend?"

"I knew nothing about the girlfriend." I finish off my drink, grabbing for the bottle. I fill mine three fingers deep this time, leaning forward and offering the same courtesy to Kristen. I sit back and try to play it cool. Kristen reaches out, covering my hand with hers.

"I'm sorry, Kat."

"I know. Me too."

"I don't want to continue talking about this if it upsets you. But I do have to address some things. I know right now you need the friend and not the publicist, but I have to let you know."

"Know what?"

"Please hear me out. Everything before you decide or make any decisions. Please."

I nod, but I know I'm not going to like where this is going.

"As your publicist, I have to let you know that there were rumors going on about you and Charlie Bates. Apparently, you claimed you two were having sex. And someone started posting about it on the Internet."

I sit up straighter. "Who? I didn't tell anyone about Chase and me." But when I dig into my brain bank who could have even known, it hits me. "Fucking Chrissy Baker."

"I don't know who that is, but the posts did come from a local account. I would assume the same."

That fucking little bitch. But then again, I should have

kept my mouth shut.

"I want you to hear it from me, since I know you don't go online. But his publicist made a statement that those allegations were false, and he didn't even know you." The liquor in my stomach churns and I close my eyes, trying to fight the urge not to throw up.

"Honey, listen to me." She reaches out for my hand, but I brush her off.

"Seriously, it's fine. He has an image to uphold and that would look bad if he attached his name to mine." I take another drink, knowing the booze is going down too fast.

"Katie, you look like you're about to lose it. It's *not* fine."

I stand up quickly, a little woozy on my feet. The three shots of whiskey find their way into my bloodstream, setting my balance off a bit. "I knew what I was getting myself into. I knew this was what would happen. I can only blame myself."

Kristen puts her drink down, standing with me. "Katie, I know you're blaming yourself for what happened, but it takes two. And you cannot take blame for the girlfriend part. You didn't know. Can you just sit? Let me finish, before you shut down on me and drown yourself in this bottle?"

I roll my eyes and fall back onto the couch. She follows suit and begins. "Pretty quickly after that statement was released Charlie or *Chase* was blowing up my office. My cell. Any place he could reach me. I thought someone had died. When I finally was able to take his call, the first thing he said was, it wasn't true. And that he did not put out that statement."

What? Well, of course he didn't, his publicist did. He took the easy way out and avoided it.

"He went on and on, honey. How he's been trying to reach you, but you won't take his call, and how he needs to speak with you. He would do anything."

You can imagine how theatrical my "pfft" was this time around. "Yeah, right. Anything? Like lie to me? Shame me on social media that he doesn't even know me?" My voice is rising. I notice my drink swishing, which means my hands have begun to shake.

"He told me that if I didn't get you to talk to him, he's pulling from the tour."

I gasp at her confession. "He said *what*?"

"He threatened to pull out if I don't convince you to take his call. One call. That's all he asks." That son of a bitch. How dare he use my best friend and all her hard work to get to me.

"I know it sounds bad. He's a little fucker for putting us both in this situation. But he's also desperate."

Pffft! "For what?"

"You."

No.

NO.

I made my peace with him. I forgave myself for the mistakes I made, and I just want to move on. I won't spend any more time dwelling on *anything* Chase Green.

"Not going to happen," I say, determined.

"And you shouldn't." Kristen nods.

"Okay. So, then it's settled."

"But…"

I *KNEW* there was a but.

"But from a business perspective, I need Charlie Bates on this tour. I'm sorry, but he trapped me in a corner. He knew I wouldn't be able to get out unless I gave him what he wanted."

What! "Are you serious? You're picking him over me?"

"No! I swear, but you have to see how this is hard for me

too. Yes, he's a total dick on a stick for what he did. I would have dropped his sorry ass right away for what he did to you. But… it's just that there is this small part of me that feels you should talk to him. He truly sounds horrible."

Pffffft! "Pffft! I don't care."

"You're right. Forget I asked." She picks up her glass, taking a sip. Good. I hope she's dropping it. "So, enough Charlie Bates talk. How are you? How's the bar? Too soon to talk about Dex?"

At that we both laugh. Dropping the *Charlie Bates* talk is for the best. I cozy up in my couch. "Dex is the same. Hot and angry." I confess my little slip-up with him in the office. She isn't too shocked to hear it and even though she pretends she doesn't think he's smokin' hot, she demands every detail. And I give it to her.

I would never regret being with Dex, but it wasn't right. He's great in bed. A beast actually. But he wasn't what I wanted. And I needed to stop sending the wrong signals because it wasn't fair for him. Kristen was right. He was probably in love with me.

We catch up on any old friends' gossip since she's an avid social media whore and fills me in on my so-called fan page. I pretend I don't really care, but then make her pull it up because I don't believe it when she tells me I have twenty-seven thousand followers. I mean, holy shit! That's like more people than the population of my hometown!

We drink more, laugh, and dance. Reliving our olden days by performing our synchronized dance to "Shoop" by Salt-n-Pepa. Once two in the morning hits, we both fall into my bed, drunk and drunker.

"Dude, I can't remember the last time I had that much

fun." Kristen sighs, snuggling into my pillow.

"Me neither. I mean, can't believe we both still remember the 'Shoop' dance."

"Katie?"

"Yup?"

"I know you're hurt. But will you consider it. Talking to him?"

I knew she'd eventually bring it back up. I know how much this tour means to her and as much as I'm done with Chase, I can't take her down with me. "I'll think about it."

"Thanks, girl."

chapter TWENTY-ONE

Kristen's phone has been buzzing all fucking morning. And since my friend is dead to the world, I'm stuck with a pillow over my head each time, until the caller gets a damn clue and hangs up. On the billionth time, I lean over and answer it.

"Kristen Miller's phone, how can I help you?" I breathe into the phone, my eyes refusing to even open yet. "Hello? Anyone there?"

"Hi, Katie Beller."

Oh, shit.

I click end and toss the phone.

Like it's on fire.

"*Ouch!*" Kristen grunts, rubbing at her forehead where her phone just hit her. "Why'd you just do that?" Her blond hair is in her face and she barely has one eye open.

Before I have a chance to even reply the phone starts buzzing again. Kristen reaches for it—

"Don't! Don't answer that." Oh, God. Why did I answer that call? His voice, it's like a drug. Just hearing it again brings me back to that high I rode night after night.

Kristen looks at her phone and back at me. "Just give him a chance. If he upsets you, hang up. He said one call. Technically that would be fulfilling his blackmailish request."

God. One call. One conversation. I can do this. *No, I can't.* Yes, I can. Before I even make a decision, Kristen swipes the call.

"Oh my god, don't, wait! It's a FaceTime—"

I lose, because there pops Chase's face onto the screen. His eyes find mine instantly.

"God, you're beautiful."

So are you.

Blink, Katie.

There's this sudden urge to fucking smack him. Hang up on him. Cry maybe or yell. But I do nothing. I stare at him, as he stares back at me. And then I realize he has to be on fucking *crack* because I take a look at myself in the upper right-hand corner and my hair is sticking up and I resemble a raccoon left for dead.

"Just stop. What do you want, Bates?" I'm going to kill Kristen.

"I'm Bates now?"

"No, you're the lying asshole who blackmailed my sweet, honest friend."

He exhales heavily, bringing his hands into his hair. "What was I supposed to do? I needed to speak to you and you wouldn't take my calls. I was out of options."

"Um, I don't know, continue with me not taking your calls?"

"Katie, please. I need you to hear me out." Oh, I've heard him out. I've replayed every single possible thing he could say to me that would talk himself out of the truth. And in my lowest times, I debated on which one of those I would actually believe. Thankfully none of them.

"There's nothing to hear, Bates."

"Stop calling me Bates! Katie, please—"

"Please what, *Chase*? Please let you explain you have a fucking girlfriend? That you played me? That I let you in. The only guy I ever gave something to and you fucking took advantage of that!" I yell, my chest beginning to heave. "How could you? Was I a joke from the beginning? A conquest? Get the one girl you would never go for in your bed? To fall in love with you?" I angrily swipe the tear that falls down my cheek.

"No. I swear to you, no. Everything I did was real."

"Yeah, sure it was."

"It was, dammit. Katie, please let me explain. Rebecca. She was my girlfriend. Yes, at one time, but she wasn't when we started what we did."

I want to cover my ears. I don't want to hear his excuses. His lies. I close my eyes, trying to hide the pain that's quickly resurfacing.

"Katie, open your eyes. Look at me."

I'm not sure why I even obey. Maybe I'm a glutton for pain.

"She's my publicist."

"Great, well, hope you and your publicist were able to work it out," I snap.

"Just here me out! Please. Her father is CEO of the minor league hockey team I play for. Before I left for the book tour, I set things straight with her. She was the exact person I was running from. The one who saw me for my fame and money. Not for who I really was. We met through her father, and she took over all my PR. The modeling, the hockey. She runs it all. And when I walked away she threatened to ruin all that. I had to be careful. Her father has a lot of power. I didn't care about the modeling. But I cared about hockey. I just wanted to play."

So, I should feel bad that he played me while he had a girlfriend because daddy dearest would be mad if he dumped his daughter? "I've heard enough," I say. I can't do this.

"I broke up with Rebecca. I wouldn't have touched you if I were in a relationship."

"Well, apparently you were! She definitely thought otherwise, showing up announcing herself as your *girlfriend*, AND you didn't say anything to justify it. You know what? I'm done—"

"I LOVE YOU!"

My breath catches and I even hear Kristen gasp.

"I love you, Katie. I meant it that night. And even more that morning. And I mean it now. Let me fix this."

I'm so confused. My heart and my brain are at battle with one another, both fighting for the complete opposite. How can Chase fix this? Do I believe him? I mean, define broken up! If he didn't get caught would he have ever told me about her?

"I have one question. That day. Someone walked into your place. You hung up on me. Why?"

His eyes close briefly. When they open, I see the guilt.

"Rebecca walked in."

That's what I thought. I didn't want to admit it, but I

knew. I attempt to swallow the lump in my throat before I ask the next question.

"If you broke up with her, why was she at your place?"

And there it is again. Guilt. It's written all over his face. "Because we live together."

chapter
TWENTY-TWO

I hung up on Chase. I refused to let him see the hurt. Shit, *I* didn't even want to see it. Kristen took cover after that. Because I was done being sad. So those feelings took the bench and anger suited up. I whipped her phone across the room, which Kristen impressively threw her arm up and caught before it smashed against Gerdie's cage. I screamed and yelled. I threw things and cussed up a storm. When I took a swift kick to my dresser, yelping in horrible pain, I finally called it quits. Mainly because I was pretty positive I broke my toe. I sat on the floor and began to cry. And we're not talking weeping. I'm talking angry sobs. What was happening to me?

Kristen first convinced me it was because I was in love and love hurts sometimes. Well, duh. Once she got me to calm down, she then convinced me to let her take me to the ER since I most likely broke something. An X-ray and a sweet boot later, I was back home.

Kristen stayed with me for a few more days while I licked my wounds, then had to get back to Chicago. Not knowing what was going to happen with Chase's attendance, she had to prepare for his absence. Then there was the discussion of mine. Was I going to stick it out or drop? I signed the contract to complete the entire tour. Kristen wouldn't personally hold me to it if I really didn't want to show, but her lawyers and her publishing company would.

She gave me the time I needed to decide and when I finally made up my mind, I told her I'd still attend. I wasn't going to hide. I had a week until the signing to get ahold of my emotions and stability. It helped that those seven days were spent at the bar working like a slave due to all the days I missed. Dex kept his distance, but he never brought up what happened. I tried to apologize again, but he shut me down every time. I hated how he was treating me like I was nobody to him, but I guess I also deserved it.

It was also a matter of time before Chrissy Baker walked into the bar and threw the Charlie Bates comment back in my face. And boy had she been practicing her swing before she strolled in, ready for me. I just wish I were ready for her.

It was a slow Monday night when Chrissy strolled in with a new sidekick, assuming Stacey is out. Sleeping with your friend's husband clearly gets you kicked out of the mean girls' club, I presume. I'm the only one on call tonight because Randy is off and on a date. I'm pouring a few draft beers for a group of college guys when they take two open seats at the bar.

"Oh, hey, Katie, didn't think you'd be popping out in public so soon."

I turn to see her smiling, resembling an ugly hairless cat.

"And why's that?" I ask, pouring foam out of the glass and refilling.

"Well, because of that whole Charlie Bates thing. Looks like you made all that up. How embarrassing. And for him to publicly admit he didn't even know you." She and her dumb friend start laughing. "I mean, you couldn't think someone like Charlie Bates would seriously go for you? And people would believe it, do you?"

Dex steps behind me, bringing his hand over mine and lifting the beer tap up since I froze, the beer overflowing the glass. "Go take a break." He leans in and softly demands in my ear.

My knuckles are white squeezing the tap. Thoughts of me losing my job and some jail time flow through my head. I should listen to Dex. But that's not what I do.

I release my death grip and wrap my hands around the two full draft beers. I make my way down the bar, right in front of Chrissy, and lean in.

"Oops, you caught me. Charlie Bates? Be into me? Ha, that *is* kinda funny, isn't it? Oh, well. I'll just have to find another guy who wouldn't think twice about someone like me and make up another hot sex scandal with. Speaking of sex scandal, how are Stacey and your husband doing? Now *that* had to burn, huh? Glad to see you're also able to show your face after *that* complete embarrassment. I mean, your best friend sleeping around with your *husband*? Wow."

Chrissy's smile is long gone, her snarl quickly taking its place.

"But hey, if you can still show your face after your ex-best friend changes her profile pic to her and your man? Then props to you, girl."

Chrissy gasps, and I smile, leaning back. Her friend is quickly pulling out her phone in search of said photo, which I totally lied about, but I don't care. I push off the bar, tell Dex I'm taking that break, and don't look back.

I go hide in the back office, and before I know it, it's been well past fifteen minutes. I'm cradled in a chair staring at the ashtray, debating on taking up smoking. People who smoke seem to love it. Constantly taking smoke breaks, sucking those sticks into their lungs one after another. Maybe it would give me a hobby outside of being a bitch. I'm just starting to calm down when Dex comes into the office.

"Just don't." I wave at him, too embarrassed to even make eye contact.

He doesn't say anything, but he does bend down and pluck me off the chair, maneuvering us so he's now sitting and I'm cradled in his lap.

"Dex, what are you doing?" I ask, a tiny smile on my face.

"Just don't talk. I thought you girls like this cuddly shit."

My smile widens and I lay my head on his chest. "I'm not really a normal girl, though."

He presses his lips to my head but doesn't follow through with his kiss. "You sure aren't."

Dex and I didn't say anything else. He allowed me the comfort I needed. I'm sure this was also him telling me he accepted my apology. We got back to work. Chrissy was long gone when I came back out and there was no mention of what happened.

Phew.

We also don't talk about the fact that I leave for New York tomorrow. The final leg of the signing tour.

For the past seven days, I've prepared. I have worn myself thin each night at the bar, allowing myself to come home and crash, then repeat. But tomorrow I can't hide behind work. I have to get on a plane, enter a world that lingers with so many memories. Good and bad. And then see Chase. I've had time to work out the emotions, and I know Kristen has made accommodations to move our tables and specifically put our rooms on opposite sides of the hotel. We should have minimal contact, and the small part we do, I can handle it.

Making it home, I see a package on my doorstep. Kristen's name by the return address, I smile and lug it inside. Dropping my keys on the table, I whistle to Gerdie that I'm home and grab for a pair of scissors.

Dropping myself onto my couch, I rip the box open and pull out a box, the Converse logo on the side and a letter.

Kat-

You're an amazing person inside and out. Don't ever think otherwise. Thank you for loving me enough to do this. I know it took a lot to agree to the tour. (Minus the whole lawyer/contract/possible lawsuit babble, of course).

I thought I'd send you a little gift to help brighten this journey for you. Plus, I may have noticed the cut-up pair of green Converse in your garbage. Thought you could use a new color in your life. It reminds me of you. Fierce.

Love you, girl.

-Kristen

I open the box to a new bright red pair of Converse.

chapter
TWENTY-THREE

During the flight, I sat next to a really nice old lady. She had three beautiful children and seventeen grandchildren. All true. I saw each single photo. All seventeen. I told myself next time I was driving, but it's frowned upon to drink and drive, and during the quick flight I've had the pleasure of two Bloody Marys. Consider it self-medication from Betty and her family tree itemization.

With a little beat to my step, I'm off the plane and heading down the terminal to baggage. I hear someone calling my name and turn to see a big sign with my name on it. And a cute little blonde holding it.

"What? What are you doing here? Don't you have to be at the hotel?" I smile, happy to see Kristen.

"Nah, welcoming you into the wonderful state of New

York is more important. Plus, I have Tara holding down the fort."

"Yikes, how mad is she?"

"Oh, that girl would sexually pleasure me if I asked. These young kids nowadays will do anything to work their way up in the publishing industry ladder."

I'm looking at her wide-eyed.

"I mean, I wouldn't ask, geez. I haven't gotten that desperate yet."

We laugh, and she tells me she'll have the driver grab my bags. Escorting me to the limo, we hop in, and she hands me a beer.

"Okay, so I'm going to go into publicist mode, really quick. I've confirmed and double confirmed. Your room will be located on the west wing. Mr. Bates will be on the east. Your room name is under Frenchy Burgess. That way if he gets sneaky he won't find your reservation."

I laugh. "Frenchy Burgess? Really?"

"Yeah, I had a dream once I was married to this guy. He was like crazy rich and took me to all these fancy places, but he kept calling me Frenchy Burgess. Hell knows why. Either way, it's now your undercover identity.

"Now for tables. You're now on the other side of the ballroom. I tried to keep it quiet as long as I could, but you know readers. They want to know where they're going. So, it's been released. Assuming Mr. Bates has gotten wind."

Like I care. And why should he? It all seems a bit silly hearing how out of the way Kristen has to go to keep me from getting my feelings hurt again. I'm honestly better and pretty over it all. Her phone rings and she looks at who's calling.

"Yep, just got wind," she says, putting her finger up to

take the call. "Kristen Miller here. Yes, Mr. Bates... I understand that, but it worked better with the layout... And I also understand that, but it's not about money. It's about better traffic flow." She's listening to whatever he's saying, her eyes forming a sadness to them. "I know and I'm sorry, but this is about business, Charlie. You know I can't ask that... I'll notify Tara of your requests." She hangs up and sticks her phone in her back pocket. Refusing to tell me what just happened, she perks back up and claps her hands together.

"Okay, so I have you doing your interviews once we get to the hotel. Learning the only way I'm going to get them is if I do them *before* the signing." She smiles humorously and as the door of the limo opens to our arrival she grabs my hand and escorts me into New York's glorious Four Seasons hotel.

It seems I was doing myself a service by skipping out on these interviews. It's one thing to fill out the forms answering each and every question, but it's another to be on the spotlight while someone drills you about anything and everything. The two most asked questions were, was I Abby, and when does my next book release. When I opened my mouth to say, what next book, Kristen stepped in and answered. And apparently, we are looking at some time next year.

We were?

"What was that about back there?" I ask as we exit the meeting room. Keeping a smile on my face because readers are everywhere, I lean into Kristen. "I'm not writing another book."

"I know, but they don't need to know that. Readers want to know you're going to give them more."

"And what I gave them wasn't enough?"

"Nope. Welcome to the world of new indie age of publishing. There are so many writers out there, if you don't keep up, you'll get lost in the shuffle. Lots of fish, big sea, kinda thing."

"Isn't it small fish? And I don't want to keep up," I say, trying to keep up with her fast pace. Kristen always being on the go clearly stays so skinny by her constant speed walking. "Dude, will you slow down! I don't plan on writing anything else. I'm done after this," I say, just as we turn the corner.

Smacking right into Chase Green, like the color, Charlie Bates, like the motel.

Fuck.

God, he looks good.

So, *so* good.

Blink, Katie.

"Hey." His voice is soft but noticeably nervous. Realizing he's holding me, he quickly lets go, jamming his hands into his pockets as if to keep himself constrained.

"Hi," I repeat, unsure what else to say or do. Kristen is *definitely* not sure, because she keeps looking back and forth between us. My skin feels on fire where his hands once touched me and my hands are starting to feel fidgety.

"Wow, you look really good. Great. I mean, better than that… You—"

"Thanks, so do you," I cut him off, saving him from wherever he was going with that. I end up following suit, jamming my own hands in my back pockets. I guess I get it now. It's so we keep our hands to ourselves. Because right now, mine want to reach out and touch him.

"Okay, well, Katie, we really need to get you checked in and to your interviews."

I turn to her. "I thought we just finish—"

She grabs my arm. "Okay! So sorry, Charlie, I need my famous author. Let me know if you need anything." She beams at him then starts pulling me away.

I pass by him, our shoulders briefly touching. The smell of his cologne seeps into my nostrils when I hear him call my name. I turn, watching him.

"It's really great to see you."

I don't reply. I slowly nod and force myself to turn, allowing Kristen to drag me away.

chapter TWENTY-FOUR

W orst night's sleep ever.

After escaping Chase's soul sucking eyes, Kristen checked me in and, taking no precautions, took me up the service elevator in case Chase was following. I rolled my eyes the whole time, saying how ridiculous it was, but she informed me she was not blind to the moment we just shared and since my hand was still shaking in hers, it was not ridiculous at all.

She told me to order room service if I didn't want to leave the room, and I agreed. I just needed to process. But with all the precautions Kristen had been taking, when I picked up the phone to order my normal pizza, I became super paranoid Chase would track me down by my infamous pizza order and spat out some random dish instead. Needless to say, the chicken parmesan went untouched.

I lay in bed attempting to watch TV, but all I could do every two fucking seconds was bring my eyes away from the screen and on to that connecting door. I was so tense, thinking that at any point it was going to open and Chase would walk through. I told myself it was impossible and to knock it off. I lasted a whole thirty-seven seconds before I finally got up and took any furniture that was light enough to move and barricaded the door.

But still, I felt no ease. Midnight rolled around, then one, then two, and it was in the crazy hours of the morning, when I had to have been so sleep deprived that I pondered ordering pizza just to see if it set off some secret buzzer notifying Chase where I was.

Once my alarm went off and I almost finished counting the specs on the ceiling, I gave up and just got up. I showered and dressed in a black dress that sat just above my knees, along with my red Converse. I left my hair down so people were less likely to see the bags under my eyes. Maybe they would focus on my pretty bright shoes instead. Kristen came and got me, and as we walked to the banquet hall, the closer we got, the more my unease set in.

"I... I don't think I can do this." I stop, waving off the sweat building in my palms.

"Kat, yes, you can. Trust me, you'll barely see him. You have a line out the door. Once you're done I'll escort you back or we can leave the hotel and go out."

I hate that this has become such a bigger deal. I don't want to admit that I secretly *do* want to see Chase. But that's just the sucker part of me. Then there's that tough guy in me that screams just rip off the Band-Aid. Just fucking deal with him and get the fuck over it.

"I know. I… I just need a minute."

She nods, and we stand there, allowing me to breathe. Two more deep breaths and I give her the okay, let's do this. But once we walk into the banquet hall, shit hits the fan.

"I swear, I had them set up the way you requested last night. I have no idea how or who got in here to move them, but I'm working to find out." Tara looks like she's going to throw up.

Kristen looks murderous, and I look, well, I look, I don't know what I look like.

We all stand there, at the table settings, the *updated* settings, to see that Charlie Bates' table has been moved directly across from mine.

"Well, who the ever-loving fuck did all this?" Kristen barks, waving her hands all over the place.

"Like I said, I'm trying to figure it out. I just called down to maintenance to have someone move them."

"*Move them*? The doors are about to open in less than two minutes!" Kristen is now yelling and other authors are looking our way. Without warning the volunteers to stall, they open the doors. And mayhem begins.

"God, Kat, I'm so sorry. I can fix—"

"Seriously, it's fine. I'll be fine," I assure her.

"Honey, no. This is *not* okay."

"Kristen, you've done way too much. I'm a grownup. I need to start acting like one. I can handle it."

And just as I vow to be the bigger person, Chase walks in, along with his assistant, smiling from ear to ear.

And Kristen attacks.

"You little—"

I grab her forearm, stopping her from jumping Chase. "Kristen, seriously. Chase and I are adults. We can work across from one another, right, Chase?"

His eyes don't leave mine. He doesn't even acknowledge the death stare from Kristen. "Yes, I promise. I'll behave. I just wanted to be close in case anything happens." He steps up to me, my body instantly on fire. "I promise I won't bother you. I just want to make sure you're safe."

Talk, Katie.

Say something.

Fucking nod!

Ugh. It takes me gulping down my emotions to finally speak. "It's fine. Just stay on your side of the pond, Bates, got it?" I force the humor out, needing this tension to wade.

I sense the hurt in his eyes when I call him Bates, but we need that separation. He can't be Chase Green to me anymore.

"Okay. Well, then, it's settled. Get on your side, Mr. Bates," Kristen snaps, then turns to me. "And if you need anything, you call for me." And with that our signing begins.

Dedication.

Holy smokes do these fans have it.

Every single signing, I've sold out of books. I don't even know how. People don't buy just one. They buy three, five, a dozen, getting books for friends, blogs, one to read and one to keep in a locked bookshelf like special autographed trophies.

And don't get me started on all the homemade fan swag. The homemade T-shirts? They were awesome. The words *Love*

Broken looked pretty badass across chests and backs. I'm now a proud owner of a few.

The signing room is packed with rows of crisp white linen tables, topped with thick books, thin books, naughty covers and sweet ones. The crazed amount of colorful swag littering in between. Pens, cups, bookmarks, the list goes on and on. And you can literally feel the vibrancy of the crowd. The chatter between friends, strangers, fans, and even tagalong husbands. It's just complete madness. And in the world of book signings, there's no time to dwell. On *anything*. Even a certain model across the way.

Due to the chaos of the day, I'm able to take my mind off Chase. For the early part of the signing, my attention is completely engrossed by readers. And who can *not* be engrossed by a bunch of people dressed in head to toe "Love Broken" riot gear. Because *that's* apparently what you get when you write a story that creates a phenomenon about women who realize they are worth more than a fake endearment and a self-indulgent slap on the ass.

These women of all ages were seeing life and love in a completely different light. They didn't want to fall for the various types of fake bullshit life was feeding them. It was complete bananas the range of stories I listened to. There was the teenager who got screwed over by the high school football star, the college girl who got taken advantage of by her long-distance boyfriend. The bartenders, the business women. The shy, the bold, the strong, the not so… They all had a story. A girl trying to be someone they weren't, just to get the guy.

The saddest thing is, that with each and every single story I listened to, I could relate. The boy in high school you spent your entire freshman year doing anything to get noticed by and, finally, at a party when he's drunk as shit, he tells you you're pretty, just to lure you into the bathroom and steal a part of you that was meant for someone special.

How about the college stories, of all girls who just want to get the guy? College being the worst stereotype when it comes to love and bullshit. It's not a place for love, it's a place where the girl doesn't not only *not* get the guy, she gets a complex and a lifelong set of insecurities and daddy issues.

We grow up just wanting forever. Guys grow up wanting the complete opposite. Now, don't get me wrong. I'm not labeling every guy on the planet. I know there are men out there, from adolescent to retired, who want nothing more than to find the same love us women do. I just have absolutely no idea where those rare species are. I've heard and read about them, but they just don't seem to run in the same circles—shit, same realm as me. As most of society.

Okay, so yeah, there was a time where I could name off a certain someone who met the endangered, perfect man, species list. At least I thought I could. And after listening to story after story about jerks, it made me put my own situation into perspective. I shouldn't be sad about how things went down with Chase and me, but should be madder. Angry. Revengeful!

With a frown now marring my face, I see him already looking my way, wearing his tender eyes and bullshit smile. As I stare back blankly, I slowly lift my hand to scratch at a fake itch on my cheek. All while conveniently placing my middle finger up at him.

Immature? Probably.

But do I feel slightly better? Absolutely.

Okay, so that *better* feeling lasts about as long as it takes me to spell *a-b-s-o-l—*

Oh, fuck it.

I was hoping the rewarding gesture would last me through the day, but as I grab another sneak peek, he's not, as I'd hope, standing there in shock, mad, devastated at my lack of affection. No. He's all Chase Green, the sweet man, who saves spiders and cries at Hallmark movies. The man who shares meals and offers you the first scoop of freshly buttered popcorn so you get the best mouthful.

He's the perfect one.

At least he used to be.

I watch him shake hands with a young girl who seems to be in tears at meeting him. I watch him sign her poster, give her a hug, and smile wide for a picture. My stupid, traitorous emotions have me swelling a wee bit with pride at how good he is with people. How kind he is. He doesn't flaunt himself like some of the other models at the signing do. He isn't pouring booze down his chest allowing crazed fans to lick it off him just to feel more popular.

It's the images of him late at night, kissing my neck, caressing my skin, and whispering words of trust and love, once a warmness in my heart, but now ruined because the *perfect man* I see before me isn't so fucking perfect. Because *those* beautiful moments are tainted by memories of his betrayal and lies.

Before I tear my eyes away, he catches me once again. A look of confusion covers his face, mostly due to the fact my facial expression is close to one of a psycho. I look away. Lucky enough, I'm greeted by another reader, and the thoughts of kicking over his table quickly fades in the background. A woman, looking to be in her late forties, comes up to me, holding half a bookstore of books in a rolling crate behind her.

"Oh boy, did you rob a bookstore before you came here?" I ask, smiling and reaching out to help take some of the load she's carrying off her hands. I put them on my table to properly shake hands and trade introductions.

"You would think. It's a damn pleasure to meet ya, darlin'. The name's Leanne."

I stick my hand out, but she goes straight for the hug.

"Sorry, where I'm from we hug. We're all friends here."

I laugh because she's right. Since the tour began I've learned that readers are lifelong friends. "Well, it's nice to meet you, Leanne. Looks like you may have enjoyed my book. Unless you're here trying to return all these," I kid. Clearly, I have no idea if someone can return a book at these things.

"Return? Hell no, darlin', you ain't getting these books back. They're like our bible now back down in Shelbyville. Our local bookstore only carries so many books, so I had to purchase all the copies they had from you. Girls from the town over were getting wind of our stock, so it was only a matter of time before the Shelbyville bookstore sold clean out of it."

"Bible?" Curious to the comparison.

"Oh, honey, the whole town practically read your book. The men dogged it, sorry to admit, them worthless pigs. But it was 'cause they were busted. Us women, oh, honey, it's changed us. For the better. No more dealings with all the bunkum shit we all put up with. Krista from the grocery store, she used to spend hours on herself fixin' to meet a man. Now? She's gotten rid of her makeup. More like clown face as some of us girls used to say, but let me tell ya'll, she's a beauty. When she stopped worrying about trying to look all done up for a man, her true self shined on right through. Found herself a nice man at church two weeks later."

236

My brows shoot up, humor filling my expression. "Oh, wow. Good for Krista," I reply.

"There's Becka who stopped hustlin' over at the local bar. Her mamma thanks you for that. Suzanne from the barbershop, she had a man, but he had more than one woman. She finally said she was better than that and kicked his filthy ass out. She's on her second date with the manager of the bank in Shelbyville."

I shake my head. These are the stories I hear all day. Outside of my little dive bar, the problem with men was a lot bigger than I thought, and these women, they just stood for so much more now.

"Honey, I don't mean to pry, but that handsome looking boy over there keeps locking his eyes over here. If I was to guess, he may be sweet on you."

I lift my head from signing one of her books to see Chase staring our way. His hands in his pockets, his eyes directly on me. Once ours meet, he smiles.

Jerk.

"Oh, don't waste your time on that guy... he's just a pretty face. I heard..." I lean in, lowering my voice. "He has major performance issues, if you know what I mean." I pull back, watching her eyes widen, taking another glance Chase's way.

"Oh my, what a shame. He sure looks like he would be just a pleasant handful in bed."

Pffft.

As if.

Totally as if... God... don't go there, Katie.

"Trust me. Girls talk. Don't get me started on the whole rash—"

"Excuse me, miss?"

We both turn to see Chase standing not two feet from us offering up his addictive smile. I take that moment to give him the death stare, while my new bestie falls right into his trap.

"Why, hello there, cute thing. We were just—"

And I accidently nudge my new friend. Both look my way. "Oops, sorry. She was just saying we were just talking about jerks and how they have no sense in the word trust and honesty."

"Well, and of course yo—"

Shit.

"Heavens, dear, why do you keep jabbing me?"

"No idea. Anyway, you can go back to your side, model boy." Please just go away.

No such luck.

"Well, since I did come all the way over here, I was hoping to get a picture with this young lady. You two look so familiar. Is this your sister, Miss Swan?"

I'm going to kill him.

Leanne blushes like a damn school girl. I believe I notice her eyelashes flutter like one too. "Oh no, you sweet thing. I'm old enough to be her mother."

Oh, *here* we go.

The theatrics on this guy are ridiculous. I watch Chase's eyebrows lift in shock, placing his palm to his chest. "No. I don't believe it."

And Leanne eats—no, she *gobbles* it all up.

"Well, I am."

"I must say, you look fantastic. Do share your secrets."

Give me a freaking break here! He needs to go. I'm not falling for this sweet guy bullshit. I can sense Leanne is about to confess to Chase all her beauty secrets, so it's time I step in.

"*Mr. Bates.* I think it's time you head on back to your table. Your fans are getting impatient."

He doesn't even look at his table. He keeps his attention all on Leanne. Pulling out his phone, he opens an app and goes in for the kill. "Not before I get a picture to remember this day. Do you mind…?"

"Oh, it's Leanne."

"Leanne. Beautiful name to match the beautiful lady."

Dead. Fucking dead.

He turns to my drooling line. "Would you mind taking a picture?" Chase asks the reader in front of the line. A small part of me hopes the girl takes his phone and runs with it like she looks like she's debating on doing.

Again, no such luck.

Dammit.

She smiles and takes his phone, raising it for the perfect shot.

Just as I step back to allow jerk face and Leanne to get their shot, Chase suddenly reaches out, grabbing my arm. "Oh, I'm gonna need you in it as well, Miss Swan. Me in between two beautiful ladies? My mother wouldn't even believe me unless I show her the picture to prove it."

Leanne sighs.

I believe I growl.

I don't know what he's trying to pull here, but it's not going to work. I look around and everyone is watching. Well, watching Chase. Leanne looks at me with the biggest smile on her face, waiting for me to step up and take the photo. *It's just a picture, Katie.* I fail at hiding my eye rolling, but I give in and step forward. I go to stand next to Leanne, but I'm pulled to the left, putting Chase between us. His arm goes around her neck and his other around mine. I can't help but stiffen at the way he's touching me. *Just a picture, Katie.* I have to remind myself, otherwise I'll put too much thought into the way he has his hand gently resting over my shoulder blade. His fingers, on purpose no less, slowly brush against my skin.

"Okay, ready?" the girl asks, preparing to take our photo.

"You bet," Chase replies and three flashes radiate from his phone. Once she's done, I start to pull away, but Chase pulls me in closer, leaning into me. I feel his breath hitting my earlobe, as his words strike. They're soft and just above a whisper, but loud enough for my heart to hear. "I miss you." He pulls away just as slowly, as if no meaning or tension just sparked between us.

He then lets me go and says his goodbyes to Leanne. He walks back to his side of the room and continues his day as if he didn't just fucking ruin mine.

I'm tired.

Hungry.

And crabby.

I signed the last four books with the wrong name, having to toss them and sign my pen name instead of my real name. If I wasn't signing Katie by accident, I was writing Abby instead. Again, tired, hungry, and crabby. I have no idea how people do this all the time. The first signing was fine because I was so busy playing googly eyes across the room with doofus during, and googly everything in the bedroom afterward. I can't really complain too much about the second signing tour because, well, I didn't make it through the whole thing. I still feel guilty at all the heat Kristen took for me cutting out halfway through.

I'm in the twilight zone staring at Amy as she restocks all my stuff onto the table, preparing for tomorrow's signing, when a shoulder bumps into me.

"Whoa there." I turn, holding out my hands to steady a drunk dude. I notice he's wearing a name badge, which means he's somehow a part of the signing. Getting a peek at his name, I realize he's Winston Mills, the model Kristen caught privates deep in a reader in the bathroom last tour.

"Whoa yourself, gorgeous." He takes a step too close, and I can smell the alcohol on his breath. I proceed to take a step back, but he grabs my forearm. "Hey now, where you going? We're just getting to know each other." He pulls my arm, causing me to trip into him. My hands fly up, unintentionally grabbing at his chest. He takes my mishap the wrong way, as I watch his sleazy eyes light up. "Well, then, how about we take this to your room and continue our introductions?"

My stomach clenches in an 'I want to vomit' sort of way. I push off him, but he doesn't let me go, which quickly irritates me. "Yeah, no, thanks, pal, but you can let me go." I try again, but he doesn't seem to get the hint.

"Feisty. Even better. Love when you women play hard to get. Did you want me to call you dirty names to get you all worked up? The last one, she—"

"I think she said she wasn't interested, man."

We both turn to see Chase, his cool factor to him, with his hands in his pockets, but there's no hiding the blaze in his eyes. I push off Drunky Douche again and this time he releases me. He eyes Chase up and down before he speaks. "Sup, man. I know you. You're the hockey player. Read some article you're about to go pro."

Eyebrows raised, I turn to Chase, waiting for his response. I didn't see or read anything about this.

Not that I was stalking or anything.

"Never believe what you read, man," he replies in a cool tone, sidestepping the question.

"Whatever you say. I bet you get tons of chicks, though. Sports and modeling at these things? I envy you, bro. We should swap stories over a beer sometime."

At that I cringe. Chase's expression darkens.

"Doubtful. Why don't you keep walking, though? I'm sure this one has to finish packing up."

Douchecanoe turns my way, taking an eyeful of me, and steps back into my personal space. "Ahh, come on, babe. Don't be shy. I'll make it just as worthwhile." He lifts his arm, his hand gunning for my cheek. Chase takes a defensive step forward as I slap Douche's hand away.

"Wow, you're a piece. Seriously. If I were into guys who reek of cheap booze and even cheaper sounding pickup lines, I'd be all over it, but this time, hard pass."

His eyes flare with anger. It's apparent he's not used to being turned down. "Whatever, bitch."

I quickly take a menacing step toward him. "What did you just call me?" I put my hand up just as Chase comes at him, warning him to stay out of this.

"I called you a bitch. I know about you. The one who thinks she's all high and mighty. One who wrote that book trashing guys. Didn't even finish the last tour. Cost a lot of readers money. Heard it was because you got played too—"

Winston is cut off by Chase shoving him from the back.

His arm goes up to swing when I step in between. "Chase, stop!" I yell and push him away. I turn to Winston, but he's already walking away, but not before pushing my books off my table. The sound makes me jump, reminding me of when that psycho attacked me, almost knocking my table over.

"Are you okay?" Chase is behind me, putting his hands over my shoulder.

I knock them off, whipping around to face him.

"I didn't need you to do that," I snap at him.

"Yeah, well, he was being a prick."

"Yeah, and I don't need you fighting my battles. I could've handled that myself."

His eyes become angry. "And I'm sure you could've, but I felt the need to step in."

"Well, next time don't," I finish and turn around, grabbing my purse and storming out of the banquet hall. Chase is on my tail, running after me, calling my name. I wish I could just click my heels and disappear. Magically be in my room so I don't have to face him.

"Katie, wait up."

I don't listen, but pick up the speed.

"Just talk to me." He tries to stop me at the elevator, but I sidestep him, trying to ignore his dominance, his anger. "Katie, for Christ's sake, stop. I fucked up, I know. But if you just hear me out, you'll understand. I swear—"

I twist, slapping the hand trying to grab for my shoulder off me. "I'm gonna *understand*? How so? As in understand that you lied? Betrayed me? Us? There's nothing to under—"

"There fucking is! Goddammit," he snaps but quickly checks himself. He's silent, trying to rein in his sudden anger. "I'm sorry. I didn't mean to yell, it's just—"

"Just what? That you fucked up?"

"Yes. More than you even know. But if you just listen…"

"I can't. And I won't. I told you how I felt. I won't lower myself and be fed more lies. I already told you, you won. You won my heart. Not sure what you do with it now, since it's in fucking pieces," I spit and turn back toward the elevator, smacking the call button for one to arrive.

Chase takes a calculated step toward me. "Katie, please. Please just let's go upstairs and talk. I promise you I won't try anything. I just want to talk."

And trick me? Lie to me more? Bury me even further into the world of pain and regret I'm already suffocating in?

"No," I say, hitting the button again. I refuse to look at him this time. I can't. I can't see the guilt in his eyes, or the torment shining in mine. And there is so much of both. There's regret that I ever let him get under my skin. Allowed him inside my simple world. Guilt that I'm so bullheaded and won't let him explain. Convince me everything I've endured the past month has been a bad dream. And God, the torment I won't give in and allow him to take me into his arms and cradle me until my heart feels whole again.

A big mistake on my part, I turn and look at him. And I know just by the pain that radiates from his beautiful green eyes that he can't do that. He won't be able to wipe away the wrong.

"Katie, please."

"Dammit, no!" I stomp my foot, squeezing my eyes shut. "What don't you get? I'm done. This, us, we're over. I don't care what you have to say." I reopen them and face him. "There's nothing you can say or do to convince me that anything you've done or said was real. You're a liar. A fake. And exactly the kind of person I despise."

I hate myself for the way the anguish seeps through his eyes. But I can't worry about how he feels. I need to worry about how I get through tonight. Tomorrow and the next day without feeling lost and broken.

"So that's it? You're just done with us? Done trying?"

"Yes." I stare back at the elevator door.

"I don't believe you. I know you love me. I know you love me just as much as I love you."

"Well, then, you're just as much a liar as you are naive." I fight not to show the emotions tearing me apart on the inside. My breaths are calculated as I count with each lungful, knowing I cannot show weakness.

"So, then there's no reason for me to bother? You want me to leave you alone?"

No. "Yes."

"And that's it? You're willing to just call it quits without even hearing me out?"

God, I want to. "Yes."

"You know… I thought our story would end with for better or worse. Not this. You said you trusted me. But it seems I was wrong."

I want to slap him for trying to turn this around on me. I don't react, but the single tear running down my cheek says enough. I want to scream I wanted forever too. But I didn't do this to us. With malice in my tone, I respond, "Our story ended the moment you betrayed us—"

"I didn't betray us! Dammit, Katie, why won't you listen!" His voice booms through the lobby, eyes turning our way. A few phones lift to snap bullshit photos, I'm sure for their Facebook gossip groups.

I turn back finally, needing this to end. "Accept what it is, Chase. You're starting to look pathetic. I'm not into you. To be honest, your bullshit did me a favor. Let it go. Let me go." My last words take everything out of me, as I press the button one last time, finally having the damn elevator hitting the lobby floor and opening. I walk into the empty elevator and turn, seeing Chase's wounded eyes. Angry. In denial maybe. I press the button for my floor and just before the doors close I speak. "Have a nice life, Chase." I watch the doors close on his beautiful, crushed face.

chapter
TWENTY-FIVE

I won't cry. I won't cry. I won't cry.

    I repeat this mantra with every sip of vodka I take.

    I will prevail. This is just a blimp in my path of self-preservation. I am stronger than this.

    I continue to chant more bullshit while I take another mini liquor bottle from the mini fridge and open it, pacing my room. My phone's gone off about a billion times since I got back. None being Chase, thank God, because I'm not sure if I could handle anything more thrown at me after what just happened downstairs. Instead, it's those annoying Facebook notifications, one after another. Ever since Kristen downloaded that damn app on my phone, it never seems to shut up. So and so posted in author group. So and so posted on author page. So and so posted AHHH! Social media just needs to die!

Not to mention, Kristen's also blowing up my phone wondering where the hell I'm at. I want to respond with in hell drinking my retirement fund in mini liquor bottles out of the hotel liquor cabinet, but that would also mean I'd have to admit I'm alive. And right about now, I'm not sure I can leave my room. And meeting her at the meet and greet she set up would entail doing just that.

I've officially diagnosed myself with real life anxiety because my palms begin to sweat just at the thought of leaving this space and running into him. Into anyone. We weren't quiet and there's no doubt we made a scene. People heard. Documented it with their stupid phones and stupid social media. It's only a matter of time before Kristen sees it and sends the troops to come find me.

So, I continue to pace my room. I pace so hard, I worry they're gonna take my deposit just to replace the carpet when I check out. I know I promised Kristen I'd make the meet and greet, but I'm not sure I can go down there. I'm fighting not to pack my bags and leave, sending a note to Kristen's room telling her I'm sorry. I know she'll be more than pissed with me, but she told me from the start she'd understand.

Another ding echoes into my room and I find myself taking down another mini bottle, before checking my phone seeing another text from Kristen. I open the message, reading her urgent plea for me to hurry and how the rampant group of fans is starting to get antsy.

"I need to do it for them. He won't even be there," I tell myself, going for my shoes and sliding a shoe up my heel. There's no way Chase would go to an author meet and greet. Especially one that my best friend is throwing just for me.

I take a few deep breaths, trying to get my shit together.

I need to rid myself of anything Chase Green and get myself back on normal ground. I brush my teeth and re-apply make-up that's worn off from the long day. I decide to change into a tight-fitting dress Randy lent me. It completely clashes with my red Converse, but I can't give a shit. I do one thing out of the norm and apply a small dab of red lip gloss. I figure I'm feeling rebellious, why not.

My phone dings again with yet another Facebook notification as I finally leave my room. "God, how do you turn these damn things off?" I mumble, pulling my phone from my back pocket. As I swipe to unlock my phone I read the most recent notification.

Carlie Lieber tagged Charlie Bates in a post in New York Author Signing Attendee group
Oh, did she now.

What the hell does *she* have to post about? I open the app and go to the group page, which takes forever since I don't even know how to use the damn thing. Once I make it to the group site I scroll until I see it. And my heart plummets.

Posted is a selfie taken of him with a pretty blonde on his lap. The attached message reads:

He smells just as yummy as his lap feels! <3 <3
I read the message two more times and stare at the picture longer than I should. That… that… *"asshole."* I hiss, kicking the wall in the hallway. I kick it again, and then kick the fake plant minding its own business in front of the elevators. He can stand there begging me to give him a chance one minute and two seconds after telling him to beat it, he's already opening his lap up to the entire female population, with open arms! Or legs, in this matter!

"What a jerk. What a fucking jerk. Jerk. Jerk. Fucking

jerk." I'm a broken record at this point. All that bullshit he fed me. Didn't take him long to get over the fact that I wouldn't succumb to his fucking bullshit. If he thinks he's going to get back at me by pulling this stunt, then he's way wrong.

I'm out of the elevator and headed toward the hotel bar like a woman on a mission. I'm a wee bit drunk, so I manage to trip over my own shoe getting out of the elevator and stumble twice more once I hit the packed bar. Kristen spots me right away and stands, waiving her hand to call me over. I use my eagle eyes to search out her surroundings when I see it. Or him. And all. Of. Them. *Deep breath. You can do this. Okay, now use your feet and walk.* I wish that was easier said than done because I sway and bump into a waitress holding a full tray.

"Shit, sorry!" I apologize to the waitress just as I make it to the seated area.

"Hey! Where the hell have you been? I've been calling and texting you."

They chose the lounge seating, which means two couches facing one another. That also means Kristen seems to be on one side with a group of people, and Chase, accompanied by a flock of fans, directly across from her.

I take a quick glance at Chase, making sure he's paying attention. "Oh, sorry. I had some people in my room for a pre-party."

Kristen has a strange expression on her face, clearly knowing I'm lying. "*Oh. Like who?* Isn't that why we're having the meet and greet?"

I shrug. "Yeah, but this was a private party, if ya know what I mean." I wink at her and throw myself onto the lounge chair.

Kristen retakes her seat next to me and flags down the waitress. The group of women surrounding Chase, some from the signing whom I met earlier today, don't even acknowledge me. They're all too busy fighting for Chase's attention. And let me tell ya, if I wasn't already agitated by him and his intentions, I'm even more so now. I lean forward, grabbing for Kristen's martini on the tiny cocktail table, but I accidently knock over a bunch of glasses.

"Whoa, careful, honey. Have you been drinking?" Kristen picks up the spilled drinks, while I ignore her and slam the rest of her martini. "Hey... slow down, killer, the night's just getting started." She takes her now empty glass and sets it down. When the waitress finally comes by Kristen orders herself a new martini and me a vodka tonic.

"Excuse me." I flag her down before she makes her getaway. "Make that a double. Actually, just bring two doubles. It's gonna be a fun one tonight." I smile and turn away from the waitress but not in the direction of Kristen's worried eyes. The bad part is the only other way to look is in front of me.

"So, Bates, who's your new lap dog?" I watch him tense, but the blonde next to him eagerly smiles. I swear she just licked her lips like a hungry animal.

"I have no idea what you're referring to, but I'm clearly just sitting here. What about you and your *room party*? What the fuck is that all about?" His eyes are on fire.

Good. I hope they burn and fall out. I lean back, feeling a bit dizzy.

"You sure you're okay?" Kristen butts in. Giving Chase the evil eye, she asks, "Did something happen?"

"Seriously, I'm fine," I snap and sit back up, the dizziness hitting me again. Thankfully the waitress shows up with our drinks, distracting Kristen from monitoring me. Grabbing both my glasses, I chug the first one, sloppily placing it back on the waitress's tray. It's when I sit back again that the dizziness hits full force. Because in front of me is a beautiful redhead now sitting next to Chase.

"You two make a great couple," I slur, raising my glass to cheers them.

Chase looks super mad, trying to brush the girl off him. "Knock it off, Katie."

"No way. You should totally go for it. Take her back up to your room. Probably should feed her too. She looks about ready to take a bite outta your neck." And boy does that bitch look hungry. Seriously, the amount of times she's licked her lips.

"I'm not taking anyone up to my room."

"You're not?" The bimbo frowns, looking as if she were just told Santa wasn't real.

"Never say never, *girlfriend*. Just tell him you're not into him and he'll make it a mission to—"

"Stop," Chase snaps.

"No, for real. She should know." I take another sip, feeling his eyes as they throw daggers at me. "Charlie Bates for the win. And I'm sure she doesn't care that you have a girlfriend either. Match made in—"

"Jesus Christ, stop! Look at you. You're drunk and making a fool of yourself."

Ouch.

But he's right.

What *am* I really accomplishing here? I need to be done. Be done playing games. Be done being hurt, being angry, being confused.

I need to be done.

I startle everyone around me when I pounce up, knocking my knee into the small drink table and shaking half the empty glasses onto the floor. I swig my drink till it's almost gone then slam it down. "All right, folks. Time to get this party started." I turn to Kristen. "Don't wait up, 'kay?" I give my back to the group and make my way to the bar. The vodka is hitting me like a freight train, so my footing is off. I get up to the bar, practically falling into it. I stick my hand up to get the bartender's attention and look around. It's difficult to see too far, but I notice some dude sitting two seats down, and he looks to be alone. I hop over until I'm seated next to him.

"Why, hello there, handsome, you alone?" Fuck, that was horrible.

The guy looks me up and down, then tends back to his full drink. "I am. What's it to you?"

Oh, I'm about to let him know. "Well, you see. I was looking for someone to take back up to my room. You wanna go back to my room and fuck like rabbits?" I know this is bad. This is not me. But I need this to end.

Shock widens his eyes at my bold offer. I may also look a wee bit surprised at how blatantly I offered him sex, but there's a lot of booze flowing through my veins and right now, I'm letting them do all the driving.

"You serious?"

"As a heart attack. My room. Now."

He debates it for another ten seconds before he slaps a twenty-dollar bill on the bar and stands. I grab for his hand, mainly for support, and tug him toward the exit. I don't bother looking back. I pull my victim out of the bar and escort him toward the elevator. It's a good thing he seems to know the way to the elevators, because seeing is not my best attribute at the moment. As I drag the man along, my mind goes back to the bar and how that stupid chick was practically sitting on his lap. He allowed her to get so close. Her small little body probably would fit perfectly in his lap. And that damn photo. Looking as if he was at ease. Enjoying himself.

My anger flares up like a raging fire. I want to turn around and go back into that bar and rip that stupid girl away from him. Then I want to stab Chase's eyes out for being him. "I fucking hate him," I spit out, forgetting my surroundings.

"What's that, sweetheart?"

I look at the blurry man beside me. I also see a bathroom door. "Oh, fuck it." I pull him to the side and drag him into the women's bathroom. Fuck waiting to get back to my room. The faster I get this over with, the faster I'll rid Chase Green from my system and feel some relief.

I get us into the bathroom stall, and he wastes no time going at it. His hands are up my waist, his sloppy tongue all over my neck, my face, my chin. I allow him free rein because I don't care at this point. I'm way over caring. I reach down, fumbling with his belt buckle, when the stall door goes crashing open. The dude jumps, ready to yell at who's interrupting us, when a fist meets his face. Everything happens so quickly. My poor victim is dragged off me and two more closed fists go flying. It's just when I'm about to start yelling, I'm thrown over Chase's shoulder and being carried out of the bathroom.

"Who do you think you are? Put me down!" I scream over his shoulder. I yell and fight him the whole way through the lobby, in the elevator and to my room. He doesn't even ask where that is. It seems he already knows.

"Put me down!" I smack him in the back, feeling dizzy

from my entire body of blood flowing to my head. He adjusts me just enough to grab for my room key that's jammed in my bra and unlocks my door. Storming inside, I go to yell some more, but before I have a chance I'm catapulted off Chase's shoulder and onto my bed.

"Are you crazy? You could have seriously hurt that guy!"

"Good. He's lucky to even be breathing right now."

How *dare* he? "That was not your business to get involved in!" I snap, trying to sit up.

His eyes go wild with fury, a side very rare for Chase. He comes at me, his dominating frame hovering above me. "It was *completely* my business. What the fuck were you thinking? Going to let that asshole touch you? Fuck you in that goddamn bathroom?"

I squint at the harshness in his tone. I would have let him do anything to get the image of Chase Green out of my mind and system. Anything to make the pain go away. "Oh, and what about bimbo Barbie? She seemed to be well on her way to having her botoxed lips around your junk. God! Newsflash, Chase, I'm not yours anymore."

"You will *always* be mine!" he booms.

His chest is heaving, his hands clenched into white fists. I want to tell him he's wrong. I'm nothing to him anymore. I'm broken and angry. I bring myself up onto my knees, gathering what wits I have left, and I lift my hand and crush my open palm against his face. The gasp that leaves my lips, startled at my own action, echoes throughout the room along with the sound of my open palm meeting his cheek. Chase's eyes widen with shock. I fight not to turn away at the reddened mark of my slap, but my lower lip begins to quiver, and the tears threaten to spill.

"Get out."

"No. I'm not leaving. I won't let you push me away again."

Push *him* away? I'm not the one who put us here. I climb off the bed. I almost fall over, but Chase is there to steady me. "Don't touch me." I slap at his hands, fighting off his warm touch. "I want you out of my room." I put some distance between us, leaning my back against the wall for support.

"Katie—"

"No! Don't you get it? I hate you. I hate you for what you did to me," I cry out. "I hate that you made me fall in love with you. For making me feel like I had a chance at happiness. You fucking broke me. And I hate you for that," I choke out my last words when he reaches out, grabbing my face, and crushes his lips to mine. I bring my hands immediately up his chest, fighting him off me. He doesn't allow it. His lips become harder against mine, parting my lips. I continue to fight him as he steals this moment.

"You don't hate me," he whispers, releasing my lips and pressing his forehead to mine. He doesn't care that my hands are in a death grip on his shirt, or that I've begun to soak both our faces with my tears. The back of his hand brushes away the wetness as he threads his fingers into my hair. "I love you, Katie."

Four words that feel like a double-edged sword digging into my heart. "No." I shake my head, needing those jaded words to not make their way into my heart. "I can't do this with you anymore." I'm no longer able to keep my emotions at bay. I push him off me, and this time he allows it. "Stop using those words to change things. You think I believe them when you spit them out? Everything you've done, you don't love me—"

"Don't." He stops me. "Don't doubt the one thing I've never been more sure of. How do I show you? Prove to you?"

"You can't. Not anymore—"

He's on me again, his lips back covering mine. "I can." He's kissing me hard. My hands are fighting against him, working up his chest until the need to have him breaks. My fingers work themselves into his hair, gripping so tight, a groan filters through his lips as he parts mine, taking his tongue inside my mouth. He presses his body hard into mine, pushing my back firmly against the wall. I feel how hard he is everywhere, and I snap. I'm kissing him back just as rough, fighting back with each violent stroke of our tongues.

His hands become just as ruthless as he tugs my dress up my thighs, grinding himself into me. The sensation it creates causes my fingers to curl. I moan, lifting my legs. Chase is right there grabbing my thighs, wrapping my legs around his waist.

"You're so damn perfect." His lips rip away from mine, taking his mouth to my neck, roughly kissing down my skin, using a hand to squeeze my breast.

I don't allow his words to sink in. I don't want to think about what's happening. Right now, I just want to feel. I drop my head against the wall, giving him free rein of my body. My skin buzzes at the feel of him touching me. On me. My hands begin to shake. I need him so bad, it's scaring me. *Just feel, Katie.* I drop a hand and fumble with his zipper. His hand is back working my dress up my thighs, pushing it past my hips. My thong is gone just as I get his zipper down. He helps me push his jeans down and then he's pushing inside of me.

I would say it was the moan heard around the world. Hot, loud. Emotional. Physical. A feeling like I just came home.

He pulls out and slams back into me pushing my back up the wall, setting off another round of sounds filtering through our lips. Again and again, until he knows he has my attention. He brings his lips back to mine, taking my mouth hard against his. His silent message telling me, showing me, this is what love feels like. Raw, vulnerable. He's baring himself in this kiss. In the way he owns my body.

"I know you feel it," he breathes, bringing me to the brink, my body in desperate need to release all the pent-up anger, sadness, need for him. I don't answer him. I fight to admit that I do feel it. In every bone in my body. It's my heart that's beating so hard in confusion. What will happen once we come down and there are no more silent words between us. I feel the tear fall from my eyelids as my orgasm comes crashing down over my body. I squeeze tightly around Chase, just as he grabs me, pressing me firmly against him. We climax together, the sounds of both our hearts, bodies, physical and emotional strain releasing.

It is only the inevitable that once we come down, reality sinks in. *Oh my God, what did we just do?* I begin shaking my head. The tears instant. I shouldn't have allowed this to happen. My mind is muddled, confused, and unsure on what to do next.

"Don't pull away from me. I can feel you wanting to."

I want to do more than pull away. I want to run so fast away if it meant not having to face what happens next. I listen. Or I tell him to leave. Two options. I open myself up to more pain at whatever he has to say, or I choose to hurt by taking him out of the equation altogether.

"This was a mistake." I wiggle out of his grip, so he has no other option but to put me down. He pulls out, leaving me feeling emptier than before. "Get out. I need you to just get out." I fight for air, knowing I'm about to lose it once again.

"No. Katie, I'm not leaving this time. I'm not allowing you to push me away anymore." He tries to console me, but my hands go up, thrusting into his chest and pushing him away from me. "Katie—"

"GET OUT."

Chase steps back, thrusting his hands through his hair. He's breathing heavily, just as I am. "No. I'm not giving up on us. I know I fucked up and, dammit, I hate myself for lying to you, but I had my reasons."

"Get out."

"No! I'm not leaving. I lied. I kept things from you. And now I need you to hear me out."

"Stop. I don't want to hear—"

"She was blackmailing me."

I stop fighting him.

"She knew things about me and was using them to keep me from breaking ties."

I look at him in disbelief. "You expect me just to believe that? Some generic excuse and I'll fall for it?"

"I expect you to believe it, because it's the truth."

I must look like such a fool to him. Everyone has dirt on people, but if he thinks… "Do you honestly take me for that big of a fool? You think just 'cause I let you fuck me I'll believe you? Newsflash—"

"I WAS IN REHAB."

His words shock me silent.

He scrubs his palms down his face and continues. "Last year I spent three months in rehab. A few months before that, six months."

That was not what I expected from Chase. "What are you talking about? Why?"

"Because I had a drinking problem. And it got really bad. I let the fame of the sport get to me. I drank to celebrate, I drank to destress, I drank just to drink. Before I knew it, there wasn't a reason, time, or place I wasn't drinking." He turns away from me, so he no longer has to face me when he talks. "I was with Rebecca during this time. She was my main cause of it. I'm not blaming her, but she wasn't helping me. She was pushing me to do the events, the parties. She was just as big of a drinker as I'd become. During one of my many occurrences where I blacked out I did something I shouldn't have. I was being scouted for the NHL and I accepted a gift, which is a big no-no. Rebecca and her father made it go away. That's when I put myself in rehab the first time." He turns back to me. "When I got out I saw a lot of things clearer. Rebecca, for one, was no good for me. Being sober allowed me to see how badly she was using me. My career benefited hers big-time. If I made it big, it was because of her. When I came home the first time, trying to break things off, she fought me on it. Convinced me to stay. She also got me to start drinking, causing me to lose my senses again."

I can see the guilt pouring from his words. There's no hiding the shame in his eyes.

"The second time I entered rehab was because I almost killed another person while driving. I was spiraling worse than before. I felt myself losing control of my life, my career. When I got home the second time, I told myself I was done. I had it out with Rebecca. I told her we were through. I wanted nothing to do with her deceptions nor her father's claws that he had so deep in my hockey career.

"She had no intentions of letting me go. She threatened to go to the media with my addiction. Tell the NHL how I'd accepted a scouting gift, which would have killed any chance of playing for the NHL." He comes close enough that I can see his hands trembling. "Rebecca never signed on to the author event. I came home and saw the paperwork. She wanted to control me and everything I did. But when I came home, I told her we were through and I left. I filled out the form myself and sent it to Kristen. It was the perfect opportunity to leave and give Rebecca the chance to move her stuff out."

"But she didn't leave."

"No." He drops his head, his hands pushing through his hair.

"Why didn't you just tell me this? Why the lies, Chase?"

He lifts his hands to touch me, then thinks twice of it and drops them. "Because who wants to meet someone and have to admit they were an alcoholic? Battling to keep my dream of playing hockey in the NHL because I fucked up."

I try and rack my brain over the past few months and it's true, I never saw Chase drink. All the times that I did, he never indulged. Oh my God, all the times I drank in front of him. All the times I blacked out. "Chase, why…"

"My addiction is my problem, not yours. I needed to prove to myself I was fighting it. If I couldn't handle being around booze and not drink, then I wasn't where I needed to be. But you… You made it bearable."

"By being a drunk in return?" God, the guilt that I'm drunk right now makes me feel like shit.

This time he does follow through, lifting his hands and cupping my face. "I kept it from you because I didn't want you to judge me. I lied to you about Rebecca because I didn't want her anywhere near the perfect thing I was building with you. She may not have accepted that we were done, but I was. She didn't own me anymore. You did."

"Chase..."

"I lied because I was ashamed. You saw this perfect guy, but in reality, I was nowhere near that."

Everything he's telling me becomes too much. The truth is not what I was expecting.

"Stop, please don't. No more crying."

I didn't even realize I'd begun to cry. Chase pulls me away, lifting me into his arms and walking us over to the bed. He lays me down, placing himself next to me. Our eyes meet once again and there's a similar look in both. Pain. Sadness. Regret.

"I don't want to be the reason you cry. Ever." He lifts his hand to wipe the fallen tear off my cheek. His eyes are pleading.

I take in a deep breath, trying to rein in my emotions.

Can everything he just confessed allow me to get past the hurt and distrust he's already imbedded in me? I stare into his shining green eyes. Ones I've gotten lost in so many times before. Seen a future in. That forever love I never thought existed.

"I'm scared," I admit. I'm scared of being naive. Allowing my heart, who wants to mend so badly, to just blanket the damage. I shake my head, the tears starting all over. I'm so damn scared. It's not until my sobs soften and my breathing levels out that the stress of the day, the alcohol, and Chase Green's confession catch up to me and I fall asleep in his arms.

chapter
TWENTY-SIX

Three months later

First loves are always messy. Remembering that boy in high school that you swore you were going to marry and live happily ever after with. And just like a rug being swept out from under your feet, you find yourself dying of heartache because he broke up with you. You know, that first true love you planned every single detail of your wedding day and the seven kids you already named? But then one day, he breaks up with you over text because college is coming up and long distance isn't in his plan. You cry and cry, asking how he could have done this to you. How you two were so madly in love. And he just... he just doesn't feel the same way anymore. You wonder how that's possible. How love is something that just turned off for him while you find yourself drowning in a sea of heartbreak and desolation. And from this moment on you swear never to love again. It hurts too much.

I woke up that morning before the sun peaked through the shades, and when Chase got up and used the bathroom, I left. I took the coward way out and chose not to see us through. I didn't even give him the chance to say goodbye. After everything he confessed, I still ran away from facing the truth, more heartache, love, and possibly my only happily ever after.

My simple world was collapsing around me ever since Chase Green fell into my life. I was struggling to recognize the person I was becoming. My once stiff backbone on love had weakened. I'd become soft. And weaknesses caused consequences. Life wasn't so simple anymore. It wasn't so easy allowing life to roll off my shoulders with no care.

I couldn't see past what was already done. Maybe I just didn't want to. I was being selfish. So, I made a decision for both of us that morning when I walked out. The last time I would have contact with him.

I came home and broke. If I didn't think I was broken before, this time I was shattered. My world had literally crumbled around me. I knew in time I would regrow the walls I allowed Chase to break down. I also knew I needed to put them up even stronger than before. But I had to leave. If it wasn't that morning, it would have been one day. This way I called the shots. He thought he loved me, but he was wrong. I chose to walk before he realized the mistake he made and crushed me all over again.

One day he would realize.

And I wouldn't be anyone's mistake. I wanted to be their forever. And I'm not sure that was ever in the cards. I know it wouldn't have been with Chase. So, I made the choice for both of us.

Little did I know, walking away that day wasn't even the hardest part. It's the memories, the struggle, the pain I feel day and night at my decision. How many times I broke down and almost called him, begging him to forgive me. To take me back if he'd have me. Confess what my heart should have long ago, that it was beating just for him. And without him, I was struggling to breathe.

It took the masochistic side of me, which will never fully allow myself to be happy, to convince myself this is how it had to be. And so, I suffered through the sobs. The guilt. The regret. And the pain. I told myself it would lessen. I would move on. And each day it did. I stopped getting sick from crying so hard. I stopped searching for signs that would lead me back to him. I stopped watching those sports channels hoping to get a glimpse.

I disconnected my phone on the third day I got home. Chase didn't give up on us like I did. He fought. My phone never stopped ringing. The messages, the voicemails. They continued for days until I called and cancelled my service. Worried he would show up at my apartment, I camped out at Randy's for almost a month. I couldn't avoid work, but with the effort he was making to talk to me, it was inevitable he would sooner or later show up at the bar. I just prayed I wouldn't be there.

It was five weeks after my devastating decision when he walked into Anchor.

I'm filling up a round of drafts, my mind in a fog. I beg for the night to end, because it's so tiring pretending that I'm this person I'm not. Happy. I'm not happy. God, I can't even remember the last time that word meant something to me.

The entrance to the bar opens, the wind bringing in a cold chill. I welcome it as it makes me feel somewhat alive, knowing I can still feel something. I don't pay attention otherwise and continue filling the glasses. It's when I feel Randy's hand on me that I snap out of my daze.

"Unless this is what you've been waiting for, I suggest you go hide in the office."

Confused, I read the look in her eyes and turn to the door. A part of me doesn't need to see him to know it's him. He's always had that pull over me. I watch Chase brush off the cold from his jacket as he looks around at his environment. The bar is wild as always. A live band playing in the back while patrons overconsume.

My heart stops at the sight of him as his vision looks around getting closer to making contact with mine. It's mere seconds. Three, two, and I'm gone. I don't wait for him to see me. I can't. The time that's passed does nothing for my healing process. My heart beats so fast I fear the result if I don't give it what it wants. I stand in the doorway of the back office as I watch him scan the bar. He notices Randy and then Dex. He stops as his eyes land at the far end of the bar. Disappointment shines in his vision when he doesn't find what he's looking for.

Go to him, Katie. Stop this nonsense.

My heart pushes me to go to him. But my feet won't move. They know better. They know that life isn't about allowing my silly heart to run the show.

I watch him make his way to the bar and flag down Randy. I fight to read what he's saying. It's when Randy makes the mistake of glancing toward the office that I know. He's asking if I'm here. I back myself farther into the corner so he can't see me. I know Randy will tell him I'm not here. She knows if I want to be noticed I would be.

"Listen, I just want to talk to her, please. I'm not here to start trouble."

"That's great, babe, but she's not here."

I watch him look back toward where Randy accidentally glanced.

"And for some reason I feel like you're lying to me. Please." Chase won't take his eyes from the corner. I swear he cannot see me, but then again. That pull between us. He knows.

"Well, I don't know what to tell ya, but she isn't here."

"Katie, please!" he yells above the crowd.

"Yeah, buddy. No need to do that. I can tell her you stopped by." Randy tries to block him from staring at the back door. She attempts to stand in his line of vision, but he sidesteps her.

He raises his voice. "Tell her that I love her."

I swipe at the tear falling down my face as I watch Randy's mouth open slightly. "Yeah... um—"

Chase cuts her off. "I know she's here. I can't leave without seeing her. Talk to her. Katie! Please. Let me just hear your voice."

Randy gasps at his statement as I choke on a sudden sob.

"Chase, I would love to help you out, but if she wanted to see—"

"You heard her. She ain't here." Dex comes out of nowhere, looking like the predator he is. He stands next to Randy, overpowering her and blocking any view of the back.

Chase puts his hands up. "Listen, man, I'm not here to cause trouble. I just want to talk to my girl."

"Oh, shit," Randy cusses under her breath.

Dex clenches his jaw, pressing his closed fists onto the bar.

The condition Dex saw me in when I came into work tonight causes him to want to murder someone. Mainly Chase. I fought it off claiming it was the flu, possibly Cryptococcal meningitis, but he knows better. He uses social media about as much as I do, but he does listen to chatter. And the bar is full of it. It's been impossible to deny every single rumor, story, speculation about why I dropped out of the signing, again.

"First off, pretty boy, she ain't your girl. She wouldn't be dumb enough to fall for your type."

Little does Dex know.

Chase's defenses go up immediately, taking a challenging step closer to the bar. "Oh, yeah? 'Cause you're her type? I'm pretty sure she deserves more than just being sex to someone."

Oh fuck. Why did I ever mention Dex to him? *I can't see Dex's expression with his back to me, but the way Randy stiffens tells me it's scary. My heart takes another hit, knowing that's gonna hurt Dex. Not that it wasn't true, but, well, we all know, truth hurts sometimes.*

"Listen, I'm not here for you. Just let me talk to her."

"Not a fucking chance. Fuck outta my bar."

I'm silently begging Chase to just leave. I've seen the damage Dex can do when he's worked up.

"I'm not leaving until I speak to her. Katie!" *He starts moving down the bar.*

I panic, afraid he'll see me, and cower farther into the corner. Once again Dex blocks him.

"I ain't askin' again."

"Then do your worst. I'm not leaving. Katie!" *He darts to the end of the bar just as I throw myself behind the door to the office.* "Katie, please. I love you, please talk to me. Please don't do this."

There's so much anguish in his voice. I can see his reflection and he looks just as bad as he sounds. His hair is a mess. His face has a layer of scruff to it. He's not his normal put together self.

"Katie, I know I hurt you. I know I lied, but I never lied about how much I love you. How much you've changed my life. I want you to know I get it. The whole love broken thing. For so long, I thought I knew what love was. The fulfillment of just having someone sleeping in your bed and the meaningless chatter. But I get it now. It's all bullshit. Because love is something you feel so deep it's not about those superficial things. It's about how my heart swells when I think about you. How my chest hurts whenever I can't be near you. Listen to the sounds you make when you sleep. When I can't be the reason why love isn't broken for you anymore.

"And to know I broke what I was helping mend. I'm a fucking mess. I hate myself. And I just wanna fix it." *He stops to inhale much needed air. He throws his hands into his unruly hair and continues.* "I need you to know I get it. I get why Abby needed to prove why it wasn't about the outside bullshit that makes love work. I lied. Abby's number one rule on why love is broken. I wanted to prove to you I'd never hurt you. And I did just that.

"I deserve all the anger, all the hate you have for me. And I'll gladly accept it. If it just meant I'd get to see you. Hear your voice. Be near you. Please. I'll take anything."

His last words break the final string that was holding me together. I shut the door to the office and ball my eyes out. The loudness of the music and bar chatter doesn't lessen the sounds of Chase yelling my name and commotion as Dex throws Chase out of his bar.

I never asked if he hurt him. I didn't want to know. I think everyone was hurting in their own way after that night. Dex wouldn't even look at me after. And I couldn't blame him. I should have never shared our personal relationship with Chase. I could tell he was hurt. I lessened what we had by Chase's comment. And not that he wasn't telling the truth, but we had more than just the bedroom. It wasn't the emotional kind like I shared with Chase. It wasn't filled with words and late-night talks, meaning, and long-term commitment. But it was unique. In its own way there was a sort of love there. Just not the kind we both needed or deserved.

I didn't know how to fix it, so I didn't. I ran away from it once again. I left that night, leaving a note on Dex's desk, quitting. I wasn't the fun, easygoing bartender anymore everyone loved to spill their beans to while drinking booze. I was angry and doubtful of everything and everyone. I wasn't easy to be around, and it affected work. My friendships. Well, the three I had.

Randy did her best to stay happy for both of us, but that gets tiring after a while. She got tired of it and ended up giving me the 'shape up or ship out' speech, and as the quitter I've become, I shipped out.

I don't know why I couldn't just bring myself to forgive Chase that night. He had a reason, and after listening, I understood why he did it. But that stubborn side of me told me to walk away. In the end, it wouldn't change things. I thought that by hearing him out, I would feel some sort of closure. Giving myself the ability to walk away easier. But that door was open wider than it was before. And let me tell you, it's so fucking cold out, I fear my heart freezing to death.

Chase left that night, and I haven't heard from him since. He may have tried to reach me, but I wouldn't know. I came home that night and packed my things. Stuff that meant something to me, which wasn't much, and I grabbed Gerdie, a rental car, and left. Where I was going I had no idea. I drove for almost two days until I made it to the end of the earth. Well, it felt that way, when I landed in a small town in Blue River, Oregon. There was nothing but forest, mountains, and time. It was exactly what I was looking for. I rented a cabin in the woods and it became my solace for the next two months. I can't really say what I did the whole time. A lot of soul-searching, I guess.

I spent most of my days sitting outside on the wraparound porch thinking about my life. Where would I be if my parents were still alive? Would I have graduated college? Been in some fancy job, free of all my bad choice tattoos and possibly married with a family? Would I be happy?

I wonder how my life would have turned out if that drunk driver didn't take it upon themselves to get on the road that night and ruin so many lives. I became angry with my parents for leaving me. Taking away the life I could have had. I cried because I wished they were here to be angry with. What I wouldn't do to be able to hug my mom just one more time. Listen to her sing while cooking dinner. Hear the laughter of my father when he finished telling a horrible joke. Acceptance is a hard feeling to conquer. Accepting that this is now your life. Accepting that they were never coming back. And the biggest, accepting that life isn't fair. Because it rarely ever is.

The one thing I did do surprisingly is sit down and write. I wrote a story about a girl who thought real love wasn't out there. She fought, bashed, and rallied against it. She wanted people to stop searching for the fake version and allow the real true love that was out there in. Because when you aren't so busy fighting against it, it tends to be something really great.

This story was about a girl who learned a valuable lesson. She learned love *was* out there. That it was messy, and it hurt. It was fulfilling but also very much scary. But if she just took a chance at it, it could be something that created this forever world of hope. That happily ever after.

In this story, the girl finds just that. But she's scared. She spent her entire life running away from love. Or at least what she knew of it. She didn't want to be hurt the way so many people were. She wanted to be guarded and safe. Until one day her life changed. She met a boy. He was kind and funny. He was gentle with her when he needed to be and rough when she wanted him that way. He made her laugh and cry. Smile more than she ever knew possible. But most importantly he made her love.

And she loved deep. It was so deep it scared her. So much that when things got tough for them she ran. She didn't want to be fooled by a love that would hurt her. She knew her heart couldn't handle it. So, she ran away from the boy who made her feel whole. Only to make herself feel even more empty.

In due time, the pain lessened. But not enough to live. To truly live. She knew people sometimes only get one chance at love. Sometimes people go through their entire lives never being able to experience the feeling of loving someone so deeply. Being loved that way in return. And she knew. That maybe she needed to face her fears. She needed to open herself up and let the unknown in. Because that unknown could just possibly be her own happily ever after.

So, she did.

She did what she was secretly scared to death to do and face the boy who once upon a time loved her. But the fearful question was if he still did.

Does time heal a broken heart? Does it change what the heart truly desires? She had those thoughts suffocating her as she made her way back to that boy for answers.

Because she was ready to face her fears. She was ready to finally open herself up. She just hoped it wasn't too late.

chapter TWENTY-SEVEN

When I finally returned home, there was a gigantic pit in my stomach on what I was returning home to. I clearly didn't have a job, and I'm sure my landlord had bolted up my door, demanding past rent. I wish I could admit I made some mistakes by taking off the way I did, but I can't. It's what needed to happen. I was spiraling. And fast. I couldn't continue to live the same life I did before Chase Green. Before the book. Before the unwanted fame that followed. Because that was no longer me. I needed a time-out. A *life* time-out. And it took me leaving to finally understand that. The time I spent at the cabin may have saved my life. Definitely my sanity. I spent it thinking about how I needed to make things right. With Dex and Randy, with Kristen, and the unbeknown anger I had toward my parents. With Chase. But I needed to clear my head before I did that.

I wrote two letters while I was hidden deep in the mountains and mailed them from the local post office in town. First one was to Dex. I started off by letting him know I was alive. Then I told him how sorry I was for up and quitting. He had been nothing but there for me since the day I stumbled into his bar, and I repaid him by leaving him high and dry. But I had to. I needed to figure out what was so wrong that I felt so cheated. I needed to fix what was so broken inside myself. And I couldn't do that staying at the bar. I loved that place. It was my second home. But as of late it wasn't that place to me anymore. But I could only blame myself for that. I tarnished that place the day I decided to publish a book.

I wrote to him how I never meant to hurt him. I know I did with Chase's comment. I couldn't go back and take those words back. But I could explain. I told him that our relationship was more than just sex to me. It was a friendship. It was something I never had. We may not have had that love we tried to work at, but we had a different kind of love. A love that bonds us closer as friends than as lovers. I did love Dex. But not like I loved Chase. I needed him to know how much he meant to me. I just hoped he did enough to forgive me.

I ended it with telling him I would be back someday and maybe we could share a drink together. I wasn't going to ask for my job back. I didn't even know if I wanted it back. But I wanted him back in my life. If he would take me. In my PS, I asked that he hug and kiss Randy for me, and tell her I missed her. And I hoped she understood why I ditched her having to deal with Ralph and his beer foamed mustache all by herself.

My next letter was to Kristen. I know I owed her a huge explanation. She did nothing but try and make me shine. She wanted nothing more than to bring me out into the world and show everyone how amazing she thought I was. Talented, smart, beautiful. All, of course, her thoughts. But all I did was piss on her efforts. I apologized for leaving. I know after the last one, there will be some legal issues. I'm sure she did her best to fight for me, but in the end, I did sign a contract, and I failed to complete the entire event. When I get home, that would be one of the first things I had to fix. Most likely just offer some jail time since the fines may be more than I'm worth.

I did my best to explain myself and hoped she got it. I spilled the beans and told her everything. All the thoughts and feelings I'd been festering for so many years. The sadness and anger about my parents. The heartache and struggle with Chase. The fight to try and find a better view on life. I apologized for my actions the last night at the bar. I know she'll forgive me. She always does, but it won't ever lessen the shame of that night. I finished with thanking her for being someone who never gave up on me. Especially when I gave up on myself.

I finally pull into the parking lot of my building. The sun has gone down and it's quiet, vacant of sounds from city life and traffic. I snatch up Gerdie and make my way inside. I'm shocked when I don't see an orange eviction notice on my door. Unlocking my door and placing the cage on the counter, I set the pile of mail that was overflowing in my mailbox on my small kitchen table.

Being back home feels strange, but good. I missed my shoebox of an apartment, the taste of real coffee and cable. You don't get to watch much TV in the boonies. Being home also reminds me of why I chose to come back. The anxiety of what I'm going to do never lessens. I've gone through every scenario over and over on what I'm going to say once I call him. What he may say in return, but it never gets easier.

I'm going to call him. I'm ready to open up. Give us a real shot. But I have to be prepared that he's moved on. He may resent me in all this, and my time may have passed. And I have to be prepared. He may not want to talk to me. It will bring up the past and the lying and it will hurt all over again, stirring up the exact reason why I spiraled out of control to begin with. But I need to try. To know if we still have a fighting chance. He will take me back or he won't. I'm just praying it's not the second option.

I picked up a pay as you go phone on my way back into town since I cancelled mine, along with bashed it to pieces. I plug it in to charge while I settle in, making Gerdie at home and getting him fed. I pass by the phone a few times while I unpack, the anxiety about what I'm about to do growing.

"Maybe I should have a drink," I suggest to myself to cool my nerves. I take a glance at the top of my fridge at my collection of hard liquor. I haven't had a drink since I left. I realized that the heavy drinking I was doing to help mask the pain was a huge part of my problem. Deciding no against drinking, I go and take a shower.

Two hours go by and I've done everything from paint my nails to clean out the fridge. I know I'm stalling. "Oh, just do it, you pussy," I talk shit to myself. I grab the small piece of paper off my dresser, snatch the phone, and plop myself down on the couch.

"Breathe, Katie."

I notice my hand is shaking when I lift the piece of paper to dial the numbers. My heart is racing, and I feel on the verge of having a heart attack. Four numbers punched in, six numbers. Come on. So close. On the seventh number, I hold my breath and squeeze my eyes shut. The call connects, followed by a beeping noise. *"The number you have reached is not in service. Please check the number and dial again..."* Again with the beeping with the repeated number. I hang up.

I double-check to make sure I dialed the right number. I did. My nerves shift to disappointment. I *definitely* didn't factor in this road block. I move down the list to what's written as house phone. With another long intake of breath, I dial.

"The number you have reached is not in service. Please check the number and dial again..."

Dammit!

My mood plummets when I make it to the last number, which is working, but ends up being a local taco joint that, from what I learn, is Chase's favorite spot for tacos. Per Jose, the owner, Chase spent a lot of time there when he wasn't traveling since he wasn't much of a cook. Unfortunately, he hadn't seen or heard from him in over a month.

I thank the nice man for the information, along with the discount if I ever come and visit and disconnect. "It's too late," I whisper as I stare at the piece of paper that holds every single number to reach Chase, which are all disconnected.

"Fuck. It's too late," I repeat almost in shock. I didn't expect this when plotting out all scenarios. All led to us at least talking. I didn't think... think... "Fuck!" I cry, ripping up the list and throwing it.

I get up, kicking my coffee table, fighting back the tears. "He just changes all his numbers?" I mean, what the hell? I swipe away at the wetness that's escaped the barriers of my lids. This, he's... I'm utterly confused. He wouldn't have changed all his numbers because of me. Would he? Did I mess up that bad? I begin to cry. I can't stop it. I finally saw clarity and know what I want, and now it's too late. He's given up. I fall onto my bed and cry. For being so stubborn. For being too afraid to follow my heart. For mostly not letting Chase in.

I cry until I've worn myself thin and expel all energy left in me. When I hear Gerdie chirping, knowing it's snack time, I pull myself up and out of bed, knowing I need to man up. Move on and accept what is. I can only blame myself for the outcome. But blaming myself doesn't solve the pain that resides where forgiveness and new comings were to be filled.

I find myself in my kitchen making a packet of hot chocolate. It's that or the tequila, and I want to wallow in my self-pity without getting loaded and vandalizing my neighborhood. I can only assume that's where it would lead to at this stage. I grab my mail and hot mug and snuggle into my couch.

Flipping through my mail, I go to my DVR and press recorded shows. If I can't indulge on my first guilty pleasure, which is vodka, it's going to be *Catfish* on MTV. *Junk, junk, junk...* God the amount of paper wasted on people trying to sell me mortgages or loans. Hello, I'm poor and I rent. "Environmental killers," I mumble and toss the mail to the ground. Flipping through more, I see the late notice from my landlord, along with bills and more bills. "God, even my mail is depressing." I take the rest of the pile and toss it on the coffee table. As they scatter across the wooden surface an envelope stands out.

Leaning forward, I push everything aside and grab for it. As I flip it over, I notice it has my name on it. The return address is labeled the NHL Corporate Center. "What the..." Setting down my mug, I slide my finger through the tiny open slot and tear the envelope open. Inside is an event ticket, nothing more. Further investigating, I realize it's to a hockey game. My eyes lock on the details, the Cleveland Barons against Chicago Blackhawks. *Who sent this?* I turn the envelope over again, but there's no further information. My address is even typed, taking away the detective work of whose handwriting it could be. Not that I know anyone's handwriting. I read the ticket again, the date of the game being... *"Today?"* I look at the small clock hanging above my television then back at the ticket. "Shit." The game started two hours ago. "Shit!"

Shit, shit, shit... What do I do? My heart is starting to pound. The ticket is shaking in my hand. I'm not sure what the ticket means. Did Chase send it? *Who else would, dummy?* "I don't know!" I start arguing with myself. I'm up and pacing my small apartment. I glance at the clock every two seconds, wondering what to do. The game is almost over. If he sent it, he probably already thinks I'm not coming. *What if he sent it so you can come and see him and his new girlfriend because he hates you now?* Oh God. That's probably true. I look back at the time with every second I use to think, tormenting me.

"If I left, I could still make the last quarter." I calculate how much time it would take me to get down to the Sports Center where the game is being held, minus downtown traffic and time to fix myself, because I look absolutely horrible, which is, "Not a lot. Oh, God!" I run to my room and practically dive into my closet.

chapter
TWENTY-EIGHT

I hate Cleveland traffic. I hope it all dies a horrible death of its own traffic hell. I curse this in my head while I run into the Center, after having to park so far away, I could have just parked at home. Traffic was horrendous and parking even worse. By the time I get into the Sports Center, the game is letting out.

"No…" I whine, fighting through the crowd. I'm like a fish trying to swim against the current, pushing through people to make it inside the arena part to the section stated on my ticket. Running up the stairs to the first level terrace, I overlook the rows and rows of empty seating below. Even the rink is absent of players.

"I'm too late," I whisper at the bare ice rink. I bring my eyes to the empty seat reserved for me. It sits below, just in front of the glass. He would have known if I showed or didn't. He'll think I didn't care. All this time and he still tried.

"Looking for someone?"

I turn, bumping into a young woman, about the same age as myself, standing behind me. "Oh, no. Well, I was. But I'm too late." Wiping a tear from my cheek, I offer her a sad smile, but fall short at hiding my emotions as another tear falls.

"Sorry to hear that." She digs in her purse, handing me a Kleenex. I silently thank her as I dry my cheeks. "Not to pry, but why do you think it's too late?" she asks, her smile so inviting. Familiar almost.

I shrug, trying to keep it together. "Because I took too long to decide. Fought too long with myself before realizing something I should have a long time ago. And now it's too late. I'm late, and he's gone." More tears. More sucking air into my suffocating lungs. "I've missed my chance, and now I... I..." I trail off because the tears become a constant flow down my face. I must look like a fool to this stranger.

She takes a step toward me, placing her comforting hand on my shoulder. "You know, my brother's in the same predicament. Feels he was too late too. Said he lost the love of his life. Missed his chance to be happy because he was scared. Maybe you two should talk sometime. You might have a lot in common."

I open my eyes and look at her. Really look. It's why her smile felt so inviting. Because it was familiar. "Wait... Are you—"

"I see you've met my sister." I whip around to see Chase standing at the bottom of the aisle, his back leaning against the arena glass. He's freshly showered and wearing a pair of form-fitting jeans and a Cleveland Barons hoodie.

"I thought… I…" He's got my tongue. I can't finish my sentence because my throat begins to lock. My eyes take him in. His beautiful face. Those eyes I've gotten lost in so many times. His hair is longer than the last time I saw him, almost tucked behind his ears. And it looks like he decided to keep the scruff, close to a full beard. "I…"

"I'm gonna leave you two alone. Chase, I'll meet you back at the hotel. Call me if you need a dinner date."

Chase nods to his sister, as she offers me a kind wave, and she's gone.

"I didn't think you'd come."

I turn back to Chase, who hasn't moved off the glass. "I didn't technically." *Ugh.* No time for jokes. "Sorry, I can't help it. I'm super nervous." I can't stop fiddling with my hands.

He's made no move to come to me, and his normal easy-going smile is missing. A rush of anxiety hits me suddenly, fearing the worst.

Finally, Chase makes his move, pushing off the glass and walking toward me, but stops at the first step, looking up at me. "And why are you nervous?"

Ten long steps separate us. "I'm not sure. I guess, just…"

"Is it because you left the hotel that morning without a word? Without giving me at least a goodbye?" As much as I deserved that, it doesn't hurt any less hearing it. "Or all the times I tried to talk to you, fight for you and nothing."

I don't know how to respond. I know he's referring to the night at the Anchor. And he has a right to be mad.

"Or how about just knowing that you gave up on us without out a second thought while I kept fighting."

My lower lip begins to tremble, my eyes filling with more tears, and still he makes no move to come to me. Missing is the normal Chase, who would scoop me into his arms and comfort me until I felt safe. Loved. That Chase is nowhere to be found. The one I see before me looks wounded. Angry maybe. His facial expression has me worried that he may return the favor and not listen to what I have to say. Fear that this is where I make my intentions clear and he tells me it's too late.

He takes one step closer. "Well? Are you going to say anything?"

There's a static in the air, with us being so close. Nine long steps separating us. A thickness to it that makes it hard not to sense the heavy emotions we're both giving off. I inhale a deep breath for strength and begin. "I'm sorry for leaving without saying goodbye that night. It was wrong of me. I made a decision for both of us. I didn't give you a chance."

He slowly nods. "You did."

God, he isn't making this easy. "I was selfish. I did it because I was only thinking of me. I never thought of you and what you were going through."

"Katie—"

"No, please listen, before you tell me to beat it." I take a second to rein in my emotions. It's taken a lot of time to be able to come to terms with everything. With myself. With being able to let go. I just needed to realize that sometimes in life, people make bad choices, but with good intentions. We can't all live life being these flawless human beings. And I know now if that's what I expected out of people, then I would forever be alone in a world surrounded by my own flaws. "I can't excuse what you did. And I can't even say that looking at you now, I still don't feel the hurt and betrayal. Because it will always hurt. But that night. There's something I never told you. I never told you that I forgave you. But I did."

He's still not budging. I know I'm losing him. The realization is slowly sinking in, my fears becoming reality.

I start to fully cry. "I was so scared to hear what you had to say that night I think I told myself that no matter what, it wouldn't have changed things. I just didn't think it mattered anymore. There was no way we would work out, and it was best I walked away from more pain that I knew I wouldn't be able to handle."

"Katie."

Again, my name falls off his lips, causing my heart to beat uncontrollably, not knowing if I've fucked this all up. I probably look super pathetic right now, but I can't stop the words from pouring out.

"I've missed you. And I'm sorry." Having him in front of me only makes my heart ache more with the need for him. How do I express in words just how badly I've messed up? How do I use the right words so he'll know just how sorry I am for not trusting in what we had, to figure us out together? I want to pretend I'm not this person who doubts and doubts. I don't want to be, but I also can't just shut that person down I've been for so long. "I'm sorry," I repeat again, because I truly am. Sorry for the hurt and pain we both caused one another. "I'm sorry I doubted us. I doubted you."

The tears are a heavy flow down my cheeks as I reach into my purse, pulling out a large stack of papers. "I did something while I was away."

Seeing that I'm trying to offer them to him, he takes the stairs two at a time, until only four steps separate us. He reaches for the papers. "Oh, yeah? What's this?"

"It's a story."

"And what's this story about?"

He doesn't look at the pages. He doesn't take his eyes off mine. I know this is where I give it my all.

I suck in a deep breath for courage and begin. "It's about a girl who doubts so much in life, she doesn't know when it's time to trust. To forgive when forgiving is needed."

A few seconds pass before he asks, "And does this girl figure out how to trust and forgive?"

I answer his question with a nod. "She learns that love isn't always how she expected it to be. You see, she finds it where she least expected it. With a person, she least expected to give her the time of day."

Another round of tormenting seconds pass. "Was this boy able to show her just how perfect he thinks she is?"

God, does he ever. The tears are making it harder now to see. "He does, but she struggles to understand why. She doesn't understand why he wants her. Because she doesn't have anything to offer back. She's lived such a hard life that she thought she didn't know how to love back. She ends up fighting his love, because she doesn't feel she's worthy of it. Until she fights it so much she ruins any chance of ever having it." I have to stop to catch my breath. I'm struggling to speak. "She hurts so much because of her choices. And she doesn't know how to fix it. She's scared of the unknown. Of taking a chance and being right, but even more scared of not taking that chance and being wrong."

Chase takes a step closer. Three steps separating us. "It sounds like this boy really loves the girl, and she should have let him in and allowed him to love her with everything he has."

With each hiccup, I reply, "And she really wants that, but

she isn't sure if it's too late or not. She ran away from him. And she acted super childish and didn't step up when it was most important. She isn't sure if he even wants her anymore."

Another step. Two steps separating us. "So how does the story end? What does she do?"

"I'm not sure because the ending isn't written yet," I tell him.

"And why not?"

"Because I don't know how it ends yet. You see, the girl finally knew what she wanted, but she had to come back home and find this boy and ask for him to give her another chance at listening and forgiving. She wasn't sure how he would react, but she prayed he hadn't given up on her as she did on them."

My heart plummets as he takes the thick stack of pages and drops it into the seat next to him. His facial expression still blank. I silently beg to see a part of the Chase I know. The kind, understanding man I fell so in love with. Right now, I fear I'm looking at a man who's given up. He places his hands back into his pockets. I hold my breath as his mouth opens.

This is it.

"It's strange, because I feel like I've heard this story before," he starts, taking another step. One step separating us. "But you're in luck because I actually know the ending."

"You do?"

Another step closer.

"Yes, I do." He's so close I can smell the freshness of his shower. The lingering scent of his cologne. The heat of his body. "See, little does this girl know, that boy has been miserable without the girl. He hates himself for what he did to her and may never stop trying to fix what he broke. This boy, he never really knew himself what love was. He was just as naive as the rest of the world in defining it as something less than what it truly was. But one day, this girl came into his life and shaped it for him. Filled his world with light, humor, beauty. And it hit him. She was the meaning of it. She may have not understood what she was doing, but piece by piece, she was owning his heart. Until one day, she had it all." He lifts his hand to brush away a strand of hair that's sticking to my wet cheek. "She was a force of nature. Just a little thing with so much love, I'm not sure she realized how much power she had over this boy. But the boy, he himself was just as scared. But their love got messy. That's when she ran away. And she had every right to."

I feel the pull in my heart at the guilt. The regret that I didn't stay and hash it out. "I'm sorry—"

"Shh… I'm not done with my story."

I can't help but nod with a small smile on my lips.

"So, this boy searched high and low for the girl, but she was nicely hidden. He was so sad that he couldn't sleep at night, even his poor dog was sad. He thought the girl was never coming home. But he swore he would never give up. Because he loved her so fiercely he knew that one day, life would bring them back together. Because this was their fairy tale. And all fairy tales have a happy ever after."

My lungs tighten as I struggle with my words. "What are you saying, Chase?"

Chase startles me when his hands leave my face and wrap around my waist. I'm up and in his arms in a blink, and he's sitting us down on the end seat of the stadium. "That the boy got his wish. She came home to him. And he told her he loved her with everything in him. That he would have never given up fighting for her."

I can't fight the sobs from overtaking me. I rest my face on his shoulder while I allow my emotions to overpower me.

"Shhh... Why are you crying?" he asks, bringing his fingers through my hair.

"I... I... thought... you had given up on me." I sob harder, soaking his sweatshirt.

Chase's chest vibrates with a soft laugh. "And here I was thinking you'd given up on me." He wraps his arms around me, holding me tighter as we share a silent moment.

Chase gently pulls my face away from his now soaked shirt, allowing our eyes to meet. He caresses my cheek. "Katie, what do I have to do to prove to you that you and I, opposites or not, there's an unstoppable force between us? No matter how much you try and deny it, it's there. It's there constantly telling us that this, us, we're real. Everything we feel. It's real. That it's not going away." He drops his forehead to mine. "I'm sorry for what I did to us."

"So am I." I pull back so I can look straight into his eyes. "The moment you fell into my life you changed me. And I didn't want that. I didn't want change. I wanted my simple life. Simple friends, simple feelings. I was perfectly fine with the life that had been laid out for me.

Then out of nowhere you showed up." I wipe the wetness from my face. "You did something to me. I probably hated you before you even gave me a reason to. You broke through the walls I had worked so hard to build. And it caused me to do the one thing I refused to ever do. I fell in love."

Chase offers me the smile that keeps my heart beating. "What if I admitted I felt so safe with you in my arms? Content. Like I'm home? I'm home anywhere you are, Katie. I want life to be beside you. You're my fuel. You're what's going to make me run. My life *is* you. I can't fix the mess I made in the beginning. But I want my love for you to help mend what pain I've caused. I want to make it right. From now until we're old, I want us. I want to be able to kiss you good night and good morning. I want to conquer your love broken motto."

I throw myself at him, that if we weren't sitting in a seat, he would go toppling over. My arms are around his neck and my lips are pressing against his. The feeling as our lips reunite is almost unexplainable. But taking a piece of Chase's words, it's like coming home.

We kiss until air becomes an issue that forces us to break apart. I rest my head on his shoulder while we let the silence comfort us.

"I have a confession to make," Chase says, pressing his chin to the top of my head.

"Am I going to want to hear this?" I ask, worried, after everything we just shared, confessed.

"It depends. You see, when you went missing in action, I was running out of ways to track you down. You turned off your phone, abandoned your place, and quit your job. I ran out of places to search for you." He stops for a moment, my nerves turning into curiosity.

I pull away and need to see his eyes. "What is it, Green? What did you do?"

"I kinda joined your fan group."

"You what?" I gasp.

"If anyone asks, Chasity Green is your biggest fan. One girl even called me a creepy stalker."

At that I bust out laughing. "Really, Green?"

"I told you. This was the inevitable. Us, you and me… and Chasity Green."

epilogue

Love isn't defined by one specific interaction or emotion. There's no rule book on it. No to-do list to make sure you're doing it right. Don't bother trying to Google "how to make all the right moves while in love." That shit just doesn't exist. Nor do the warning signs about how scary it is. How it's messy, never to the point, and firsthand, it makes people crazy. But then again, if it doesn't, then you're probably not in love.

Let's not get me started on the types. Because there's not just one type of love. There's infinite love. Short-lived love. There's love that's so powerful, it hurts. So consuming you struggle to understand its beauty. It can be unexpected and confusing. The love you feel the moment your paths cross at a young age, or love that comes with a lot of struggle, time, and ups and downs before presenting the beauty of itself. But all types lead to a love that's beautiful, passionate, and worthwhile.

My love story didn't come all wrapped up in a neat pretty bow. It wasn't your perfect, storybook material. My love got so messy, it should have come with a cleaning kit. To say it was a bit turbulent at times was an understatement. I thought I knew so much about the four-letter word. Boy, was I wrong.

When I wrote *Love Broken*, I wrote it for the people who needed a lesson on real love. Little did I know I was one of them. Maybe those people who came through that bar knew about love, just needed to understand the importance of it. That sometimes when times get tough, don't give up on it. When you feel like you will never have a real shot at it, just remember you *are* worth the love you're looking for. Maybe… just maybe, those cheesy pickup lines are some people's way of trying and *hoping* to find it.

As they say, ignorance was bliss. And that's the name tag I wore for a while after the book. Because I wasn't any better at being able to define what it was, than anyone else was. All I knew was that everyone deserves it. That not a single person will have the same love as the other. Each definition of it will differ. Not everyone loves the same way. And that's okay.

I accepted Chase's love and vowed not to diagnose it. I would never be able to compare it to anything else. Because his love wasn't from a how-to book. It was built just for me. I didn't want to compare stories and have someone tell me "their love did the same thing." I wanted our days and nights, our talks and experiences to be ours. And with that said, I stopped analyzing love.

I threw in the towel and decided I was going to ride out

the one I had. And no, I don't mean that kind of riding-it-out. At least not in this context. Because lots of riding since that day has been had.

Chase Green made me see love for what it truly was. Flawed and beautiful. He proved to me that the oldest saying in the book may have had some truth to it. That opposites do attract. Because goddammit, us together, we were destined for an amazing life.

He also taught me the most important attribute of the four-letter word. And that was trust. He made me promise that day that no matter what bumps we hit, I would do one thing, and that was to trust in him. In us that the love we had would beat it. No matter what the obstacle. And with a shed of unstoppable tears, I promised.

It's been five years and that promise is going strong. Because so is our love. Chase Green gave me something I never thought I was destined for. A life where my heart and soul felt completely full. I won't deny that it gets overwhelming at times. Because if anything, Chase Green is a lot to handle. When you have a man who thinks his destiny is to make you feel safe and jam-packed with endearments, I won't deny that sometimes I want to jam one of his hockey pucks in his mouth. The smile I provide just thinking of the exact memory.

"Chase, seriously, stop!" I scream, trying to run around the couch to avoid his hands. "If you don't stop tickling me, I'm going to murder you!" A simple demand that if he didn't stop telling me how beautiful I was, I was going to shove his hockey puck down his throat. Last week it was up his ass. I was running out of places to threaten to shove it.

Another dodge, as he reaches over, trying to grab me. "You wouldn't. Who would rub your feet?"

"Casey. She's old enough to understand the word rub."
Chase laughs and dashes to the right, trying to catch me.

I dodge another large hand as I take a swift right and dash it down the hallway. I start to scream because I can hear his laughter and feet right behind me. I know I don't stand a chance.

I barely make it through the threshold of our bedroom, before I'm up and cradled in his arms. "Chase! Don't, please. You're gonna make me pee myself again!"

"Well, we wouldn't want that, babe, now, would we?" He kisses my forehead and places me in his lap and sits down on our gigantic king-sized bed. He brushes my hair out of my face, smiling at the scowl I'm holding. "Now, now. Why the face?"

"Because I told you to stop calling me beautiful."

"I can't do that. I think you're a sight, always."

I scowl again, wanting to cry. "I'm not. I'm ugly and huge."

Chase lifts his hand, caressing my belly. "You have never been more beautiful to me. And as much as you threaten me, I'm not staying quiet about it." Just then Chase starts yelling.

"I have the most beautiful wife! I love my beautiful, perfect, pregnant, grouchy wife!"

I use my elbow to nudge him in the ribs. It's mid fall, but due to the crazy weather, we have all our windows open. Mr. Bigsley, the neighbor, is outside picking at his garden.

"Seriously, Chase. Shut up. The windows are open!"

"Mr. Bigsley! Did you know that my wife is the most amazing person ALIVE!"

I give another elbow to his chest again, but Chase just laughs it off. Mr. Bigsley just shakes his head and goes back to tending to his garden.

"Stop. Please."

His eyes are always so tender when he looks at me. "I can't.

Because you are. And I will keep telling you until we're old and wrinkling and my tongue falls out."

I go for a third nudge, but this time he smartens up and catches my elbow. He lifts my arm and kisses the inside of my upper arm, then my forearm. One soft press to the inside of my wrist, taking my hand and placing it over his heart.

"You have it workin' extra hard today."

"And why's that?" I ask, choking on my out of whack emotions.

"Because you're in my arms."

I laugh. "Chase, I'm always in your arms. You never leave me alone."

"True, because you're addictive. But also, because you're mine and I still can't believe it."

I have to close my eyes and rein in my emotions. I've been extremely emotional lately, and I'm shocked he's willing to handle another "Katie the cuckoo" breakdown.

"Well, it's your lucky day. I'm all yours. Every single mood swing," I reply.

He takes his hand and rubs at my gigantic belly. "I hope she's just like you."

"You mean you want another Casey? So she can debate that grass should be inside?" Just the reminder of how I turned my back for a second and our four-year-old daughter dragged the bag of grass clippings inside and spread them all over our living room, smiling and telling us she "made outside."

"Well, I hope this one doesn't want to be a scientist. Having to teach this one about how the eggs in our fridge aren't actually baby chickens and watch her cry for four days was enough for me." At that we both laugh. Poor Casey and her toddler theories are going to be the end of us.

"I just want her to have your determination. Your beauty. Your fire."

Dammit, he has me on that one. My eyes begin to tear up, but of course, he's there to save the day, wiping away each tear.

"You say all this as if you know it's going to be another girl."

Chase bends down, pressing a kiss to my stomach. We both have our suspicions. I say girl and so does Chase. My delightful mood swings all align with my pregnancy with Casey.

"Well, then if it's a boy, he's going to be handsome, with his mother's eyes hopefully, and he's going to be one hell of a hockey player."

We had a boy. Benjamin was born just hours before Chase had to be on the ice, thankfully at a home game. We were all on pins and needles worried that I would have to deliver by myself. We got lucky with Casey since she was born on Chase's off season. The birth was easy. Chase cried like a baby. He also played the best game of his entire career that night.

Five years ago, I wrote a story about a girl who fought to understand love. She was so scared to let something so powerful in, knowing it had the potential to destroy her. But it was only when she almost lost it that she realized how much she truly needed it. Needed him. And it was the boy who captured her heart who saved her. Just when she thought she may have missed out on her own chance for that happily ever after, that boy showed her love doesn't just fade. Especially not for them. He showed her their love would mend the mistakes they made. Heal the hardships both have faced. It would also give her peace. And that boy was right.

Chase and I worked out our differences. We talked and talked until there were no more secrets, insecurities, and questions about us and our future. I explained my hiatus and every single doubt I had festering inside me. I learned that while I was trying to find myself, Chase was super busy. He had finally obtained a lawyer able to outsmart Rebecca and clear himself of any wrongdoings with the league. He chose to come clean and confess, risking losing any spot with the NHL. But he said it was his only way to be free and clear of her. With the help of his lawyer, he paid a hefty fine and no wrongdoings were noted with the league. It seemed after further investigation, Chase technically didn't accept anything. With his faulty memory and only the word of Rebecca once sober, they came to learn Chase didn't officially accept anything. It was Rebecca. This left him free of her and her father.

What he told me next almost threw me off his lap. He went on to explain that he had a deal in the works for months now. When that schmuck at the signing mentioned a NHL deal, he was telling the truth. Chase had officially signed on to play for the NHL. The 'throw me out of my seat' part of it? He signed with the Cleveland Barons. He told me that no matter how long it took me to come around he wanted to be close when I did. He also told me he passed on three other offers. Because hockey had become second on his list of importance, next to his number one. That one was me.

A lot has happened in the last five years. Reconciliation was just the beginning for us. Marriage. Two beautiful kids. Life was unstoppable for us. Chase's dream was in full force. He was one of the top five best players in the NHL. When he was asked what made him so good, his answer always stayed the same. Because he did what he loved. Little did they know that saying had a double meaning. And every time his interviews were live, and he looked in the camera and said he "did what he loved," I would chuckle at my man. Because in bed when it was just us, he would turn to me and tell me how much he loooved doing what he loved. If you haven't caught on, he loved doing me.

Chase Green and his wit.

Within the last five years, I became part owner of Anchor. Dex had been looking for a partner and I had nothing but love for the bar. I knew it inside and out, and it helped that I was also the best bartender. At first, I didn't go back to the bar. I needed to do something for myself first. I went back to school. Not to the whole college shebang. I took online classes and finally got my degree. I needed to do it to prove to myself that my life didn't need to end a certain way. I needed to prove to myself that even if my life didn't change that night that took my parents, I would have still landed exactly where I needed to be.

This also helped with the bar. I took over the books and business aspect. Dex loved it because it was less on his plate, and I loved it because I was actually really good at it. Not to mention, as well as the bar has been prospering the past couple of years, as of two days ago, we just signed a lease for Anchor's Two. The second bar plans to open early next year.

In case you were wondering, I didn't end up having to do any time behind bars, walking out with any jailhouse tattoos for ditching out on the signings and my contract. Kristen, bless her heart, was able to work out a deal. Bless my man's heart because he was my ticket to freedom. It seems the Director of Romance Association was a huge Charlie Bates fan. An even bigger Chase Green fan. It's amazing what a signed autograph and season tickets will get someone out of. Two weeks of Hard Knox for me, apparently. Kristen's career continued to blossom. She forgave my unstableness as I knew she would but made me promise one thing. To continue to be myself. Beautiful with a little bit of crazy.

Life couldn't have ended up any more perfect. Even though I hate that word. Because nothing in life is truly that way. Perfection will always be the downfall of everything. Every person who can't find the perfect love, the perfect job, the perfect life. Because, then you ask yourself, does perfect really exist? And if it did, would you want it?

And for the record, love is still broken. It's still flawed in so many ways, but with Chase, it will always still be beautiful. He told me once in an argument, and yes, our imperfect marriage has them, the only thing that love will never do again is destroy us. We will always forgive, and we will always understand. Because love in the end will never let us down.

I told that to my parents' grave when I visited them right before my wedding. I told them how I got it. That I didn't need to find the same love as they had. Because no love is identical. But I found something that was irreplaceable. Because there was no one like Chase Green in this world. My heart can attest to that.

I'm sure one thing you're dying to know is what came of my writing career. The last book I wrote was the start of my real life. When I truly started to live. I guess you would say the girl got the boy.

And that night, I knew there was no more denying the bond we shared. That unspoken feeling that's almost bigger than love. While I lay in Chase's arms, listening to the constant beat of his heart. I asked him about his version of the story he told me and if it had a name.

His reply?

"Yeah, it did, babe. I named it *The Story of Us.*"

the
END

acknowledgements

First, and most importantly, I'd like to thank myself. It's not easy having to drink all the wine in the world and sit in front of a computer writing your heart out, drinking your liver off and crying like a buffoon because part of the job is being one with your characters. You truly are amazing and probably the prettiest person in all the land. Keep doing what you're doing.

Thanks to my husband who supports me, but also thinks I should spend less time on the computer and more time doing my own laundry.

Thanks to all my eyes and ears. Having a squad who has your back is the utmost important when creating a masterpiece. From betas, to proofers, to PA's to my dog, Jackson who just got me when I didn't get myself, thank you. This success is a solo mission. It comes with an entourage of awesome people who got my back. So, shout out to Amy Wiater, Ashley Cestra, Rachel Schneider, Jenny Hanson, Kristi Webster, Amber Higbie, and anyone who I may have forgotten! I appreciate you all!

Thank you to my editor Emily for helping bring this story to where it needed to be.

Thank you to Sarah Hansen at Okay Creations for creating my amazing cover. A cover is the first representation of a story and she nailed it.

Thank you to my awesome reader group, Club JD. All your constant support for what I do warms my heart. I appreciate all the time you take in helping my stories come to life within this community.

A big hug and wine clink to Stacey at Champagne Formats for always making my books look so pretty.

Thank you to the team at Enticing Journey for all your hard work in promoting this book!

And most importantly every single reader and blogger! THANK YOU for all that you do. For supporting me, reading my stories, spreading the word. It's because of you that I get to continue in this business. And for that I am forever grateful.

Cheers. This big glass of wine is for you.

about

THE AUTHOR

Creative designer, mother, wife, writer, part time superhero…

J.D. Hollyfield is a creative designer by day and superhero by night. When she is not trying to save the world one happy ending at a time, she enjoys the snuggles of her husband, son and three doxies. With her love for romance, and head full of book boyfriends, she was inspired to test her creative abilities and bring her own story to life.

J.D. Hollyfield lives in the Midwest, and is currently at work on blowing the minds of readers, with the additions of her new books and series, along with her charm, humor and HEA's.

Read MORE of J.D. Hollyfield

My So Called Life
Life Next Door
Life in a Rut, Love not Included
Life as we Know it
Faking It
Unlocking Adeline
Sinful Instincts
Passing Peter Parker

CONNECT WITH J.D. Hollyfield

Website: authorjdhollyfield.com
Facebook: www.facebook.com/authorjdhollyfield
Twitter: @jdhollyfield
Newsletter: http://eepurl.com/Wf7gv
Pinterest: www.pinterest.com/jholla311
Instagram: instagram.com/jdhollyfield

Made in the USA
Lexington, KY
05 March 2018